"A witty, concise and delightfully logical guide for the high-tech entrepreneur. Everything you need to know, but not a line more. I'm already recommending it to the faculty, students and business colleagues who are starting companies."

Lita Nelsen
Director, Technology Licensing Office
Massachusetts Institute of Technology
Cambridge, Massachusetts

"*Financial Statements* brings to the non-financial manager an innovative and painless approach to understanding financial statements. Recommended reading for all my clients and their lawyers and bankers."

F. Grant Waite, *CPA*
Partner, Richard A. Eisner & Company
Cambridge, Massachusetts

"Well-organized and easy to read, *Financial Statements* is a great tool for the novice...makes accounting simple and enjoyable."

William Rodgers
President, Hamilton Consultants, Inc.
Cambridge, Massachusetts

"After reading *Financial Statements,* executives will no longer have to pretend that they understand what financial statements mean. A great introductory book."

Timothy D. MacLellan, CPA, PFS
Partner, Morgan & Morgan, PC
Hingham, Massachusetts

"I wish this book were around when I started my first company. The entrepreneur can learn in one evening's reading what it took me two years of learning-by-doing! I plan on giving a copy to every CEO in our venture fund's portfolio."

Gordon B. Baty
Partner, Zero Stage Capital
Cambridge, Massachusetts

"Finally, a handbook that takes the mystery out of accounting principles. I recommend this book to any "non-financial" type who sits at the head of the table—boardroom or kitchen."

Margi Gandolfi
Vice President, Strategic Programs / Clinical Services
New York Blood Center, New York, New York

Financial Statements

A Step-by-Step Guide to Understanding and Creating Financial Reports

Financial Statements

A Step-by-Step Guide to Understanding and Creating Financial Reports

By
Thomas R. Ittelson

CAREER PRESS
3 Tice Road
P.O. Box 687
Franklin Lakes, NJ 07417
1-800-CAREER-1
201-848-0310 (NJ and outside U.S.)
Fax: 201-848-1727

FINANCIAL STATEMENTS

Cover design by The Hub Graphics Corp.

Printed in the U.S.A. by Book-mart Press

To order this title, please call toll-free 1-800-CAREER-1 (NJ and Canada: 201-848-0310) to order using VISA or MasterCard, or for further information on books from Career Press.

Library of Congress Cataloging-in-Publication Data

Ittelson, Thomas R., 1946-
    Financial statements : a step-by-step guide to understanding and
creating financial reports / by Thomas R. Ittelson.
        p.   cm.
    Includes index.
    ISBN 1-56414-341-4 (pbk.)
    1. Financial statements.   I. Title.
HF5681.B2I74   1998
657'.32--dc21

                                                97-49104
                                                CIP

I dedicate this book to my daughter, Alice Dagmar.
May her assets always exceed her liabilities.

Acknowledgments

Many people have helped make this book possible. My special thanks go to Isay Stemp who first showed me that knowing a little finance and accounting could be fun; to my agent, Michael Snell, who taught me how to write a book proposal; and to Theresa Bonar for her thoughtful critiques and encouragement as this book passed through its several versions.

Many thanks to my publisher, Ronald Fry of Career Press, for seeing promise in a preliminary version of this book, to Betsy Sheldon, for editing my sometimes confusing and overblown prose and to Ellen Scher for her guiding of this book through to publication. I am indebted to my colleague, Jack Turner, for his thoughtful review of the words and numbers in this book.

These clients, colleagues and friends at one time or another helped me to develop (whether they realized it or not) the concepts presented in this book. My thanks to Bob Aldrich, Robert Ames, Timothy Barberich, Judy Bowman, Jean Devine, James Dwyer, Margi Gandolfi, Norman and Allan Shapiro, Cavas Gobhai, Carl Good, Adrian Gropper, Jack Haley, James and Bobbi Hope, Bruce Jacobs, John Kimbell, Elliot Lebowitz, John O'Leary, Mel Platte, Chris Simmons, Sally Seaver, Rolf Stutz, Ben Van Vort, Grant Waite and Gene Zurlo.

And of course, my thanks to Darcy, Brenden, Sara and Charlie.

Thomas Ittelson

Contents

Section A. Financial Statements: Structure & Vocabulary

Much of what passes for complexity in accounting and financial reporting is just a specialized vocabulary and a simple numeric structure. This section will introduce the words, the basic accounting principles and the structure of the main financial statements.

Accountants have some basic rules upon which all their work in preparing financial statements is based. Who makes these rules? The simple answer is that the "FASB" makes the rules and they are called "GAAP." Got that?

The Balance Sheet is one of the two main financial statements of a business ...the other is the Income Statement. The Balance Sheet states the basic equation of accounting at an instant in time: *What you have minus what you owe is what you're worth.*

One of the two main financial statements of a business...the other is the Balance Sheet. The Income Statement gives one significant perspective on the health of the enterprise, *its profitability.*

Where the company gets cash and where that cash goes. The Cash Flow Statement tracks *the movement of cash* through the business *over a defined period of time.*

The financial statements are connected; an entry in one may well affect each of the others. This interlocking flow of numbers allows the three statements together to form a cohesive picture of the company's financial position.

A. Balance Sheet Connections
B. Sales Cycle
C. Expense Cycle
D. Investment Cycle
E. Asset Purchase & Depreciation Cycle

Section B. Transactions: Exploits of AppleSeed Enterprises, Inc.

With our knowledge of the three main financial statements, we will now draft the books of a hypothetical company, AppleSeed Enterprises, Inc. We will report the common and everyday actions that AppleSeed takes as it goes about its business of making and selling applesauce. Accounting for these "transactions" *(T1 through T31 below)* is the subject of the rest of this book. We will describe the Balance Sheet, Income Statement and Cash Flow entries for business actions from selling common stock, to shipping product, to paying the owners a dividend.

Welcome to our little business, AppleSeed Enterprises, Inc. Imagine that you are AppleSeed's entrepreneurial CEO. You also double as Treasurer and Chief Financial Officer (CFO).

T1. Sell 150,000 shares of AppleSeed's common stock (par value $1) for $10 per share.

T2. Pay yourself your first month's salary. Book all payroll-associated fringe benefits and taxes.

T3. Borrow $1 million to buy a building. Terms of this 10 year mortgage are 10% per annum.

T4. Pay $1.5 million for a building to be used for office, manufacturing and warehouse space. Set up a depreciation schedule.

T5. Hire administrative and sales staff. Pay first month's salaries and book fringe benefits and taxes.

T6. Pay employee health, life and disability insurance premiums plus FICA, unemployment and withholding taxes.

Now begins the fun stuff. In a few short weeks we will be producing thousands of cases of the best applesauce the world has ever tasted.

T7. Order $250,000 worth of manufacturing machinery. Pay one-half down now.

T8. Receive and install manufacturing machinery. Pay the remaining $125,000 due.

T9. Hire production workers; capitalize first month's salary and wages.
- Prepare bill of materials and establish labor requirements.
- Set up plant and machinery depreciation schedules.
- Plan monthly production schedule and set standard costs.

T10. Place standing orders for raw materials with suppliers; receive 1 million jar labels.

We are ready to start producing applesauce. The machinery is up and running, the workers are hired and we are about to receive a supply of raw materials.

T11. Receive two months' supply of raw materials.

T12. Start up production. Pay workers and supervisor for the month.

T13. Book depreciation and other manufacturing overhead costs for the month.

T14. Pay for the labels received in Transaction 10 in Chapter 7.

T15. Finish manufacturing 19,500 cases of applesauce and move them into finished goods inventory.

T16. Scrap 500 cases' worth of work-in-process inventory.

  • Manufacturing variances: what can go wrong, what can go right.

T17. Pay for the two months' supply of raw materials received in Transaction 11 above.

T18. Manufacture another month's supply of applesauce.

A wise old consultant once said, "...really, all you need to be in business is a customer."

T19. Produce product advertising fliers and T-shirt giveaways.

  • Product pricing; break-even analysis

T20. A new customer orders 1,000 cases of applesauce. Ship 1,000 cases at $15.90 per case.

T21. Take an order (on credit) for 15,000 cases of applesauce at a discounted price of $15.66 per case.

T22. Ship and invoice customer for 15,000 cases of applesauce ordered in Transaction 21 above.

T23. Receive payment of $234,900 for the shipment made in Transaction 22 above and pay the broker's commission.

T24. OOPS! customer goes bankrupt. Write off cost of 1,000 cases as a bad debt.

We've been busy making and selling our delicious applesauce. But having been in business for three months, it is time to attend to some important administrative tasks.

T25. Pay this year's general liability insurance.

T26. Make principal and interest payments on three months' worth of building debts.

T27. Pay payroll-associated taxes and insurance benefit premiums.

T28. Pay some suppliers...especially the mean and hungry ones.

We've had a very good first year of operations. We will determine our profit for the year, compute the taxes we owe, declare a dividend and issue our first Annual Report to Shareholders.

T29. Fast-forward through the rest of the year. Record summary transactions.

T30. Book income taxes payable.

T31. Declare a $0.375 per-share dividend and pay to common shareholders.

- Cash Flow Statement: Changes in Financial Position format.
- AppleSeed Enterprises, Inc. Annual Report to Shareholders.
- What is AppleSeed worth? How to value a business.

Section C. Financial Statements: Construction & Analysis

Journals and ledgers are where accountants scribble transaction entries. A journal is a book (or computer memory) in which all financial events are recorded in chronological order. A ledger is a book of accounts. An account is simply any grouping of like-items that we want to keep track of.

- Keeping Track with Journals and Ledgers: *Cash Ledger, Accounts Payable Ledger, Accrued Expenses Ledger, Accounts Receivable Ledger*

Often in judging the financial condition of an enterprise, it is not so much the absolute amount of sales, costs, expenses and assets that are important, but rather the relationships between them.

- Common Size Statements: *Income Statement, Balance Sheet*
- Liquidity Ratios: *Current Ratio, Quick Ratio*
- Asset Management Ratios: *Inventory Turn, Asset Turn, Receivable Days*
- Profitability Ratios: *Return on Assets, Return on Equity, Return on Sales, Gross Margin*
- Leverage Ratios: *Debt-to-Equity, Debt Ratio*
- Industry and Company Comparisons

Various alternative accounting policies and procedures are completely legal and widely used, but may result in significant differences in the values reported on a company's financial statements. Conservative? Aggressive? Some people would call this chapter's topic "creative accounting."

"Cooking the books" means intentionally hiding or distorting the real financial performance or financial condition of a company. Cooking is most often accomplished by incorrectly and fraudulently moving Balance Sheet items onto the Income Statements and vise versa. Outright lying is also a favorite technique.

⌐

Preface

We needed to hire an accountant to keep the books at a venture-capital backed, high-technology startup of which I was a founder and CEO. I interviewed a young woman—just out of school—for the job and asked her why she wanted to become an accountant. Her answer was a surprise to all of us,

"Because accounting is so symmetrical, so logical, so beautiful and it always comes out right," she said.

We hired her on the spot, thinking it would be fun to have almost-a-poet keeping our books. She worked out fine.

I hope you take away from this book a part of what my young accountant saw. Knowing a little accounting and financial reporting can be very satisfying. Yes, it does all come out right at the end and there is real beauty and poetry in its structure.

~

But, let's discuss perhaps the real reason you've bought and are now reading this book. My bet is that it has to do with power. You want the power you see associated with knowing how numbers flow in business.

Be it poetry or power, this accounting and financial reporting stuff is not rocket science. You've learned all the math required to master accounting by the end of the fourth grade—mostly addition and subtraction with a bit of multiplication and division thrown in to keep it lively.

The specialized vocabulary, on the other hand, can be confusing. You will need to learn the accounting definitions of revenue, income, cost and expense. You'll also need to understand the structure and appreciate the purpose of the three major numeric statements that describe a company's financial condition.

Here's a hint: Watch where the money flows; watch where goods and services flow. Documenting these movements of cash and product is all that financial statements do. It is no more complicated than that. Everything else is details.

But why is it all so boring, you ask? Well, it's only boring if you do not understand it. Yes, the day-to-day repetitive accounting tasks are boring. However, how to finance and extract cash from the actions of the enterprise is not boring at all. It is the essence of business and the generation of wealth.

Not boring at all.

Introduction

Many non-financial managers have an accounting phobia...a financial vertigo that limits their effectiveness. If you think "inventory turn" means rotating stock on the shelf, and that "accrual" has something to do with the Wicked Witch of the East...then this book's for you.

Financial Statements: A Step-by-Step Guide to Understanding and Creating Financial Statements is designed for those business professionals: (1) who know very little about accounting and financial statements, but feel they should, and (2) who need to know a little more, but for whom the normal accounting and financial reporting texts are mysterious and unenlightening. In fact, the above two categories make up the majority of all people in business. You are not alone.

Financial Statements: A Step-by-Step Guide to Understanding and Creating Financial Statements is a transaction-based, business training tool with clarifying, straightforward, real-life examples of how financial statements are built and how they interact to present a true financial picture of the enterprise.

We will not bog down in details that get in the way of conceptual understanding. Just as it is not necessary to know how the microchip in your electric calculator works to multiply a few numbers, it's not necessary to be a Certified Public Accountant (CPA) to have a working knowledge of the "accounting model of the enterprise."

~

Transactions. This book describes a sequence of "transactions" of our sample company, AppleSeed Enterprises Inc., as it goes about making and selling delicious applesauce. We will sell stock to raise money, buy machinery to make our product, and then satisfy our customers by shipping wholesome applesauce. We'll get paid and we will hope to make a profit.

Each step along the way will generate account "postings" on AppleSeed's books. We'll discuss each transaction to get a hands-on feel for how a company's financial statements are constructed. We'll learn how to report using the three main financial statements of a business—the

"Accounting is a language, a means of communicating among all the segments of the business community. It assumes a reference base called the *accounting model of the enterprise*. While other models of the enterprise are possible, this accounting model is the accepted form, and is likely to be for some time.

"If you don't speak the language of accounting or feel intuitively comfortable with the accounting model, you will be at a severe disadvantage in the business world. Accounting is a fundamental tool of the trade."

Gordon B. Baty,
Entrepreneurship for the Nineties,
Prentice Hall, Englewood Cliffs, NJ, 1990

Financial Statements

Balance Sheet, Income Statement and Cash Flow Statement—for these common business dealings:

1. selling stock
2. borrowing money
3. receiving orders
4. shipping goods
5. invoicing customers
6. receiving payments
7. paying sales commissions
8. writing off bad debts
9. prepaying expenses
10. ordering equipment
11. paying deposits
12. receiving raw materials
13. scrapping damaged product
14. paying suppliers
15. booking variances in manufacturing
16. depreciating fixed assets
17. valuing inventory
18. hiring staff and paying salary, wages and payroll taxes
19. computing profit
20. paying income taxes
21. issuing dividends
22. and more

By the end of this book, you'll know your way around the finances of our applesauce-making company, AppleSeed Enterprises, Inc.

Goals. My goal in writing this book is to help people in business master the basics of accounting and financial reporting. This book is especially directed at those managers, scientists and sales-people who should know how a Balance Sheet, Income Statement and Cash Flow work…but don't.

Your goal is to gain knowledge of accounting and finance, to assist you in your business dealings. You want the power that comes from understanding financial manipulations. You must know how the score is kept in business. You recognize, as Gordon Baty says, you must "feel intuitively comfortable with the accounting model" to succeed in business.

~

This book is divided into three main sections, each with a specific teaching objective:

Section A. Financial Statements: Structure & Vocabulary will introduce the three main financial statements of the enterprise and define the special vocabulary that is necessary to understand the books and to converse with accountants.

Section B. Transactions: Exploits of AppleSeed Enterprises, Inc., will take us through 31 business transactions showing how to report financial impact of each on the Balance Sheet, Income Statement and Cash Flow Statement of AppleSeed Enterprises.

Section C. Financial Statements: Construction & Analysis will subject the financial statement of our sample company to a rigorous analysis using common ratio analysis techniques. Then finally we will touch on how to "cook the books," why someone would want to, and how to detect financial fraud.

"…even if it's boring and dull and soon to be forgotten, continue to learn double-entry bookkeeping. People think I'm joking, but I'm not. You should love the mathematics of business."

Kenneth H. Olsen,
founder and former CEO,
Digital Equipment Corporation

With your newly acquired understanding of the structure and flow of money in business, you will appreciate these important business quandaries:

- How an enterprise can be rapidly growing, highly profitable and out of money all at the same time...and why this state of affairs is fairly common.

- Why working capital is so important and which management actions lead to more, which lead to less.

- The difference between cash in the bank and profit on the bottom line and how the two are interrelated.

- When in the course of business affairs a negative cash flow is a sign of good things happening...and when it's a sign of impending catastrophe.

- Limits of common product costing systems and when to apply (and, more importantly, when to ignore) the accountant's definition of cost.

- Why a development investment made today must return a much greater sum to the coffers of the company in later years.

- How discounts drop right to the bottom line as lost profits and why they are so dangerous to a company's financial health.

To be effective in business, you must understand accounting and financial reporting. Don't become an accountant, but do "speak the language" and become intuitively comfortable with the accounting model of the enterprise.

Read on.

Section A. Financial Statements: Structure & Vocabulary

About this Section

This book is written for people who need to use financial statements in their work but have no formal training in accounting and financial reporting. Don't feel bad if you fall into this category. My guess is that 95 percent of all non-financial managers are financially illiterate when it comes to understanding the company's books. Let us proceed toward some enlightenment.

∽

This section is about financial statement structure and about the specialized vocabulary of financial reporting. We will learn both together. It's easier that way.

Much of what passes as complexity in accounting and financial reporting is just specialized (sometimes counterintuitive) vocabulary and basically simple reporting structure that gets confusing only in the details.

Vocabulary. In accounting, some important words may have meanings that are different than what you think. The box below shows some of this confusing vocabulary. It's absolutely essential to use these words correctly when discussing financial statements. You'll just have to learn them. It's really not much, but it is important. Look at these examples:

1. *Sales* and *revenue* are synonymous and refer to the top line of the Income Statement; the money that comes in from customers.

2. *Profits, earnings* and *income* are all synonymous and mean the "bottom line," or what is left over from revenue after all the costs and expenses spent in generating that revenue are subtracted.

Note that *revenue* and *income* have different meanings. *Revenue* is the "top line" and *income* is the "bottom line" of the Income Statement. Got that?

3. *Costs* are money spent making a product. *Expenses* are money spent to develop it, to sell it, to account for it and to manage this whole making and selling process.

Sales and **revenue** mean the same thing.
Profits, earnings and **income** mean the same thing.
Now, **revenue** and **income** *do not* mean the same thing.

Costs are different from **expenses.**
Expenses are different from **expenditures.**

Sales are different from **orders** but are the same as **shipments.**

Profits are different from **cash.**
Solvency is different from **profitability.**

---

4. Both costs and expenses become *expenditures* when money is actually sent to vendors to pay for them.

5. *Orders* are placed by customers and signify a request for the future delivery of products. *Orders* do not have an impact on any of the financial statements in any way until the products are actually shipped. At this point these *shipments* become sales. *Shipments* and *sales* are synonyms.

6. *Solvency* means having enough money in the bank to pay your bills. Profitability means that your sales are greater than your costs and expenses. You can be *profitable* and *insolvent* at the same time. You are making money but still do not have enough cash to pay your bills.

Financial Statements. Once you understand the specialized accounting vocabulary, you can appreciate financial statement structure. For example, there will be no confusion when we say that *revenue* is at the top of an Income Statement and *income* is at the bottom.

In this section we will learn vocabulary and financial statement structure simultaneously. Then follows a chapter on each one of the three main financial statements: the Balance Sheet, the Income Statement and the Cash Flow Statement. To end the section we'll discuss how these three statements interact and when changing a number in one necessitates changing a number in another.

~

Chapter 1 will lay some ground rules for financial reporting—starting points and assumptions that accounting professionals require to let them make sense of a company's books. In **Chapter 2** we'll discuss the Balance Sheet...what you own and what you owe. Then next in **Chapter 3** comes the Income Statement reporting on the enterprise's product selling activities and whether there is any money left over after all these operations are done and accounted for.

The last statement, but often the most important in the short term, is the Cash Flow discussed in **Chapter 4** Look at this statement as a simple check register with deposits being cash-in and any payments cash-out.

Chapter 5 puts all three financial statements together and shows how they work in concert to give a true picture of the enterprise's financial health.

Chapter 1. Twelve Basic Principles

Accountants have some basic rules and assumptions upon which rests all their work in preparing financial statements. These rules and assumptions tell accountants *what* financial items to measure and *when* and *how* to measure them. As you'll see by the end of this discussion, it is important to have at least an appreciation for these rules and assumptions. So, following are 12 very important ones:

1. the accounting entity
2. going concern
3. measurement
4. units of measure
5. historical cost
6. materiality
7. estimates and judgments
8. consistency
9. conservatism
10. periodicity
11. substance over form
12. accrual basis of presentation

These rules and assumptions define and qualify all that accountants do and all that financial reporting reports. We will deal with each in turn.

1. Accounting Entity. The *accounting entity* is the business unit (regardless of the legal business form) for which the financial statements are being prepared. This principal states that there is a "business entity" separate from its owners...a fictional "person" called a corporation for which the books can be written.

2. Going Concern. Unless there is evidence to the contrary, accountants assume that the life of the business entity is infinitely long. Obviously this assumption can not be verified and is hardly ever true. But, this assumption does greatly simplify the presentation of the financial position of the firm and aids in the preparation of financial statements.

3. Measurement. Accounting deals with things that can be *quantified*— resources and obligations upon which there is an agreed-upon value. Accounting only deals with things that can be measured and quantified.

This assumption leaves out many very valuable company "assets." For example, loyal customers, while necessary for company success, still cannot be quantified and assigned a value and thus are not stated in the books.

A set of financial statements contains only measures of assets (what the business owns), liabilities (what the business owes) and the difference between the two equaling owner's equity.

4. Units of Measure. U.S. dollars are the units of value reported in the financial statements of United States companies. Results of any foreign subsidiaries are translated into dollars for consolidated reporting of results. As exchange rates vary, so do the values of any foreign currency denominated assets and liabilities.

5. Historical Cost. What a company owns and what it owes are recorded at their original (historical) cost with no adjustment for inflation.

A company can own a building valued at $50 million yet carry it on the books at its $5 million original purchase price (less accumulated depreciation), a gross understatement of value.

This assumption can greatly understate the value of some assets purchased in the past and depreciated to a very low amount on the books. Why, you ask, do accountants demand that we obviously understate assets? Basically, it is the easiest thing to do. You do not have to appraise and reappraise all the time.

6. Materiality. Materiality refers to the relative importance of financial information. Here accountants don't sweat the small stuff. But all transactions must be reported if they would materially effect the financial condition of the company.

Remember, what is material for a corner drug store is not material for IBM (lost in the rounding errors). Materiality is a straightforward judgment call.

7. Estimates and Judgments. Complexity and uncertainty make any measurements less than exact. Estimates and judgments must often be made for financial reporting. It is okay to guess if: (1) that is the best you can do and (2) the expected error would not matter much anyway. You should use the same guessing method for each period. Be consistent in your guesses.

8. Consistency. Sometimes identical transactions could be accounted for differently. You could do it this way or that way, depending upon preference. The principal of consistency states that each individual enterprise must choose a single method of reporting and use it consistently over time. You cannot switch back and forth. Measurement techniques must be consistent from one fiscal period to another.

9. Conservatism. Accountants have a downward measurement bias, preferring understatement to overvaluation. For example, losses are recorded when you feel that they have a great probability of occurring, not later, when they actually do occur. Conversely, the recording of a gain is postponed until it *actually* occurs, not when it is only anticipated.

10. Periodicity. Accountants assume that the life of a corporation can be divided into periods of time for which profits and losses can be reported, usually a month, quarter or year.

What is so special about a month, quarter or year? They are just convenient periods; short enough so that management can remember what has happened, long enough to have meaning and not just be random fluctuations. These periods are called "fiscal" periods. For example a "fiscal year" could extend from October 1 in one year till September 30 in the next year.

11. Substance Over Form. Accountants report the economic "substance" of a transaction rather than just its form. For example, an equipment lease that is

---

"Lines" are perhaps not as important as principals, but they can be confusing if you don't know how accountants use them in financial statements. Financial statements often have two types of lines to indicate types of numeric computations.

Single lines on a financial statement indicate that a calculation (addition or subtraction) has been made on the numbers just preceding in the column.

The ***double underline*** is saved for last. That is, use of a double underline signifies the very last figure in the statement.

Note that while all the numbers in the statement represent currency, only the top line and the bottom line normally show a dollar sign.

a	SALES [$]
b	COST OF GOODS
$a-b=c$	GROSS MARGIN
d	SALES & MARKETING
e	R&D
f	G&A
$d+e+f=g$	TOTAL EXPENSES
h	INTEREST INCOME
i	INCOME TAXES
$c-g+h-i=j$	NET INCOME [$]

FASB[1] makes the rules and they are called GAAP.[2]

[1]Financial Accounting Standards Board; [2]Generally Accepted Accounting Principals

---

really a purchase, dressed in a costume, is booked as a purchase and not as a lease on financial statements. This rule states that if it's a duck...then you must report it as a duck.

12. Accrual Basis. This concept is important. Accountants translate into dollars of profit or loss the money-making (or losing) activities that take place in a fiscal period. In accrual accounting, this documentation is accomplished by matching for presentation: (1) the revenue received in selling product and (2) the costs to make the specific product sold. Fiscal period expenses such as selling, legal, administrative and so forth are then added.

Key to accrual accounting is. (1) when you may report a sale on the financial statements, (2) matching and then reporting the appropriate costs of the sale, and (3) using a systematic and rational method of allocating of all the other costs of being in business for the period. We will deal with each point separately:

Revenue recognition. In accrual accounting, a sale is recorded when all the necessary activities to provide the good or service have been completed regardless when cash changes hands. A customer just ordering a product has not yet generated any revenue. Revenue is recorded when the product is shipped.

Matching principal. In accrual accounting the costs associated with making products (Cost of Goods Sold) are recorded at the same time the matching revenue is recorded.

Allocation. Many costs are not specifically associated with a product. These costs must be allocated to fiscal periods in a reasonable fashion. For example, each month can be charged with one-twelfth of the general business insurance policy even though the policy was paid in full at the beginning of the year. Other expenses are recorded when they arise (period expenses).

Note that all businesses with inventory must use the accrual basis of accounting. Other businesses may use a "cash basis" if they desire. Cash basis financial statements are just like the Cash Flow Statement or a simple checkbook. We'll describe features of accrual accounting in the chapters that follow.

~

Who makes these rules? The simple answer is that FASB makes the rules and they are called GAAP. Note also that FASB is made up of CPAs.

Financial statements in the United States must be prepared according to the accounting profession's set of rules and guiding principals called the *Generally Accepted Accounting Principals,* GAAP for short. Other countries use different rules.

GAAP is a series of conventions, rules and procedures for preparing financial statements. The *Financial Accounting Standards Board*, FASB for short, lays out the GAAP conventions, rules and procedures.

CPAs are, of course, Certified Public Accountants. These exalted individuals, are specially trained in college, and have practiced auditing companies both public and private for a number of years. In addition, they have passed a series of exams testing their clear understanding of accounting principles and auditing procedures.

Chapter 2. The Balance Sheet

One of the two main financial statements of a business...

the other is the *Income Statement.*

The Basic Equation of Accounting

- The basic equation of accounting states: "What you *have* minus what you *owe* is what you're worth."

     Assets - Liabilities = Worth

     "have"   *"owe"*   *"value to owners"*

- *Worth, net worth, equity, owners' equity* and *shareholders' equity* all mean the same thing—the value of the enterprise belonging to its owners.

The Balance Sheet

- The Balance Sheet presents the basic equation of accounting in a slightly rearranged form:

     Assets = Liabilities + Worth

     "have"   *"owe"*   *"value to owners"*

- By definition, this equation must always be "in balance" with assets equaling the sum of liabilities and worth.

- So, if you add an asset to the left side of the equation, you must also increase the right side by adding a liability or increasing worth. Two entries are required to keep the equation in balance.

Balance Sheet Format
as of a specific date

ASSETS	LIABILITIES & EQUITY
CASH	ACCOUNTS PAYABLE
ACCOUNTS RECEIVABLE	ACCRUED EXPENSES
INVENTORY	CURRENT PORTION OF DEBT
PREPAID EXPENSES	INCOME TAXES PAYABLE
CURRENT ASSETS	CURRENT LIABILITIES
OTHER ASSETS	LONG-TERM DEBT
FIXED ASSETS AT COST	CAPITAL STOCK
ACCUMULATED DEPRECIATION	RETAINED EARNINGS
NET FIXED ASSETS	SHAREHOLDERS' EQUITY
TOTAL ASSETS	TOTAL LIABILITIES & EQUITY

The Balance Sheet—a snapshot in time.

- The Balance Sheet presents the financial picture of the enterprise on *one particular day, an instant in time, the date it was written.*

- The Balance Sheet presents:

  what the enterprise *has* today: **assets**
  how much the enterprise *owes* today: **liabilities**
  what the enterprise *is worth* today: **equity**

- The Balance Sheet reports:

  Has today = Owes today + Worth today
  assets *liabilities* *shareholders' equity*

Balance Sheet Format
as of a specific date

ASSETS

CASH	A
ACCOUNTS RECEIVABLE	B
INVENTORY	C
PREPAID EXPENSES	D
CURRENT ASSETS	A + B + C + D = E
OTHER ASSETS	F
FIXED ASSETS AT COST	G
ACCUMULATED DEPRECIATION	H
NET FIXED ASSETS	G - H = I
TOTAL ASSETS	E + F + I = J

What are Assets?

- **Assets** are everything you've got—cash in the bank, inventory, machines, buildings—all of it.

- **Assets** are also certain "rights" you own that have a monetary value...like the right to collect cash from customers who owe you money.

- **Assets** are *valuable* and this value must be *quantifiable* for an asset to be listed on the Balance Sheet. Everything in a company's financial statements must be translated into dollars and cents.

Balance Sheet Format

as of a specific date

most liquid asset

ASSETS

CASH	A
ACCOUNTS RECEIVABLE	B
INVENTORY	C
PREPAID EXPENSES	D
CURRENT ASSETS	A + B + C + D = E
OTHER ASSETS	F
FIXED ASSETS AT COST	G
ACCUMULATED DEPRECIATION	H
NET FIXED ASSETS	**G - H = I**
TOTAL ASSETS	E + F + I = J

least liquid asset

Grouping Assets for Presentation

- **Assets** are grouped for presentation on the Balance Sheet according to their characteristics:

  > *very liquid assets* ..... cash and securities
  > *productive assets* ..... plant and machinery
  > *assets for sale* .... inventory

- **Accounts receivable** are a special type of asset group —the obligations of customers of a company to pay the company for goods shipped to them on credit.

- **Assets** are displayed in the asset section of the Balance Sheet in the *descending order of liquidity (the ease of convertibility into cash)*. Cash itself is the most liquid of all assets; fixed assets are normally the least liquid.

Balance Sheet Format
as of a specific date

ASSETS

CASH	A
ACCOUNTS RECEIVABLE	B
INVENTORY	C
PREPAID EXPENSES	D
CURRENT ASSETS	A + B + C + D = E
OTHER ASSETS	F
FIXED ASSETS AT COST	G
ACCUMULATED DEPRECIATION	H
NET FIXED ASSETS	G - H = I
TOTAL ASSETS	E + F + I = J

Current Assets

- By definition, **current assets** are those assets that are expected to be converted into cash in less than 12 months.

- **Current asset** groupings are listed in order of liquidity with the most easy to convert into cash listed first:

  1. Cash
  2. Accounts receivable
  3. Inventory

- The money the company will use to pay its bills in the near term (within the year) will come when its **current assets** are converted into cash (that is, inventory is sold and accounts receivable are paid).

Balance Sheet Format
as of a specific date

ASSETS

CASH	A
ACCOUNTS RECEIVABLE	B
INVENTORY	C
PREPAID EXPENSES	D
CURRENT ASSETS	$A + B + C + D = E$
OTHER ASSETS	F
FIXED ASSETS AT COST	G
ACCUMULATED DEPRECIATION	H
NET FIXED ASSETS	$G - H = I$
TOTAL ASSETS	$E + F + I = J$

Current Assets: Cash

- **Cash** is the ultimate liquid asset: on-demand deposits in a bank as well as the dollars and cents in the petty cash drawer.

- When you write a check to pay a bill you are taking money out of **cash** assets.

- Like all the rest of the Balance Sheet, **cash** is denominated in U.S. dollars for corporations in the United States. A U.S. company with foreign subsidiaries would convert the value of any foreign currency it holds (and also other foreign assets) into dollars for financial reporting.

Balance Sheet Format
as of a specific date

ASSETS

CASH	A
ACCOUNTS RECEIVABLE	**B**
INVENTORY	C
PREPAID EXPENSES	D
CURRENT ASSETS	A + B + C + D = E
OTHER ASSETS	F
FIXED ASSETS AT COST	G
ACCUMULATED DEPRECIATION	H
NET FIXED ASSETS	G - H = I
TOTAL ASSETS	E + F + I = J

Current Assets: Accounts Receivable

- When the enterprise ships a product to a customer on credit, the enterprise acquires *a right* to collect money from that customer at a specified time in the future.

- These collection rights are totaled and reported on the Balance Sheet as **accounts receivable.**

- **Accounts receivable** are owed to the enterprise from customers (called "accounts") who were shipped goods but have not yet paid for them. Credit customers—most business between companies is done on credit—are commonly given payment terms that allow 30 or 60 days to pay.

Balance Sheet Format
as of a specific date

ASSETS

CASH	A
ACCOUNTS RECEIVABLE	B
INVENTORY	C
PREPAID EXPENSES	D
CURRENT ASSETS	A + B + C + D = E
OTHER ASSETS	F
FIXED ASSETS AT COST	G
ACCUMULATED DEPRECIATION	H
NET FIXED ASSETS	G - H = I
TOTAL ASSETS	E + F + I = J

Current Assets: Inventory

- **Inventory** is both finished products for ready sale to customers and also materials to be made into products. A manufacturer's **inventory** includes three groupings:

  1. Raw material inventory is unprocessed materials that will be used in manufacturing products.

  2. Work-in-process inventory is partially finished products in the process of being manufactured.

  3. Finished goods inventory is completed products ready for shipment to customers when they place orders.

- As *finished goods inventory* is sold it becomes an *accounts receivable* and then *cash* when the customer pays.

Balance Sheet Format
as of a specific date

ASSETS

CASH	A
ACCOUNTS RECEIVABLE	B
INVENTORY	C
PREPAID EXPENSES	**D**
CURRENT ASSETS	A + B + C + D = E
OTHER ASSETS	F
FIXED ASSETS AT COST	G
ACCUMULATED DEPRECIATION	H
NET FIXED ASSETS	G - H = I
TOTAL ASSETS	E + F + I = J

Current Assets: Prepaid Expenses

- **Prepaid expenses** are bills the company has already paid...but for services not yet received.

- **Prepaid expenses** are things like prepaid insurance premiums, prepayment of rent, deposits paid to the telephone company, salary advances, etc.

- **Prepaid expenses** are current assets not because they can be turned into cash, but because the enterprise will not have to use cash to pay them in the near future. They have been paid already.

Current Asset Cycle

- **Current assets** are said to be "working assets" because they are in a constant cycle of being converted into cash. The repeating **current asset cycle** of a business is shown below:

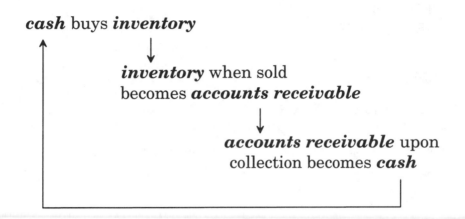

cash buys *inventory*

inventory when sold
becomes *accounts receivable*

accounts receivable upon
collection becomes *cash*

More asset types

- In addition to a company's current assets, there are two other major asset groups listed on the Balance Sheet: **Other assets** and **fixed assets.** These so-called *"non-current assets"* are not converted into cash during the normal course of business.

- **Other assets** is a catchall category that includes intangible assets such as the value of patents, trade names and so forth.

- The company's **fixed assets** (so-called *property, plant and equipment* or *PP&E)* is generally the largest and most important non-current asset grouping.

Balance Sheet Format

as of a specific date

ASSETS

CASH	A
ACCOUNTS RECEIVABLE	B
INVENTORY	C
PREPAID EXPENSES	D
CURRENT ASSETS	A + B + C + D = E
OTHER ASSETS	F
FIXED ASSETS AT COST	G
ACCUMULATED DEPRECIATION	H
NET FIXED ASSETS	G - H = I
TOTAL ASSETS	E + F + I = J

Fixed Assets

- **Fixed assets** are productive assets not intended for sale. They will be used over and over again to manufacture the product, display it, warehouse it, transport it and so forth.

- **Fixed assets** commonly include land, buildings, machinery, equipment, furniture, automobiles, trucks, etc.

- **Fixed assets** are normally reported on the Balance Sheet as *net fixed assets*—valued at original cost minus an allowance for depreciation. See the *depreciation* discussion following.

Balance Sheet Format
as of a specific date

ASSETS

CASH	A
ACCOUNTS RECEIVABLE	B
INVENTORY	C
PREPAID EXPENSES	D
CURRENT ASSETS	A + B + C + D = E
OTHER ASSETS	F
FIXED ASSETS AT COST	G
ACCUMULATED DEPRECIATION	**H**
NET FIXED ASSETS	G - H = I
TOTAL ASSETS	E + F + I = J

Depreciation

- **Depreciation** is an *accounting convention* reporting *(on the Income Statement)* the decline in useful value of a fixed asset due to wear and tear from use and the passage of time.

- **Depreciating** an asset means spreading the cost to acquire the asset over the asset's whole useful life. **Accumulated depreciation** *(on the Balance Sheet)* is the sum of all the depreciation charges taken since the asset was first acquired.

- **Depreciation** charges taken in a period do lower *profits* for the period, but do not lower *cash*. Cash was required to purchase the fixed asset originally.

Balance Sheet Format
as of a specific date

ASSETS

CASH	A
ACCOUNTS RECEIVABLE	B
INVENTORY	C
PREPAID EXPENSES	D
CURRENT ASSETS	A + B + C + D = E
OTHER ASSETS	F
FIXED ASSETS AT COST	G
ACCUMULATED DEPRECIATION	H
NET FIXED ASSETS	**G - H = I**
TOTAL ASSETS	E + F + I = J

Net Fixed Assets

- The **net fixed assets** of a company are the sum of its fixed assets' purchase prices *("fixed assets @ cost")* minus the depreciation charges taken on the Income Statement over the years *("accumulated depreciation").*

- The so-called *book value* of an asset—its value as reported on the books of the company—is the asset's purchase price minus its accumulated depreciation.

- Note that depreciation does not necessarily relate to an actual decrease in value. In fact, some assets appreciate in value over time. However, such appreciated assets are *by convention* still reported on the Balance Sheet at their lower book value.

Balance Sheet Format
as of a specific date

ASSETS

CASH	A
ACCOUNTS RECEIVABLE	B
INVENTORY	C
PREPAID EXPENSES	D
CURRENT ASSETS	A + B + C + D = E
OTHER ASSETS	**F**
FIXED ASSETS AT COST	G
ACCUMULATED DEPRECIATION	H
NET FIXED ASSETS	G - H = I
TOTAL ASSETS	E + F + I = J

Other Assets

- The **other asset** category on the Balance Sheet includes assets of the enterprise that cannot be properly classified into *current asset* or *fixed asset* categories.

- *Intangible assets* (a major type of other assets) are things owned by the company that have value but are not tangible (that is, not physical property) in nature.

  For example, a patent, a copyright, or a brand name can have considerable value to the enterprise, yet these are not *tangible* like a machine or inventory is.

- *Intangible assets* are valued by management according to various accounting conventions too complex, arbitrary and confusing to be of interest here.

Balance Sheet Format
as of a specific date

	LIABILITIES & EQUITY
K	ACCOUNTS PAYABLE
L	ACCRUED EXPENSES
M	CURRENT PORTION OF DEBT
N	INCOME TAXES PAYABLE
K + L + M+ N = O	CURRENT LIABILITIES
P	LONG-TERM DEBT
Q	CAPITAL STOCK
R	RETAINED EARNINGS
Q - R = S	SHAREHOLDERS' EQUITY
O + P + S = T	TOTAL LIABILITIES & EQUITY

What are Liabilities?

- **Liabilities** are economic obligations of the enterprise such as money that the corporation owes to lenders, suppliers, employees, etc.

- **Liabilities** are categorized and grouped for presentation on the balance sheet by: (1) to whom the debt is owed and (2) whether the debt is payable within the year *(current liabilities)* or is a long-term obligation.

- *Shareholders' equity* is a very special kind of **liability**. It represents the value of the corporation that belongs to its owners. However, this "debt" will never be repaid in the normal course of business.

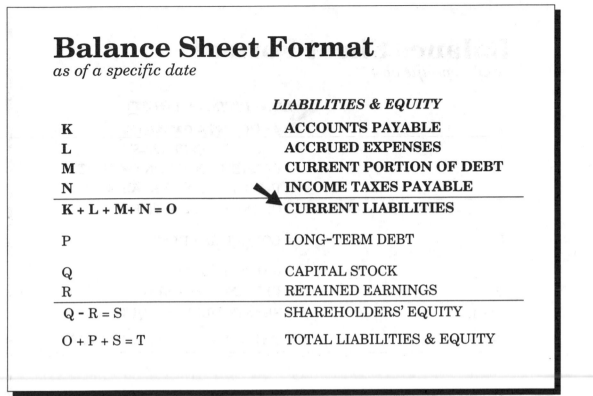

Balance Sheet Format
as of a specific date

	LIABILITIES & EQUITY
K	ACCOUNTS PAYABLE
L	ACCRUED EXPENSES
M	CURRENT PORTION OF DEBT
N	INCOME TAXES PAYABLE
K + L + M+ N = O	CURRENT LIABILITIES
P	LONG-TERM DEBT
Q	CAPITAL STOCK
R	RETAINED EARNINGS
Q − R = S	SHAREHOLDERS' EQUITY
O + P + S = T	TOTAL LIABILITIES & EQUITY

Current Liabilities

- **Current liabilities** are bills that must be paid within *one year* of the date of the Balance Sheet. **Current liabilities** are a reverse of current assets:

  > *current assets*...provide cash within 12 months
  > *current liabilities*...take cash within 12 months.

- The cash generated from current assets is used to pay **current liabilities** as they become due.

- **Current liabilities** are grouped depending on to whom the debt is owed: (1) *accounts payable* owed to suppliers, (2) *accrued expenses* owed to employees and others for services, (3) *current debt* owed to lenders and (4) *taxes* owed to the government.

Balance Sheet Format
as of a specific date

	LIABILITIES & EQUITY
K	ACCOUNTS PAYABLE
L	ACCRUED EXPENSES
M	CURRENT PORTION OF DEBT
N	INCOME TAXES PAYABLE
K + L + M + N = O	CURRENT LIABILITIES
P	LONG-TERM DEBT
Q	CAPITAL STOCK
R	RETAINED EARNINGS
Q - R = S	SHAREHOLDERS' EQUITY
O + P + S = T	TOTAL LIABILITIES & EQUITY

Current Liabilities: Accounts Payable

- **Accounts payable** are bills, generally to other companies for materials and equipment bought on credit, that the corporation must pay soon.

- When it receives materials, the corporation can either pay for them immediately with cash or wait and let what is owed become an **account payable**.

- Business-to-business transactions are most often done on credit. Common trade payment terms are usually 30 or 60 days with a discount for early payment like 2% off if paid within 10 days, or the total due in 30 days *("2% 10; net 30")*.

Balance Sheet Format
as of a specific date

	LIABILITIES & EQUITY
K	ACCOUNTS PAYABLE
L	ACCRUED EXPENSES
M	CURRENT PORTION OF DEBT
N	INCOME TAXES PAYABLE
K + L + M+ N = O	CURRENT LIABILITIES
P	LONG-TERM DEBT
Q	CAPITAL STOCK
R	RETAINED EARNINGS
Q - R = S	SHAREHOLDERS' EQUITY
O + P + S = T	TOTAL LIABILITIES & EQUITY

Current Liabilities: Accrued Expenses

- **Accrued expenses** are monetary obligations similar to accounts payable. The business uses one or the other classification depending on to whom the debt is owed.

- *Accounts payable* is used for debts to regular suppliers of merchandise or services bought on credit.

- Examples of **accrued expenses** are salaries earned by employees but not yet paid to them; lawyers' bills not yet paid; interest due but not yet paid on bank debt and so forth.

Balance Sheet Format
as of a specific date

	LIABILITIES & EQUITY
K	ACCOUNTS PAYABLE
L	ACCRUED EXPENSES
M	**CURRENT PORTION OF DEBT**
N	INCOME TAXES PAYABLE
K + L + M + N = O	CURRENT LIABILITIES
P	**LONG-TERM DEBT**
Q	CAPITAL STOCK
R	RETAINED EARNINGS
Q - R = S	SHAREHOLDERS' EQUITY
O + P + S = T	TOTAL LIABILITIES & EQUITY

Current Debt and Long Term Debt

- Any *notes payable* and the *current portion of long-term debt* are both components of current liabilities and are listed on the Balance Sheet under **current portion of debt.**

- If the enterprise owes money to a bank and the terms of the loan say it must be repaid in less than 12 months, then the debt is called a *note payable* and is a current liability.

- A loan with an overall term of more than 12 months from the date of the Balance Sheet is called **long-term debt.** A mortgage on a building is a common example.

  The so-called *current portion of long-term debt* is that amount due for payment within 12 months and is a current liability listed under **current portion of debt.**

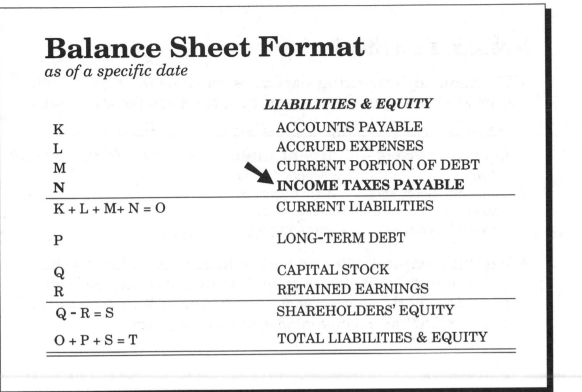

Balance Sheet Format
as of a specific date

	LIABILITIES & EQUITY
K	ACCOUNTS PAYABLE
L	ACCRUED EXPENSES
M	CURRENT PORTION OF DEBT
N	**INCOME TAXES PAYABLE**
K + L + M+ N = O	CURRENT LIABILITIES
P	LONG-TERM DEBT
Q	CAPITAL STOCK
R	RETAINED EARNINGS
Q − R = S	SHAREHOLDERS' EQUITY
O + P + S = T	TOTAL LIABILITIES & EQUITY

Current Liabilities: Taxes Payable

- Every time the company sells something and makes a profit on the sale, a percentage of the profit will be owed the government as *income taxes.*

- **Income taxes payable** are income taxes that the company owes the government but that the company has not yet paid.

- Every three months or so the company will send the government a check for the income taxes owed. For the time between when the profit was made and the time that the taxes are actually paid, the company will show the amount to be paid as **income taxes payable** on the Balance Sheet.

Working Capital

- The company's **working capital** is the amount of money left over after you subtract current liabilities from current assets.

"the good stuff"	*"the less good stuff"*	*"the great stuff"*
Current Assets -	**Current Liabilities** =	**Working Capital**
Cash	Accounts Payable	
Accounts Receivable	Accrued Expenses	
Inventory	Current Debt	
Prepaid Expenses	Taxes Payable	

- **Working capital** is the amount of money the enterprise has to "work with" in the *short-term*. **Working capital** feeds the operations of the enterprise with dollar bills. **Working capital** is also called *"net current assets"* or simply *"funds."*

Sources and Uses of Working Capital

- **Sources** of working capital are ways working capital *increases* in the normal course of business. This increase in working capital happens when:

   1. current liabilities decrease and/or
   2. current assets increase

- **Uses** of working capital (also called *applications*) are ways working capital *decreases* during the normal course of business. For example when:

   1. current assets decrease and/or
   2. current liabilities increase

- With lots of working capital it will be easy to pay your "current" financial obligations...bills that come due in the next 12 months.

Balance Sheet Format

as of a specific date

	LIABILITIES & EQUITY
K	**ACCOUNTS PAYABLE**
L	**ACCRUED EXPENSES**
M	**CURRENT PORTION OF DEBT**
N	**INCOME TAXES PAYABLE**
K + L + M + N = O	**CURRENT LIABILITIES**
P	**LONG-TERM DEBT**
Q	CAPITAL STOCK
R	RETAINED EARNINGS
Q - R = S	SHAREHOLDERS' EQUITY
O + P + S = T	TOTAL LIABILITIES & EQUITY

Total Liabilities

- A company's **total liabilities** are just the sum of its *current liabilities* and its *long-term debt*.

- *Long-term debt* is any loan to the company to be repaid more than 12 months after the date of the Balance Sheet.

  Common types of long-term debt include mortgages for land and buildings and so-called *chattel mortgages* for machinery and equipment.

- There is not a separate line for **total liabilities** in most Balance Sheet formats.

Balance Sheet Format
as of a specific date

	LIABILITIES & EQUITY
K	ACCOUNTS PAYABLE
L	ACCRUED EXPENSES
M	CURRENT PORTION OF DEBT
N	INCOME TAXES PAYABLE
K + L + M + N = O	CURRENT LIABILITIES
P	LONG-TERM DEBT
Q	CAPITAL STOCK
R	RETAINED EARNINGS
Q - R = S	**SHAREHOLDERS' EQUITY**
O + P + S = T	TOTAL LIABILITIES & EQUITY

Shareholders' Equity

- If you subtract what the company owes *(Total Liabilities)* from what it has *(Total Assets)* you are left with companies value to its owners...its **shareholders' equity.**

- **Shareholders' equity** has two components:

    1. *Capital Stock.* The original amount of money the owners contributed as their investment in the stock of the company.

    2. *Retained Earnings.* All the earnings of the company that have been retained, that is, not paid out as dividends to owners.

- Note: Both *"net worth"* and *"book value"* mean the same thing as **shareholders' equity.**

Balance Sheet Format
as of a specific date

	LIABILITIES & EQUITY
K	ACCOUNTS PAYABLE
L	ACCRUED EXPENSES
M	CURRENT PORTION OF DEBT
N	INCOME TAXES PAYABLE
K + L + M + N = O	CURRENT LIABILITIES
P	LONG-TERM DEBT
Q	**CAPITAL STOCK**
R	RETAINED EARNINGS
Q - R = S	SHAREHOLDERS' EQUITY
O + P + S = T	TOTAL LIABILITIES & EQUITY

Capital Stock

- The original money to start and any add-on money invested in the business is represented by shares of **capital stock** held by owners of the enterprise.

- So-called **common stock** is the regular *"denomination of ownership"* for all corporations. All companies issue common stock, but they may issue other kinds of stock, too.

- Companies often issue **preferred stock** that have certain contractual rights or *"preferences"* over the common stock. These rights may include a specified dividend and/or a preference over common stock to receive company assets if the company is liquidated.

Balance Sheet Format
as of a specific date

	LIABILITIES & EQUITY
K	ACCOUNTS PAYABLE
L	ACCRUED EXPENSES
M	CURRENT PORTION OF DEBT
N	INCOME TAXES PAYABLE
K + L + M + N = O	CURRENT LIABILITIES
P	LONG-TERM DEBT
Q	CAPITAL STOCK
R	**RETAINED EARNINGS**
Q - R = S	SHAREHOLDERS' EQUITY
O + P + S = T	TOTAL LIABILITIES & EQUITY

Retained Earnings

- All of the company's profits that have not been returned to the shareholders as dividends are called **retained earnings.**

  retained earnings = sum of all profits - sum of all dividends

- **Retained earnings** can be viewed as a *"pool"* of money from which future dividends could be paid. In fact, dividends cannot be paid to shareholders unless sufficient retained earnings are on the Balance Sheet to cover the total amount of the dividend checks.

- If the company has not made a profit but rather has sustained losses, it has *"negative retained earnings"* that are called its accumulated deficit.

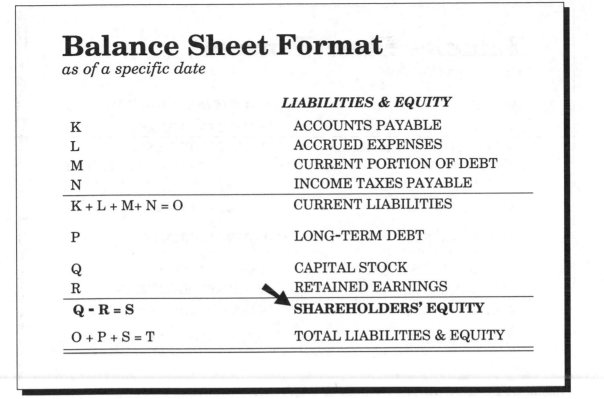

Balance Sheet Format
as of a specific date

	LIABILITIES & EQUITY
K	ACCOUNTS PAYABLE
L	ACCRUED EXPENSES
M	CURRENT PORTION OF DEBT
N	INCOME TAXES PAYABLE
K + L + M+ N = O	CURRENT LIABILITIES
P	LONG-TERM DEBT
Q	CAPITAL STOCK
R	RETAINED EARNINGS
Q - R = S	**SHAREHOLDERS' EQUITY**
O + P + S = T	TOTAL LIABILITIES & EQUITY

Changes in Shareholders' Equity

• **Shareholders' equity** is just the sum of the investment made in the stock of the company plus any profits (less any losses) minus any dividends that have been paid to shareholders.

• The value of **shareholders' equity** increases when the company: (1) *makes a profit,* thereby increasing retained earnings, or (2) *sells new stock* to investors, thereby increasing capital stock.

• The value of **shareholders' equity** decreases when the company: (1) *has a loss,* thereby lowering retained earnings, or (2) *pays dividends* to shareholders, thereby lowering retained earnings.

Balance Sheet Format
as of a specific date

ASSETS	LIABILITIES & EQUITY
CASH	ACCOUNTS PAYABLE
ACCOUNTS RECEIVABLE	ACCRUED EXPENSES
INVENTORY	CURRENT PORTION OF DEBT
PREPAID EXPENSES	INCOME TAXES PAYABLE
CURRENT ASSETS	CURRENT LIABILITIES
OTHER ASSETS	LONG-TERM DEBT
FIXED ASSETS AT COST	CAPITAL STOCK
ACCUMULATED DEPRECIATION	RETAINED EARNINGS
NET FIXED ASSETS	SHAREHOLDERS' EQUITY
TOTAL ASSETS	TOTAL LIABILITIES & EQUITY

Balance Sheet Summary

- The **Balance Sheet** presents the financial picture of the enterprise on one particular day, an instant in time.

    "have today" *"owe today"* *"worth today"*

    Assets = Liabilities + Shareholders' Equity

- By definition, this equation must always be *in balance* with assets equaling the sum of liabilities and equity.

- The **Balance Sheet** along with the **Income Statement** form the two major financial statements of the company.

Chapter 3. The Income Statement

One of the two main financial statements

of a business...the other is the *Balance Sheet.*

Income Statement Format

for the period x through y

NET SALES	A
COST OF GOODS	B
GROSS MARGIN	A - B = C
SALES & MARKETING	D
RESEARCH & DEVELOPMENT	E
GENERAL & ADMINISTRATIVE	F
OPERATING EXPENSES	D + E + F = G
INCOME FROM OPERATIONS	C - G = H
INTEREST INCOME	I
INCOME TAXES	J
NET INCOME	H + I - J = K

The Income Statement

- The **Income Statement** gives one important perspective on the health of a business—its *profitability*.

- Note: The **Income Statement** does not tell the whole picture about a company's financial health.

  The **Balance Sheet** reports on *assets, liabilities and equity*.

  The **Cash Flow Statement** reports on *cash movements*.

- Also note: The **Income Statement** says nothing about when the company receives cash or how much cash it has on hand.

The Income Statement (continued)

- The **Income Statement** reports on making and selling activities of a business *over a period of time:*

what's **sold** in the period

minus

what it **cost** to make

minus

selling & general **expenses** for the period

equals

income for the period.

- The **Income Statement** documents for a specific period (a month, quarter or year) the *second basic equation of accounting:*

Sales - Costs & Expenses = Income

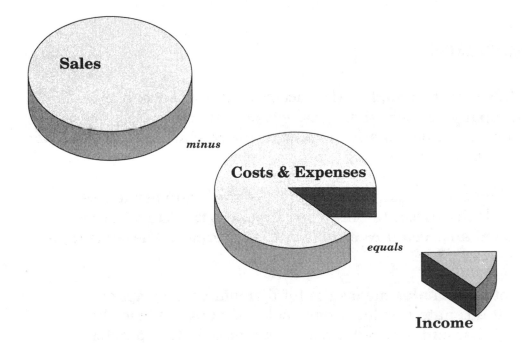

Income Statement Format
for the period x through y

NET SALES	A
COST OF GOODS	B
GROSS MARGIN	A - B = C
SALES & MARKETING	D
RESEARCH & DEVELOPMENT	E
GENERAL & ADMINISTRATIVE	F
OPERATING EXPENSES	D + E + F = G
INCOME FROM OPERATIONS	C - G = H
INTEREST INCOME	I
INCOME TAXES	J
NET INCOME	H + I - J = K

Net Sales

- **Sales** are recorded on the Income Statement when the company actually ships products to customers. Customers now have an obligation to pay for the product and the company has the right to collect.

- When the company ships a product to a customer it also sends an invoice (a bill). The company's right to collect is called an *account receivable* and is entered on the company's Balance Sheet.

- Note: **Net sales** means the total amount the company will ultimately collect from a sale—that is, list price less any discounts offered to the customer to induce purchase.

Sales vs. Orders

- A **sale** is made when the company actually ships a product to a customer. **Orders**, however, are something different.

- **Orders** become **sales** only when the products ordered have left the company's loading dock and are en route to the customer.

- When a **sale** is made, *income is generated* on the Income Statement. **Orders** only increase the "backlog" of products to be shipped and do not have an impact on the Income Statement in any way. Simply receiving an order does not result in income.

Costs

- **Costs** are expenditures for raw materials, workers' wages, manufacturing overhead and so forth. **Costs** are what you spend when you buy (or make) products for inventory.

- When this inventory is sold, that is, shipped to customers, its total **cost** is taken out of inventory and entered in the Income Statement as a special type of expense called *cost of goods sold.*

- **Costs** lower cash and increase inventory values on the Balance Sheet. Only when inventory is sold does its value move from the Balance Sheet to the Income Statement as *cost of goods sold.*

Income Statement Format

for the period x through y

NET SALES	A
COST OF GOODS	**B**
GROSS MARGIN	A - B = C
SALES & MARKETING	D
RESEARCH & DEVELOPMENT	E
GENERAL & ADMINISTRATIVE	F
OPERATING EXPENSES	D + E + F = G
INCOME FROM OPERATIONS	C - G = H
INTEREST INCOME	I
INCOME TAXES	J
NET INCOME	H + I - J = K

Cost of Goods Sold

- When a product is shipped and a sale is booked, the company records the total cost of manufacturing the product as **cost of goods sold** on the Income Statement.

- Remember: When the company made the product, it took all the product's costs and added them to the value of inventory.

- The costs to manufacture products are accumulated in inventory until the products are sold. Then these costs are *"expensed"* through the Income Statement as **cost of goods sold.**

Income Statement Format
for the period x through y

NET SALES	A
COST OF GOODS	B
GROSS MARGIN	**A - B = C**
SALES & MARKETING	D
RESEARCH & DEVELOPMENT	E
GENERAL & ADMINISTRATIVE	F
OPERATING EXPENSES	D + E + F = G
INCOME FROM OPERATIONS	C - G = H
INTEREST INCOME	I
INCOME TAXES	J
NET INCOME	H + I - J = K

Gross Margin

- **Gross margin** is the amount left over from sales after product manufacturing costs (cost of goods sold) are taken out. **Gross margin** is sometimes called *"gross profit"* or the company's *"manufacturing margin."*

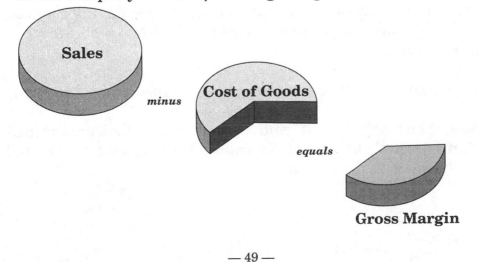

Sales *minus* Cost of Goods *equals* Gross Margin

Cost vs. Expense

- Two different terms, **cost** and **expense**, are used to describe how the company spends its money:

  Manufacturing expenditures to build inventories are called ***costs***.

  All other business expenditures are called ***expenses***.

- Note: Using the terms **"cost"** and **"expense"** correctly will make it easier to understand how the Income Statement and Balance Sheet work together.

- Also note: An *"expenditure"* can be either a cost or an expense. Expenditure simply means the use of cash to pay for an item purchased.

Expenses

- **Expenses** pay for developing and selling products and for running the "general and administrative" aspects of the business.

- Examples of **expenses** are paying legal fees; paying a sales person's salary; buying chemicals for the R&D laboratory and so forth.

- **Expenses** directly lower *income* on the Income Statement.

- Note: The words *"profit"* and *"income"* mean the same thing. That is, what's left over from sales after you have subtracted all the costs and expenses.

Income Statement Format

for the period x through y

NET SALES	A
COST OF GOODS	B
GROSS MARGIN	A − B = C
SALES & MARKETING	D
RESEARCH & DEVELOPMENT	E
GENERAL & ADMINISTRATIVE	F
OPERATING EXPENSES	**D + E + F = G**
INCOME FROM OPERATIONS	C − G = H
INTEREST INCOME	I
INCOME TAXES	J
NET INCOME	H + I − J = K

Operating Expenses

- **Operating expenses** are those expenditures (that is, cash out) that a company makes to generate income.

- Common groupings of **operating expense** are:
    1. Sales & Marketing expense,
    2. Research & Development ("R&D") expenses, and
    3. General & Administrative ("G&A") expenses.

- **Operating expenses** are also called "SG&A" expenses, meaning *"sales, general and administrative expense."*

Income or (Loss)

- If *sales* exceed *costs plus expenses* (as reported on the Income Statement), the business has earned **income.** If costs plus expenses exceed sales, then a **loss** has occurred.

- The terms *"income"* and *"profit"* and *"earnings"* all have the same meaning—what's left over when you subtract expenses plus costs from sales.

  Note: The Income Statement is often referred to as the *"Profit & Loss Statement,"* the *"Earnings Statement,"* or simply the *"P&L."*

- Remember: **Income** is the difference between two very large numbers: *sales* less *costs and expenses.* Slightly lower *sales* and/or slightly higher *costs and expenses* can eliminate any expected profit and result in a **loss**.

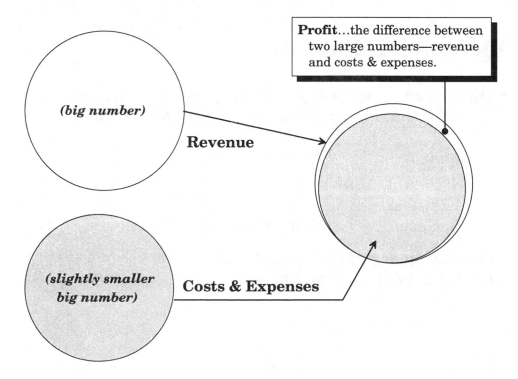

Profit...the difference between two large numbers—revenue and costs & expenses.

(big number)

Revenue

(slightly smaller big number)

Costs & Expenses

Income Statement Format

for the period x through y

NET SALES	A
COST OF GOODS	B
GROSS MARGIN	A - B = C
SALES & MARKETING	D
RESEARCH & DEVELOPMENT	E
GENERAL & ADMINISTRATIVE	F
OPERATING EXPENSES	D + E + F = G
INCOME FROM OPERATIONS	**C - G = H**
INTEREST INCOME	I
INCOME TAXES	J
NET INCOME	H + I - J = K

Income From Operations

- A manufacturing company's *operations* are all its actions taken in making and selling products, resulting in both expenses and costs. The term **income from operations** refers to what is left over after expenses and costs are subtracted from sales.

- Note: Companies can also generate income and have expenses from financial (non-operating) activities.

Income Statement Format

for the period x through y

NET SALES	A
COST OF GOODS	B
GROSS MARGIN	A - B = C
SALES & MARKETING	D
RESEARCH & DEVELOPMENT	E
GENERAL & ADMINISTRATIVE	F
OPERATING EXPENSES	D + E + F = G
INCOME FROM OPERATIONS	C - G = H
INTEREST INCOME	**I**
INCOME TAXES	**J**
NET INCOME	H + I - J = K

Non-operating Income & Expense

- Paying interest on a loan is a so-called **non-operating expense**. Likewise, receiving interest on cash balances in the company's bank account is **non-operating income.**

- Because it is from non-operating sources, interest income (or expense) is reported on the Income Statement just below the *Income from Operations* line. Likewise taxes.

- Note: A company's operations can be producing income but the company as a whole can still show an overall loss. This sad state of affairs comes about when **non-operating expenses** (such as very high interest expenses) exceed the total operating income.

Income Statement Format

for the period x through y

NET SALES	A
COST OF GOODS	B
GROSS MARGIN	A - B = C
SALES & MARKETING	D
RESEARCH & DEVELOPMENT	E
GENERAL & ADMINISTRATIVE	F
OPERATING EXPENSES	D + E + F = G
INCOME FROM OPERATIONS	C - G = H
INTEREST INCOME	I
INCOME TAXES	J
NET INCOME	**H + I - J = K**

Net Income

- **Income** is the difference between two large numbers: *(1) sales* and *(2) costs plus expenses*. More *costs plus expenses* than *sales* and the company will show a loss. Less *costs plus expenses* than sales and the company will show a profit.

- Remember: **Income** is not cash. In fact, a very profitable company with lots of **net income** can also be insolvent, that is with no cash left to pay its bills.

- Often rapidly growing companies are short of cash...even though they are highly profitable. They simply cannot supply out of earnings the capital required for such rapid growth.

Income Statement Format
for the period x through y

NET SALES	A
COST OF GOODS	B
GROSS MARGIN	A - B = C
SALES & MARKETING	D
RESEARCH & DEVELOPMENT	E
GENERAL & ADMINISTRATIVE	F
OPERATING EXPENSES	D + E + F = G
INCOME FROM OPERATIONS	C - G = H
INTEREST INCOME	I
INCOME TAXES	J
NET INCOME	H + I - J = K

Income *(Profits)* vs. Sales *(Revenue)*

- The words **income** and **revenue** are often confused. They mean very different things:

   "Profit" and *"income"* do mean the same thing.

   "Sales" and *"revenue"* do mean the same thing.

- **Income** (also called **profits**) is at the BOTTOM of the Income Statement. **Sales** (also called **revenue**) is at the TOP of the Income Statement.

- **Income** is often referred to as *the bottom line* because it is the last line of the Income Statement.

- **Sales** is often referred to as *the top line* because it is at the top of the Income Statement.

Income Statement Format

for the period x through y

NET SALES	A
COST OF GOODS	B
GROSS MARGIN	A - B = C
SALES & MARKETING	D
RESEARCH & DEVELOPMENT	E
GENERAL & ADMINISTRATIVE	F
OPERATING EXPENSES	D + E + F = G
INCOME FROM OPERATIONS	C - G = H
INTEREST INCOME	I
INCOME TAXES	J
NET INCOME	H + I - J = K

Income Statement Summary

- The **Income Statement** summarizes and displays the financial impact of:

   movement of goods to customers **(sales)**

   minus

   efforts to make and sell those goods **(costs and expenses)**

   equals

   any value created in the process **(income)**

- All business activities that generate income or result in a loss for a company—*that is, all transactions that change the value of shareholders' equity*—are recorded on the Income Statement.

Accrual Basis vs. Cash Basis

- The two major ways of running a company's books—**cash basis** or **accrual basis**—differ on when the company records expenses and income.

- If income is measured *when cash is received* and expenses are measured *when cash is spent*, the business is said to be operating on a **cash basis**.

- If income and expenses are measured *when the transactions occur*—regardless of the physical flow of cash—the business is said to be operating on an **accrual basis.**

Cash Basis

- **Cash basis** books are the simplest...functioning just like the proverbial cookie jar. When the books are on a **cash basis**, accounting transactions are triggered only by the movement of cash.

- With the books on a **cash basis**, the *Income Statement* and the *Cash Flow Statement* are the same.

- In general, people run their lives on a **cash basis** but most businesses run their books on an **accrual basis.** All businesses that maintain inventories of product for sale must use accrual accounting to report income...so says the IRS.

Accrual Basis

- In **accrual basis** accounting the Income Statement does not reflect the movement of cash, but rather, the generation of obligations (payables) to pay cash in the future.

- With **accrual basis** accounting, expenses occur when the company incurs the obligation to pay, not when it actually parts with the cash. In **accrual basis** accounting, sales and costs are recorded when the goods are shipped and customers incur the obligation to pay, not when they actually pay.

- For example, under **accrual basis** accounting you would lower your net worth when you use your charge card rather than when you ultimately paid the bill.

Income Statement & Balance Sheet

- The enterprise's **Income Statement** and **Balance Sheet** are inexorably linked:

  If the enterprise's **Income Statement** shows income, then retained earnings are *increased* on the **Balance Sheet.**

  Then, also, either the enterprise's *assets* must increase or its *liabilities* decrease for the **Balance Sheet** to remain in balance.

- Thus, the **Income Statement** shows for a period all the actions taken by the enterprise to either *increase assets* or *decrease liabilities* on the **Balance Sheet.**

Chapter 4. Cash Flow Statement

Where the company gets cash

...and whcre that cash goes

Cash Flow Statement Format
for the period x through y

BEGINNING CASH BALANCE	A
CASH RECEIPTS	B
CASH DISBURSEMENTS	C
CASH FROM OPERATIONS	B - C = D
FIXED ASSET PURCHASES	E
NET BORROWINGS	F
INCOME TAXES PAID	G
SALE OF STOCK	H
ENDING CASH BALANCE	A + D - E + F - G + H = I

Cash Flow Statement

- The **Cash Flow Statement** tracks the *movement of cash* through the business over a *period of time.*

- A company's **Cash Flow Statement** is just like a check register...recording all the company's transactions that use cash *(checks)* or supply cash *(deposits).*

- The **Cash Flow Statement** shows:

    cash on hand at the start of a period
    plus
    cash received in the period
    minus
    cash spent in the period
    equals
    cash on hand at the end of the period.

Cash Transactions

- So-called **cash transactions** affect cash flow. For example:

  Paying salaries lowers **cash.**
  Paying for equipment lowers **cash.**
  Paying off a loan lowers **cash.**

  Receiving money borrowed from a bank raises **cash.**
  Receiving money from investors for stock raises **cash.**
  Receiving money from customers raises **cash.**

- Notice the use of the words "paying" and "receive money" in those transactions where cash actually changes hands.

Non-cash Transactions

- So-called **non-cash transactions** are company activities where no cash moves into or out of the company's accounts. **Non-cash transactions** have no effect on the *Cash Flow Statement* but they can affect the *Income Statement* and *Balance Sheet*.

- Examples of **non-cash transactions** include: shipping product to a customer; receiving supplies from a vendor and receiving raw materials required to make the product.

- Note: Cash comes into the company when the customer pays for the product, not when the company ships it. Cash moves out of the company when it pays for materials, not when the company orders or receives them.

Cash Flow

- A **positive cash flow** for a period means that the company *has more cash at the end of the period than at the beginning.*

- A **negative cash flow** for a period means that the company has *less cash at the end of the period than at the beginning.*

- If a company has a continuing negative **cash flow**, it runs the risk of running out of cash and not being able to pay its bills when due—just another way of saying:

   broke...tapped-out...insolvent.

Sources and Uses of Cash

- **Cash** comes into the business (***sources***) in two major ways:
   1. *Operating activities* such as receiving payment from customers.
   2. *Financing activities* such as selling stock or borrowing money.

- **Cash** goes out of the business (***uses***) in four major ways:
   1. *Operating activities* such as paying suppliers and employees.
   2. *Financial activities* such as paying interest and principal on debt or paying dividends to shareholders.
   3. Making major *capital investments* in long-lived productive assets like machines.
   4. *Paying income taxes* to the government.

Cash Flow Statement Format
for the period x through y

BEGINNING CASH BALANCE	A
CASH RECEIPTS	B
CASH DISBURSEMENTS	C
CASH FROM OPERATIONS	**B - C = D**
FIXED ASSET PURCHASES	E
NET BORROWINGS	F
INCOME TAXES PAID	G
SALE OF STOCK	H
ENDING CASH BALANCE	A + D - E + F - G + H = I

Cash from Operations

- The normal day-to-day business activities (making and selling product) of a business are called its *"operations."*

- The Cash Flow Statement shows **cash from operations** separately from other cash flows.

- *Cash receipts* are inflows of money coming from operating the business.

- *Cash disbursements* are outflows of money used in operating the business.

- *Cash receipts* (money in) minus *cash disbursements* (money out) equals **cash from operations.**

Cash Flow Statement Format
for the period x through y

BEGINNING CASH BALANCE	A
CASH RECEIPTS	**B**
CASH DISBURSEMENTS	C
CASH FROM OPERATIONS	B - C = D
FIXED ASSET PURCHASES	E
NET BORROWINGS	F
INCOME TAXES PAID	G
SALE OF STOCK	H
ENDING CASH BALANCE	A + D - E + F - G + H = I

Cash Receipts

- **Cash receipts** (also called *collections* or simply *receipts)* come from collecting money from customers.

- **Cash receipts** increase the amount of cash the company has on hand.

  Note: Receiving cash from customers decreases the amount that is due the company as accounts receivable shown on the *Balance Sheet.*

- **Cash receipts** are not profits. Profits are something else altogether. Don't confuse the two. Profits are reported on the *Income Statement.*

Cash Flow Statement Format

for the period x through y

BEGINNING CASH BALANCE	A
CASH RECEIPTS	B
CASH DISBURSEMENTS	**C**
CASH FROM OPERATIONS	B - C = D
FIXED ASSET PURCHASES	E
NET BORROWINGS	F
INCOME TAXES PAID	G
SALE OF STOCK	H
ENDING CASH BALANCE	A + D - E + F - G + H = I

Cash Disbursements

- A **cash disbursement** is writing a check to pay for the rent, for inventory and supplies or for a worker's salary. **Cash disbursements** *lower* the amount of cash the company has on hand.

  Note: **Cash disbursements** (payments) to suppliers lower the amount the company owes as reported in *accounts payable* on the *Balance Sheet*.

- **Cash disbursements** are also called *payments* or simply *disbursements*.

Other elements of cash flow

- **Cash from operations** reports the flow of money into and out of the business from the making and selling of products.

- **Cash from operations** is a good measure of how well the enterprise is doing in its day-to-day business activities, its so-called *"operations."*

- But remember, **cash from operations** is just one of the important elements of cash flow. Other major cash flows are:

    1. *Investment in fixed assets* such as buying a manufacturing facility and machinery to make product.

    2. *Financial activities* such as selling stock to investors; borrowing money from banks, paying dividends; or paying taxes to the government.

Cash Flow Statement Format
for the period x through y

BEGINNING CASH BALANCE	A
CASH RECEIPTS	B
CASH DISBURSEMENTS	C
CASH FROM OPERATIONS	B - C = D
FIXED ASSET PURCHASES	**E**
NET BORROWINGS	F
INCOME TAXES PAID	G
SALE OF STOCK	H
ENDING CASH BALANCE	A + D - E + F - G + H = I

Fixed Asset Purchases

- Money spent to buy *property, plant and equipment* ("PP&E") is an investment in the long-term capability of the company to manufacture and sell product.

- Paying for PP&E is not considered part of operations and thus is not reported in *cash disbursements from operations*. Cash payments for PP&E are reported on a separate line on the Cash Flow Statement. PP&E purchases are *investments* in productive assets.

- Needless to say, after paying for PP&E the business has less cash. Cash is used when the PP&E is purchased originally. Note however, when the enterprise *depreciates* a fixed asset it does not use any cash at that time. No check is written to anyone.

Cash Flow Statement Format
for the period x through y

BEGINNING CASH BALANCE	A
CASH RECEIPTS	B
CASH DISBURSEMENTS	C
CASH FROM OPERATIONS	B - C = D
FIXED ASSET PURCHASES	E
NET BORROWINGS	F
INCOME TAXES PAID	G
SALE OF STOCK	H
ENDING CASH BALANCE	A + D - E + F - G + H = I

Net Borrowings

- Borrowing money *increases* the amount of cash the company has on hand.

- Conversely, paying back a loan *decreases* the company's supply of cash on hand.

- The difference between any new borrowings in a period and the amount paid back in the period is called **net borrowings**. **Net borrowings** are reported for the period on a separate line in the *Cash Flow Statement*.

Cash Flow Statement Format
for the period x through y

BEGINNING CASH BALANCE	A
CASH RECEIPTS	B
CASH DISBURSEMENTS	C
CASH FROM OPERATIONS	B - C = D
FIXED ASSET PURCHASES	E
NET BORROWINGS	F
INCOME TAXES PAID	G
SALE OF STOCK	H
ENDING CASH BALANCE	A + D - E + F - G + H = I

Income Taxes Paid

- Owing **income taxes** is different from paying them. The business owes some more **income tax** every time it sells something for a profit.

- But just owing taxes does not reduce cash; *only writing a check to the government and thus paying the taxes due actually reduces the company's cash on hand.*

- Paying **income taxes** to the government decreases the company's supply of cash. **Income taxes paid** are reported on the *Cash Flow Statement*.

Cash Flow Statement Format

for the period x through y

BEGINNING CASH BALANCE	A
CASH RECEIPTS	B
CASH DISBURSEMENTS	C
CASH FROM OPERATIONS	B - C = D
FIXED ASSET PURCHASES	E
NET BORROWINGS	F
INCOME TAXES PAID	G
SALE OF STOCK	**H**
ENDING CASH BALANCE	A + D - E + F - G + H = I

Sale of Stock: New Equity

- When people invest in a company's **stock** they exchange one piece of paper for another: real U.S. currency for a fancy stock certificate.

- When a company sells **stock** to investors, it receives money and increases the amount of cash it has on hand.

- Selling **stock** is the closest thing to *printing money* that a company can do...and it's perfectly legal—unless you mislead widows and orphans as to the real value of the **stock**, in which case the S.E.C. (U.S. Securities and Exchange Commission) will send you to jail. Really.

Cash Flow Statement Format

for the period x through y

BEGINNING CASH BALANCE	A
CASH RECEIPTS	B
CASH DISBURSEMENTS	C
CASH FROM OPERATIONS	B - C = D
FIXED ASSET PURCHASES	E
NET BORROWINGS	F
INCOME TAXES PAID	G
SALE OF STOCK	H
ENDING CASH BALANCE	A + D - E + F - G + H = I

Ending Cash Balance

- The beginning cash balance at the start of the period plus or minus all cash transactions that took place during the period equals the **ending cash balance.**

- Thus: *beginning* **cash** *on hand*

    plus **cash** *received*

    minus **cash** *spent*

    equals ending **cash** *on hand.*

Cash Flow Statement Format
for the period x through y

BEGINNING CASH BALANCE	A
CASH RECEIPTS	B
CASH DISBURSEMENTS	C
CASH FROM OPERATIONS	B - C = D
FIXED ASSET PURCHASES	E
NET BORROWINGS	F
INCOME TAXES PAID	G
SALE OF STOCK	H
ENDING CASH BALANCE	A + D - E + F - G + H = I

Cash Flow Statement Summary

- Think of the company's **Cash Flow Statement** as a check register reporting all the company's payments *(cash outflows)* and deposits *(cash inflows)* for a period of time.

- If no actual cash changes hands in a particular transaction, then the **Cash Flow Statement** is not changed.

  Note, however, that the *Balance Sheet* and *Income Statement* may be changed by a *noncash transaction*.

  Note also that cash transactions—those reported on the **Cash Flow Statement**—usually do have some effect on the *Income Statement* and *Balance Sheet* as well.

Chapter 5. Connections

These pages will begin our formal study of how the three major financial statements interact...how they work in concert to give a true picture of the enterprise's financial health.

In the prior chapters, we studied separately the vocabulary and structure of each of the three main financial statements. What follows here is an opportunity to put the statements together as a financial reporting tool. We will see how the *Income Statement* relates to the *Balance Sheet* and vice versa and how changes to each can effect the *Cash Flow Statement*.

Remember the fundamental reporting function of each of the three main financial statements:

1. *The Income Statement* shows the manufacturing and selling actions of the enterprise that result in profit or loss.
2. *The Cash Flow Statement* details the movements of cash into and out of the coffers of the enterprise.
3. *The Balance Sheet* records what the company owns and what it owes, including the owner's stake.

Each statement views the enterprise's financial health from a different—and very necessary—perspective. And also, each statement relates to the other two. Review these examples of the natural "connections" between the three financial statements.

Balance Sheet Connections. First shown are several structural connections between the Balance Sheet and the other two statements.

Sales Cycle. Next shown is the sales cycle describing those repeating financial statement entries that the company must make in order to report a sale and receive payment.

Expense Cycle. Then follows the documenting entries for SG&A expenses and their subsequent payment.

Investment Cycle. Next shown are the connection entries relating to the investment of capital and debt.

Asset Purchase/Depreciation. Last shown are entries for asset purchase and depreciation.

~

Here is a hint for you as you study the following connections pages: Watch the reporting of two things entering or leaving the business (and the statements):

1. *Watch the flow of cash money.*
2. *Watch the flow of goods and services.*

Fundamentally, the financial statements document the movement of cash and the movement of goods and services into and out of the enterprise. That is all that financial statements are about. It is no more complicated. Everything else is in the details. Don't sweat the details.

Read on. We're making real progress.

Income Statement
for the period

	1	NET SALES	$3,055,560
	2	COST OF GOODS SOLD	2,005,830
1 - 2 = 3		GROSS MARGIN	1,049,730
	4	SALES & MARKETING	328,523
	5	RESEARCH & DEVELOPMENT	26,000
	6	GENERAL & ADMINISTRATIVE	203,520
4 + 5 + 6 = 7		OPERATING EXPENSE	558,043
3 - 7 = 8		INCOME FROM OPERATIONS	491,687
	9	NET INTEREST INCOME	(100,000)
	10	INCOME TAXES	139,804
8 + 9 - 10 = 11		NET INCOME	$251,883

Cash Flow Statement
for the period

	a	BEGINNING CASH BALANCE	$155,000
	b	CASH RECEIPTS	2,584,900
	c	CASH DISBURSEMENTS	2,796,438
b - c = d		CASH FLOW FROM OPERATIONS	(211,538)
	e	PP&E PURCHASE	1,750,000
	f	NET BORROWINGS	900,000
	g	INCOME TAXES PAID	0
	h	SALE OF CAPITAL STOCK	1,550,000
a + d - e + f - g + h = i		ENDING CASH BALANCES	$643,462

> **Balance Sheet Connections**

> **ENDING CASH** on the *Cash Flow Statement* always equals **CASH** on the *Balance Sheet.*

Balance Sheet
as of period end

	A	CASH	$643,462
	B	ACCOUNTS RECEIVABLE	454,760
	C	INVENTORIES	414,770
	D	PREPAID EXPENSES	0
A + B + C + D = E		CURRENT ASSETS	1,512,992
	F	OTHER ASSETS	0
	G	FIXED ASSETS @ COST	1,750,000
	H	ACCUMULATED DEPRECIATION	78,573
G - H = I		NET FIXED ASSETS	1,671,427
E + F + I = J		TOTAL ASSETS	$3,184,419
	K	ACCOUNTS PAYABLE	$236,297
	L	ACCRUED EXPENSES	26,435
	M	CURRENT PORTION OF DEBT	100,000
	N	INCOME TAXES PAYABLE	139,804
K + L + M + N = O		CURRENT LIABILITIES	502,536
	P	LONG-TERM DEBT	800,000
	Q	CAPITAL STOCK	1,550,000
	R	RETAINED EARNINGS	331,883
Q + R = S		SHAREHOLDERS' EQUITY	1,881,883
O + P + S = T		TOTAL LIABILITIES & EQUITY	$3,184,419

> According to the basic equation of accounting, **TOTAL ASSETS** equals **TOTAL LIABILITIES** plus **SHAREHOLDERS' EQUITY.** Then by definition, the *Balance Sheet* must always be "in balance."

Income Statement
for the period

1	NET SALES	$3,055,560
2	COST OF GOODS SOLD	2,005,830
1 - 2 = 3	GROSS MARGIN	1,049,730
4	SALES & MARKETING	328,523
5	RESEARCH & DEVELOPMENT	26,000
6	GENERAL & ADMINISTRATIVE	203,520
4 + 5 + 6 = 7	OPERATING EXPENSE	558,043
3 - 7 = 8	INCOME FROM OPERATIONS	491,687
9	NET INTEREST INCOME	(100,000)
10	INCOME TAXES	139,804
8 + 9 - 10 = 11	NET INCOME	$251,883

Cash Flow Statement
for the period

a	BEGINNING CASH BALANCE	$155,000
b	CASH RECEIPTS	2,584,900
c	CASH DISBURSEMENTS	2,796,438
b - c = d	CASH FLOW FROM OPERATIONS	(211,538)
e	PP&E PURCHASE	1,750,000
f	NET BORROWINGS	900,000
g	INCOME TAXES PAID	0
h	SALE OF CAPITAL STOCK	1,550,000
a + d - e + f - g + h = i	ENDING CASH BALANCES	$643,462

> **Balance Sheet Connections**

Balance Sheet
as of period end

A	CASH	$643,462
B	ACCOUNTS RECEIVABLE	454,760
C	INVENTORIES	414,770
D	PREPAID EXPENSES	0
A + B + C + D = E	CURRENT ASSETS	1,512,992
F	OTHER ASSETS	0
G	FIXED ASSETS @ COST	1,750,000
H	ACCUMULATED DEPRECIATION	78,573
G - H = I	NET FIXED ASSETS	1,671,427
E + F + I = J	TOTAL ASSETS	$3,184,419
K	ACCOUNTS PAYABLE	$236,297
L	ACCRUED EXPENSES	26,435
M	CURRENT PORTION OF DEBT	100,000
N	INCOME TAXES PAYABLE	139,804
K + L + M + N = O	CURRENT LIABILITIES	502,536
P	LONG-TERM DEBT	800,000
Q	CAPITAL STOCK	1,550,000
R	RETAINED EARNINGS	331,883
Q + R = S	SHAREHOLDERS' EQUITY	1,881,883
O + P + S = T	TOTAL LIABILITIES & EQUITY	$3,184,419

> For the *Balance Sheet* to stay "in balance," when you **subtract** from an asset account, you must also...

> ...either **add** the same amount to another asset account
> **or**
> **subtract** it from a liability account.

Income Statement

for the period

1		NET SALES	$3,055,560
2		COST OF GOODS SOLD	2,005,830
1 - 2 = 3		GROSS MARGIN	1,049,730
4		SALES & MARKETING	328,523
5		RESEARCH & DEVELOPMENT	26,000
6		GENERAL & ADMINISTRATIVE	203,520
4 + 5 + 6 = 7		OPERATING EXPENSE	558,043
3 - 7 = 8		INCOME FROM OPERATIONS	491,687
9		NET INTEREST INCOME	(100,000)
10		INCOME TAXES	139,804
8 + 9 - 10 = 11		NET INCOME	$251,883

Cash Flow Statement

for the period

a		BEGINNING CASH BALANCE	$155,000
b		CASH RECEIPTS	2,584,900
c		CASH DISBURSEMENTS	2,796,438
b - c = d		CASH FLOW FROM OPERATIONS	(211,538)
e		PP&E PURCHASE	1,750,000
f		NET BORROWINGS	900,000
g		INCOME TAXES PAID	0
h		SALE OF CAPITAL STOCK	1,550,000
a + d - e + f - g + h = i		ENDING CASH BALANCES	$643,462

Balance Sheet

as of period end

A		CASH	$643,462
B		ACCOUNTS RECEIVABLE	454,760
C		INVENTORIES	414,770
D		PREPAID EXPENSES	0
A + B + C + D = E		CURRENT ASSETS	1,512,992
F		OTHER ASSETS	0
G		FIXED ASSETS @ COST	1,750,000
H		ACCUMULATED DEPRECIATION	78,573
G - H = I		NET FIXED ASSETS	1,671,427
E + F + I = J		TOTAL ASSETS	$3,184,419
K		ACCOUNTS PAYABLE	$236,297
L		ACCRUED EXPENSES	26,435
M		CURRENT PORTION OF DEBT	100,000
N		INCOME TAXES PAYABLE	139,804
K + L + M + N = O		CURRENT LIABILITIES	502,536
P		LONG-TERM DEBT	800,000
Q		CAPITAL STOCK	1,550,000
R		RETAINED EARNINGS	331,883
Q + R = S		SHAREHOLDERS' EQUITY	1,881,883
O + P + S = T		TOTAL LIABILITIES & EQUITY	$3,184,419

Balance Sheet Connections

NET INCOME from the *Income Statement* is added to RETAINED EARNINGS on the Balance Sheet and thus SHAREHOLDERS' EQUITY increases.

Income Statement
for the period

1	NET SALES	$3,055,560	
2	COST OF GOODS SOLD	2,005,830	
1 - 2 = 3	GROSS MARGIN	1,049,730	
4	SALES & MARKETING	328,523	
5	RESEARCH & DEVELOPMENT	26,000	
6	GENERAL & ADMINISTRATIVE	203,520	
4 + 5 + 6 = 7	OPERATING EXPENSE	558,043	
3 - 7 = 8	INCOME FROM OPERATIONS	491,687	
9	NET INTEREST INCOME	(100,000)	
10	INCOME TAXES	139,804	
8 + 9 - 10 = 11	NET INCOME	$251,883	

❶ Sales Cycle

When a sale is made on credit, NET SALES increases at the top of the *Income Statement* and ACCOUNTS RECEIVABLE increases on the *Balance Sheet* by the same amount.

Cash Flow Statement
for the period

a	BEGINNING CASH BALANCE	$155,000
b	CASH RECEIPTS	2,584,900
c	CASH DISBURSEMENTS	2,796,438
b - c = d	CASH FLOW FROM OPERATIONS	(211,538)
e	PP&E PURCHASE	1,750,000
f	NET BORROWINGS	900,000
g	INCOME TAXES PAID	0
h	SALE OF CAPITAL STOCK	1,550,000
a + d - e + f - g + h = i	ENDING CASH BALANCES	$643,462

Balance Sheet
as of period end

A	CASH	$643,462
B	ACCOUNTS RECEIVABLE	454,760
C	INVENTORIES	414,770
D	PREPAID EXPENSES	0
A + B + C + D = E	CURRENT ASSETS	1,512,992
F	OTHER ASSETS	0
G	FIXED ASSETS @ COST	1,750,000
H	ACCUMULATED DEPRECIATION	78,573
G - H = I	NET FIXED ASSETS	1,671,427
E + F + I = J	TOTAL ASSETS	$3,184,419
K	ACCOUNTS PAYABLE	$236,297
L	ACCRUED EXPENSES	26,435
M	CURRENT PORTION OF DEBT	100,000
N	INCOME TAXES PAYABLE	139,804
K + L + M + N = O	CURRENT LIABILITIES	502,536
P	LONG-TERM DEBT	800,000
Q	CAPITAL STOCK	1,550,000
R	RETAINED EARNINGS	331,883
Q + R = S	SHAREHOLDERS' EQUITY	1,881,883
O + P + S = T	TOTAL LIABILITIES & EQUITY	$3,184,419

Income Statement
for the period

1	NET SALES	$3,055,560
2	COST OF GOODS SOLD	2,005,830
1 - 2 = 3	GROSS MARGIN	1,049,730
4	SALES & MARKETING	328,523
5	RESEARCH & DEVELOPMENT	26,000
6	GENERAL & ADMINISTRATIVE	203,520
4 + 5 + 6 = 7	OPERATING EXPENSE	558,043
3 - 7 = 8	INCOME FROM OPERATIONS	491,687
9	NET INTEREST INCOME	(100,000)
10	INCOME TAXES	139,804
8 + 9 - 10 = 11	NET INCOME	$251,883

2

Sales Cycle
When a sale is made, product value is moved from **INVENTORY** on the *Balance Sheet* to **COST OF GOODS** on the *Income Statement*.

Cash Flow Statement
for the period

a	BEGINNING CASH BALANCE	$155,000
b	CASH RECEIPTS	2,584,900
c	CASH DISBURSEMENTS	2,796,438
b - c = d	CASH FLOW FROM OPERATIONS	(211,538)
e	PP&E PURCHASE	1,750,000
f	NET BORROWINGS	900,000
g	INCOME TAXES PAID	0
h	SALE OF CAPITAL STOCK	1,550,000
a + d - e + f - g + h = i	ENDING CASH BALANCES	$643,462

Balance Sheet
as of period end

A	CASH	$643,462
B	ACCOUNTS RECEIVABLE	454,760
C	INVENTORIES	414,770
D	PREPAID EXPENSES	0
A + B + C + D = E	CURRENT ASSETS	1,512,992
F	OTHER ASSETS	0
G	FIXED ASSETS @ COST	1,750,000
H	ACCUMULATED DEPRECIATION	78,573
G - H = I	NET FIXED ASSETS	1,671,427
E + F + I = J	TOTAL ASSETS	$3,184,419
K	ACCOUNTS PAYABLE	$236,297
L	ACCRUED EXPENSES	26,435
M	CURRENT PORTION OF DEBT	100,000
N	INCOME TAXES PAYABLE	139,804
K + L + M + N = O	CURRENT LIABILITIES	502,536
P	LONG-TERM DEBT	800,000
Q	CAPITAL STOCK	1,550,000
R	RETAINED EARNINGS	331,883
Q + R = S	SHAREHOLDERS' EQUITY	1,881,883
O + P + S = T	TOTAL LIABILITIES & EQUITY	$3,184,419

Income Statement
for the period

1	NET SALES	$3,055,560
2	COST OF GOODS SOLD	2,005,830
1 - 2 = 3	GROSS MARGIN	1,049,730
4	SALES & MARKETING	328,523
5	RESEARCH & DEVELOPMENT	26,000
6	GENERAL & ADMINISTRATIVE	203,520
4 + 5 + 6 = 7	OPERATING EXPENSE	558,043
3 - 7 = 8	INCOME FROM OPERATIONS	491,687
9	NET INTEREST INCOME	(100,000)
10	INCOME TAXES	139,804
8 + 9 - 10 = 11	NET INCOME	$251,883

Cash Flow Statement
for the period

a	BEGINNING CASH BALANCE	$155,000
b	CASH RECEIPTS	2,584,900
c	CASH DISBURSEMENTS	2,796,438
b - c = d	CASH FLOW FROM OPERATIONS	(211,538)
e	PP&E PURCHASE	1,750,000
f	NET BORROWINGS	900,000
g	INCOME TAXES PAID	0
h	SALE OF CAPITAL STOCK	1,550,000
a + d - e + f - g + h = i	ENDING CASH BALANCES	$643,462

3 Sales Cycle
When the customer pays for products shipped, the **ACCOUNT RECEIVABLE** on the *Balance Sheet* becomes a **CASH RECEIPT** in the *Cash Flow Statement*.

Balance Sheet
as of period end

A	CASH	$643,462
B	ACCOUNTS RECEIVABLE	454,760
C	INVENTORIES	414,770
D	PREPAID EXPENSES	0
A + B + C + D = E	CURRENT ASSETS	1,512,992
F	OTHER ASSETS	0
G	FIXED ASSETS @ COST	1,750,000
H	ACCUMULATED DEPRECIATION	78,573
G - H = I	NET FIXED ASSETS	1,671,427
E + F + I = J	TOTAL ASSETS	$3,184,419
K	ACCOUNTS PAYABLE	$236,297
L	ACCRUED EXPENSES	26,435
M	CURRENT PORTION OF DEBT	100,000
N	INCOME TAXES PAYABLE	139,804
K + L + M + N = O	CURRENT LIABILITIES	502,536
P	LONG-TERM DEBT	800,000
Q	CAPITAL STOCK	1,550,000
R	RETAINED EARNINGS	331,883
Q + R = S	SHAREHOLDERS' EQUITY	1,881,883
O + P + S = T	TOTAL LIABILITIES & EQUITY	$3,184,419

Income Statement

for the period

	1	NET SALES	$3,055,560
	2	COST OF GOODS SOLD	2,005,830
1 - 2 = 3		GROSS MARGIN	1,049,730
	4	SALES & MARKETING	328,523
	5	RESEARCH & DEVELOPMENT	26,000
	6	GENERAL & ADMINISTRATIVE	203,520
4 + 5 + 6 = 7		OPERATING EXPENSE	558,043
3 - 7 = 8		INCOME FROM OPERATIONS	491,687
	9	NET INTEREST INCOME	(100,000)
	10	INCOME TAXES	139,804
8 + 9 - 10 = 11		NET INCOME	$251,883 ↑

Cash Flow Statement

for the period

	a	BEGINNING CASH BALANCE	$155,000
	b	CASH RECEIPTS	2,584,900
	c	CASH DISBURSEMENTS	2,796,438
b - c = d		CASH FLOW FROM OPERATIONS	(211,538)
	e	PP&E PURCHASE	1,750,000
	f	NET BORROWINGS	900,000
	g	INCOME TAXES PAID	0
	h	SALE OF CAPITAL STOCK	1,550,000
a + d - e + f - g + h = i		ENDING CASH BALANCES	$643,462

> **4** **Sales Cycle**
> When a sale is entered
> on the *Income Statement*
> **NET INCOME (LOSS)** is
> generated and is added
> to **RETAINED EARNINGS**
> on the Balance Sheet.

Balance Sheet

as of period end

	A	CASH	$643,462
	B	ACCOUNTS RECEIVABLE	454,760
	C	INVENTORIES	414,770
	D	PREPAID EXPENSES	0
A + B + C + D = E		CURRENT ASSETS	1,512,992
	F	OTHER ASSETS	0
	G	FIXED ASSETS @ COST	1,750,000
	H	ACCUMULATED DEPRECIATION	78,573
G - H = I		NET FIXED ASSETS	1,671,427
E + F + I = J		TOTAL ASSETS	$3,184,419
	K	ACCOUNTS PAYABLE	$236,297
	L	ACCRUED EXPENSES	26,435
	M	CURRENT PORTION OF DEBT	100,000
	N	INCOME TAXES PAYABLE	139,804
K + L + M + N = O		CURRENT LIABILITIES	502,536
	P	LONG-TERM DEBT	800,000
	Q	CAPITAL STOCK	1,550,000
	R	RETAINED EARNINGS	331,883 ↑
Q + R = S		SHAREHOLDERS' EQUITY	1,881,883
O + P + S = T		TOTAL LIABILITIES & EQUITY	$3,184,419

Income Statement

for the period

1	NET SALES	$3,055,560	
2	COST OF GOODS SOLD	2,005,830	
1 - 2 = 3	GROSS MARGIN	1,049,730	
4	SALES & MARKETING	328,523	⬆
5	RESEARCH & DEVELOPMENT	26,000	⬆
6	GENERAL & ADMINISTRATIVE	203,520	⬆
4 + 5 + 6 = 7	OPERATING EXPENSE	558,043	
3 - 7 = 8	INCOME FROM OPERATIONS	491,687	
9	NET INTEREST INCOME	(100,000)	
10	INCOME TAXES	139,804	
8 + 9 - 10 = 11	NET INCOME	$251,883	⬇

Cash Flow Statement

for the period

a	BEGINNING CASH BALANCE	$155,000
b	CASH RECEIPTS	2,584,900
c	CASH DISBURSEMENTS	2,796,438
b - c = d	CASH FLOW FROM OPERATIONS	(211,538)
e	PP&E PURCHASE	1,750,000
f	NET BORROWINGS	900,000
g	INCOME TAXES PAID	0
h	SALE OF CAPITAL STOCK	1,550,000
a + d - e + f - g + h = i	ENDING CASH BALANCES	$643,462

Balance Sheet

as of period end

A	CASH	$643,462	
B	ACCOUNTS RECEIVABLE	454,760	
C	INVENTORIES	414,770	
D	PREPAID EXPENSES	0	
A + B + C + D = E	CURRENT ASSETS	1,512,992	
F	OTHER ASSETS	0	
G	FIXED ASSETS @ COST	1,750,000	
H	ACCUMULATED DEPRECIATION	78,573	
G - H = I	NET FIXED ASSETS	1,671,427	
E + F + I = J	TOTAL ASSETS	$3,184,419	
K	ACCOUNTS PAYABLE	$236,297	⬆
L	ACCRUED EXPENSES	26,435	
M	CURRENT PORTION OF DEBT	100,000	
N	INCOME TAXES PAYABLE	139,804	
K + L + M + N = O	CURRENT LIABILITIES	502,536	
P	LONG-TERM DEBT	800,000	
Q	CAPITAL STOCK	1,550,000	
R	RETAINED EARNINGS	331,883	⬇
Q + R = S	SHAREHOLDERS' EQUITY	1,881,883	
O + P + S = T	TOTAL LIABILITIES & EQUITY	$3,184,419	

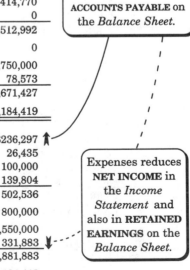

❶ Expense Cycle
EXPENSES, when incurred and entered in the *Income Statement,* become **ACCOUNTS PAYABLE** on the *Balance Sheet.*

Expenses reduces **NET INCOME** in the *Income Statement* and also in **RETAINED EARNINGS** on the *Balance Sheet.*

Income Statement
for the period

	1	NET SALES	$3,055,560
	2	COST OF GOODS SOLD	2,005,830
1 - 2 = 3		GROSS MARGIN	1,049,730
	4	SALES & MARKETING	328,523
	5	RESEARCH & DEVELOPMENT	26,000
	6	GENERAL & ADMINISTRATIVE	203,520
4 + 5 + 6 = 7		OPERATING EXPENSE	558,043
3 - 7 = 8		INCOME FROM OPERATIONS	491,687
	9	NET INTEREST INCOME	(100,000)
	10	INCOME TAXES	139,804
8 + 9 - 10 = 11		NET INCOME	$251,883

Cash Flow Statement
for the period

	a	BEGINNING CASH BALANCE	$155,000
	b	CASH RECEIPTS	2,584,900
	c	CASH DISBURSEMENTS	2,796,438
b - c = d		CASH FLOW FROM OPERATIONS	(211,538)
	e	PP&E PURCHASE	1,750,000
	f	NET BORROWINGS	900,000
	g	INCOME TAXES PAID	0
	h	SALE OF CAPITAL STOCK	1,550,000
a + d - e + f - g + h = i		ENDING CASH BALANCES	$643,462

Balance Sheet
as of period end

	A	CASH	$643,462
	B	ACCOUNTS RECEIVABLE	454,760
	C	INVENTORIES	414,770
	D	PREPAID EXPENSES	0
A + B + C + D = E		CURRENT ASSETS	1,512,992
	F	OTHER ASSETS	0
	G	FIXED ASSETS @ COST	1,750,000
	H	ACCUMULATED DEPRECIATION	78,573
G - H = I		NET FIXED ASSETS	1,671,427
E + F + I = J		TOTAL ASSETS	$3,184,419
	K	ACCOUNTS PAYABLE	$236,297
	L	ACCRUED EXPENSES	26,435
	M	CURRENT PORTION OF DEBT	100,000
	N	INCOME TAXES PAYABLE	139,804
K + L + M + N = O		CURRENT LIABILITIES	502,536
	P	LONG-TERM DEBT	800,000
	Q	CAPITAL STOCK	1,550,000
	R	RETAINED EARNINGS	331,883
Q + R = S		SHAREHOLDERS' EQUITY	1,881,883
O + P + S = T		TOTAL LIABILITIES & EQUITY	$3,184,419

2

Expense Cycle
When paid, ACCOUNTS PAYABLE on the *Balance Sheet* become CASH DISBURSEMENTS and lower CASH.

Income Statement

for the period

	1	NET SALES	$3,055,560
	2	COST OF GOODS SOLD	2,005,830
1 - 2 = 3		GROSS MARGIN	1,049,730
	4	SALES & MARKETING	328,523
	5	RESEARCH & DEVELOPMENT	26,000
	6	GENERAL & ADMINISTRATIVE	203,520
4 + 5 + 6 = 7		OPERATING EXPENSE	558,043
3 - 7 = 8		INCOME FROM OPERATIONS	491,687
	9	NET INTEREST INCOME	(100,000)
	10	INCOME TAXES	139,804
8 + 9 - 10 = 11		NET INCOME	$251,883

Cash Flow Statement

for the period

	a	BEGINNING CASH BALANCE	$155,000
	b	CASH RECEIPTS	2,584,900
	c	CASH DISBURSEMENTS	2,796,438
b - c = d		CASH FLOW FROM OPERATIONS	(211,538)
	e	PP&E PURCHASE	1,750,000
	f	NET BORROWINGS	900,000 ⬆
	g	INCOME TAXES PAID	0
	h	SALE OF CAPITAL STOCK	1,550,000
a + d - e + f - g + h = i		ENDING CASH BALANCES	$643,462 ⬆

① Investment Cycle

NET BORROWINGS, when entered on the *Cash Flow Statement,* increase both CASH and DEBT on the *Balance Sheet.*

Balance Sheet

as of period end

	A	CASH	$643,462 ⬆
	B	ACCOUNTS RECEIVABLE	454,760
	C	INVENTORIES	414,770
	D	PREPAID EXPENSES	0
A + B + C + D = E		CURRENT ASSETS	1,512,992
	F	OTHER ASSETS	0
	G	FIXED ASSETS @ COST	1,750,000
	H	ACCUMULATED DEPRECIATION	78,573
G - H = I		NET FIXED ASSETS	1,671,427
E + F + I = J		TOTAL ASSETS	$3,184,419
	K	ACCOUNTS PAYABLE	$236,297
	L	ACCRUED EXPENSES	26,435
	M	CURRENT PORTION OF DEBT	100,000 ⬆
	N	INCOME TAXES PAYABLE	139,804
K + L + M + N = O		CURRENT LIABILITIES	502,536
	P	LONG-TERM DEBT	800,000 ⬆
	Q	CAPITAL STOCK	1,550,000
	R	RETAINED EARNINGS	331,883
Q + R = S		SHAREHOLDERS' EQUITY	1,881,883
O + P + S = T		TOTAL LIABILITIES & EQUITY	$3,184,419

Repayment in *less* than one year

or

Repayment in *more* than one year

Income Statement
for the period

1		NET SALES	$3,055,560
2		COST OF GOODS SOLD	2,005,830
1 - 2 = 3		GROSS MARGIN	1,049,730
4		SALES & MARKETING	328,523
5		RESEARCH & DEVELOPMENT	26,000
6		GENERAL & ADMINISTRATIVE	203,520
4 + 5 + 6 = 7		OPERATING EXPENSE	558,043
3 - 7 = 8		INCOME FROM OPERATIONS	491,687
9		NET INTEREST INCOME	(100,000)
10		INCOME TAXES	139,804
8 + 9 - 10 = 11		NET INCOME	$251,883

Cash Flow Statement
for the period

a		BEGINNING CASH BALANCE	$155,000
b		CASH RECEIPTS	2,584,900
c		CASH DISBURSEMENTS	2,796,438
b - c = d		CASH FLOW FROM OPERATIONS	(211,538)
e		PP&E PURCHASE	1,750,000
f		NET BORROWINGS	900,000
g		INCOME TAXES PAID	0
h		SALE OF CAPITAL STOCK	1,550,000 ↑
a + d - e + f - g + h = i		ENDING CASH BALANCES	$643,462 ↑

❷ Investment Cycle
Selling stock increases both **CASH** and **CAPITAL STOCK** on the *Balance Sheet*.

Balance Sheet
as of period end

A		CASH	$643,462 ↑
B		ACCOUNTS RECEIVABLE	454,760
C		INVENTORIES	414,770
D		PREPAID EXPENSES	0
A + B + C + D = E		CURRENT ASSETS	1,512,992
F		OTHER ASSETS	0
G		FIXED ASSETS @ COST	1,750,000
H		ACCUMULATED DEPRECIATION	78,573
G - H = I		NET FIXED ASSETS	1,671,427
E + F + I = J		TOTAL ASSETS	$3,184,419
K		ACCOUNTS PAYABLE	$236,297
L		ACCRUED EXPENSES	26,435
M		CURRENT PORTION OF DEBT	100,000
N		INCOME TAXES PAYABLE	139,804
K + L + M + N = O		CURRENT LIABILITIES	502,536
P		LONG-TERM DEBT	800,000
Q		CAPITAL STOCK	1,550,000 ↑
R		RETAINED EARNINGS	331,883
Q + R = S		SHAREHOLDERS' EQUITY	1,881,883
O + P + S = T		TOTAL LIABILITIES & EQUITY	$3,184,419

Income Statement
for the period

1	NET SALES	$3,055,560
2	COST OF GOODS SOLD	2,005,830
1 - 2 = 3	GROSS MARGIN	1,049,730
4	SALES & MARKETING	328,523
5	RESEARCH & DEVELOPMENT	26,000
6	GENERAL & ADMINISTRATIVE	203,520 ⬆
4 + 5 + 6 = 7	OPERATING EXPENSE	558,043
3 - 7 = 8	INCOME FROM OPERATIONS	491,687
9	NET INTEREST INCOME	(100,000)
10	INCOME TAXES	139,804
8 + 9 - 10 = 11	NET INCOME	$251,883

> Over time, depreciation expenses in the *Income Statement* increases **ACCUMULATED DEPRECIATION**, lowering **NET FIXED ASSET** value

Cash Flow Statement
for the period

a	BEGINNING CASH BALANCE	$155,000
b	CASH RECEIPTS	2,584,900
c	CASH DISBURSEMENTS	2,796,438
b - c = d	CASH FLOW FROM OPERATIONS	(211,538)
e	PP&E PURCHASE	1,750,000 ⬆
f	NET BORROWINGS	900,000
g	INCOME TAXES PAID	0
h	SALE OF CAPITAL STOCK	1,550,000
a + d - e + f - g + h = i	ENDING CASH BALANCES	$643,462 ⬇

> When equipment **(PP&E)** is purchased, **FIXED ASSETS @ COST** increases and **CASH** decreases.

Balance Sheet
as of period end

A	CASH	$643,462 ⬇
B	ACCOUNTS RECEIVABLE	454,760
C	INVENTORIES	414,770
D	PREPAID EXPENSES	0
A + B + C + D = E	CURRENT ASSETS	1,512,992
F	OTHER ASSETS	0
G	FIXED ASSETS @ COST	1,750,000 ⬆
H	ACCUMULATED DEPRECIATION	78,573 ⬆
G - H = I	NET FIXED ASSETS	1,671,427 ⬇
E + F + I = J	TOTAL ASSETS	$3,184,419
K	ACCOUNTS PAYABLE	$236,297
L	ACCRUED EXPENSES	26,435
M	CURRENT PORTION OF DEBT	100,000
N	INCOME TAXES PAYABLE	139,804
K + L + M + N = O	CURRENT LIABILITIES	502,536
P	LONG-TERM DEBT	800,000
Q	CAPITAL STOCK	1,550,000
R	RETAINED EARNINGS	331,883
Q + R = S	SHAREHOLDERS' EQUITY	1,881,883
O + P + S = T	TOTAL LIABILITIES & EQUITY	$3,184,419

> **Fixed Asset Cycle**

Section B. Transactions:
Exploits of AppleSeed Enterprises, Inc.

About This Section

We are now at the heart of learning how financial statements work. In the previous section we reviewed financial statement structure and vocabulary and saw samples of how the three main financial statements interact.

> To give a real-life flavor to our study of accounting and financial reporting, we will draft the books of a hypothetical company, *AppleSeed Enterprises, Inc.*

The following pages chronicle 31 specific business transactions in AppleSeed's financial life. We'll show how AppleSeed constructs and maintains its books to accurately report the company's financial position. Also, we will discuss additional financial terms and then show examples of applying financial concepts required to keep a company's books.

Each new business action means new "postings" to AppleSeed's financial statements as our company goes about its business of making and selling delicious applesauce. As we discuss each transaction you'll get a hands-on feel for how a company's books are constructed. Each transaction is described in a two-page spread. See the "annotated" transaction spread on the next two pages.

Right-Hand Page. The right-hand page of each two-page transaction spread describes an AppleSeed business transaction, discussing both business rationale and financial effect. Note that numbered shadowboxes are placed beside descriptions of specific, required financial postings for the transaction. These shadowboxes correspond to the entries beside the smaller numbered shadowboxes on the left-hand page showing the company's three main financial statements.

As you begin to study each new transaction, first read and understand the right-hand page description, then go to the left-hand page to see the actual postings to AppleSeed's three financial statements.

Left-Hand Page. The left-hand page of each of the transaction spreads shows AppleSeed's Income Statement, Balance Sheet and Cash Flow Statement *prior* to the transaction and then *after* the transaction. Depending on the type of transaction, all three financial statements may change, or just two, or one or none may change.

Individual account changes are shown on left-hand pages this way:

1. The *first numeric column* shows all prior account values as of the last transaction.

2. The *second numeric column* shows the individual account entries and values that will be posted for this transaction.

3. The *third numeric column* shows the account values after the transaction has been posted, that is, after the second column numbers are added to the first.

Note these last values are those that will appear as the "prior" values for the next transaction.

~

That is all there is to accounting and financial reporting. It is really not rocket science at all, just a little addition and subtraction. With some effort and this book you will understand.

But remember, our analysis is just an overview. If you need details (and there are many), just ask an accountant associate a question, based upon the knowledge you learned from this book. They will be so happy to get an intelligent question from a non-financial type, they will bend over backwards to answer.

Welcome to AppleSeed Enterprises!

Financial Statements

*Transaction Spread
Left-Hand Page*

Amounts to be posted for each account in this transaction.

Account values prior to posting this transaction.

Account values after posting this transaction

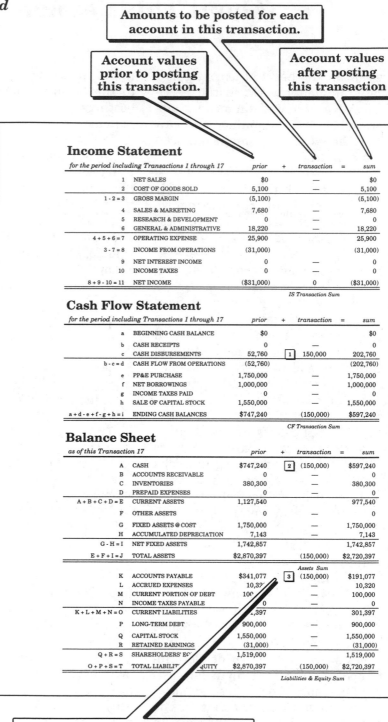

Income Statement

for the period including Transactions 1 through 17

			prior	+	transaction	=	sum
1	NET SALES		$0		—		$0
2	COST OF GOODS SOLD		5,100		—		5,100
1 - 2 = 3	GROSS MARGIN		(5,100)				(5,100)
4	SALES & MARKETING		7,680		—		7,680
5	RESEARCH & DEVELOPMENT		0		—		0
6	GENERAL & ADMINISTRATIVE		18,220		—		18,220
4 + 5 + 6 = 7	OPERATING EXPENSE		25,900				25,900
3 - 7 = 8	INCOME FROM OPERATIONS		(31,000)				(31,000)
9	NET INTEREST INCOME		0		—		0
10	INCOME TAXES		0		—		0
8 + 9 - 10 = 11	NET INCOME		($31,000)		0		($31,000)

IS Transaction Sum

Cash Flow Statement

for the period including Transactions 1 through 17

			prior	+	transaction	=	sum
a	BEGINNING CASH BALANCE		$0				$0
b	CASH RECEIPTS		0		—		0
c	CASH DISBURSEMENTS		52,760		[1] 150,000		202,760
b - c = d	CASH FLOW FROM OPERATIONS		(52,760)				(202,760)
e	PP&E PURCHASE		1,750,000		—		1,750,000
f	NET BORROWINGS		1,000,000		—		1,000,000
g	INCOME TAXES PAID		0		—		0
h	SALE OF CAPITAL STOCK		1,550,000		—		1,550,000
a + d - e + f - g + h = i	ENDING CASH BALANCES		$747,240		(150,000)		$597,240

CF Transaction Sum

Balance Sheet

as of this Transaction 17

			prior	+	transaction	=	sum
A	CASH		$747,240		[2] (150,000)		$597,240
B	ACCOUNTS RECEIVABLE		0		—		0
C	INVENTORIES		380,300		—		380,300
D	PREPAID EXPENSES		0		—		0
A + B + C + D = E	CURRENT ASSETS		1,127,540				977,540
F	OTHER ASSETS		0		—		0
G	FIXED ASSETS @ COST		1,750,000		—		1,750,000
H	ACCUMULATED DEPRECIATION		7,143		—		7,143
G - H = I	NET FIXED ASSETS		1,742,857				1,742,857
E + F + I = J	TOTAL ASSETS		$2,870,397		(150,000)		$2,720,397

Assets Sum

			prior	+	transaction	=	sum
K	ACCOUNTS PAYABLE		$341,077		[3] (150,000)		$191,077
L	ACCRUED EXPENSES		10,32?		—		10,320
M	CURRENT PORTION OF DEBT		10?		—		100,000
N	INCOME TAXES PAYABLE		0		—		0
K + L + M + N = O	CURRENT LIABILITIES		,397				301,397
P	LONG-TERM DEBT		900,000		—		900,000
Q	CAPITAL STOCK		1,550,000		—		1,550,000
R	RETAINED EARNINGS		(31,000)		—		(31,000)
Q + R = S	SHAREHOLDERS' EC?		1,519,000				1,519,000
O + P + S = T	TOTAL LIABILIT? ?UITY		$2,870,397		(150,000)		$2,720,397

Liabilities & Equity Sum

Amounts to be posted as described on the facing page beside the corresponding shadowbox number.

> **At the top of right-handed pages the
> transactions are described in detail.**

T17. Pay for a portion of the raw materials received in Transaction 11.

With our first month's production successfully placed in our finished goods warehouse, we throw a company picnic in celebration.

Halfway through the first hot dog an important telephone call comes in. The president of the Apple and Jar Supply Incorporated, our apple and jar supplier, is on the line. He is calling to see how we are doing and when we plan to pay our bill for apples and jars. He suggests $150,000 or so would be appreciated.

Because we want to remain on good terms with this important supplier, we tell him, "The check is in the mail," and rush back to our offices to put it there.

Looking at our listing of current accounts payable, we note that we owe Acme: $79,200 for apples, $184,000 for jars, and $33,200 for jar caps—a total of $296,400 outstanding.

Take out the checkbook and write the check.

Transaction: Pay a major supplier a portion of what is due for apples and jars. Cut a check for $150,000 in partial payment.

1 Cut a check for $150,000 to pay the supplier. Increase CASH DISBURSEMENTS by that amount in the *Cash Flow Statement*.

2 Lower CASH by $150,000 in the assets section of the *Balance Sheet*.

3 Lower ACCOUNTS PAYABLE in the liabilities section of the *Balance Sheet* by the $150,000 that we no longer owe ... since we just paid as described above.

Note: Actually paying for raw materials does not affect our inventory value in any way. Inventory value increased when we received the raw material and we created an accounts payable.

~

Inventory Valuation Worksheet	RAW MATERIAL	WORK IN PROCESS	FINISHED GOODS
INVENTORY VALUES FROM T16.	$181,400	$0	$198,900
J. Pay for raw materials received in T11.	$0	$0	$0
SUBTOTAL (AS OF THIS TRANSACTION)	$181,400	$0	$198,900
	TOTAL	INVENTORY	$380,300

> **Read these account posting descriptions.
> Then refer to the account changes shown
> beside the corresponding shadowboxes in the
> financial statements on the left-hand page.**

Chapter 6. Startup Financing and Staffing

Welcome to our little business—AppleSeed Enterprises, Inc. Imagine that you are AppleSeed's entrepreneurial CEO. You also double as treasurer and chief financial officer.

You have just incorporated (in Delaware) and invested $50,000 of your own money into the company—well, actually it's your Great Aunt Lillian's money. You're going to need much more capital to get into production, but these initial transactions start up the business. Follow along...we have a lot to do.

~

Transaction 1. Sell 150,000 shares of AppleSeed's common stock ($1 par value) for $10 per share.

Transaction 2. Pay yourself your first month's salary. Book all payroll-associated fringe benefits and taxes.

Transaction 3. Borrow $1 million to buy a building. Terms for this 10-year mortgage are 10% per annum.

Transaction 4. Pay $1.5 million for a building to be used for office, manufacturing and warehouse space. Set up a depreciation schedule.

Transaction 5. Hire administrative and sales staff. Pay first-month salaries and book fringe benefits and taxes.

Transaction 6. Pay employee health, life and disability insurance premiums plus FICA, unemployment and withholding taxes.

Income Statement

for the period including Transactions 1 through 1		prior	+	transaction	=	sum
1	NET SALES	$0		—		$0
2	COST OF GOODS SOLD	0		—		0
1 - 2 = 3	GROSS MARGIN	0				0
4	SALES & MARKETING	0		—		0
5	RESEARCH & DEVELOPMENT	0		—		0
6	GENERAL & ADMINISTRATIVE	0		—		0
4 + 5 + 6 = 7	OPERATING EXPENSE	0				0
3 - 7 = 8	INCOME FROM OPERATIONS	0				0
9	NET INTEREST INCOME	0		—		0
10	INCOME TAXES	0		—		0
8 + 9 - 10 = 11	NET INCOME	$0		0		$0

IS Transaction Sum

Cash Flow Statement

for the period including Transactions 1 through 1		prior	+	transaction	=	sum
a	BEGINNING CASH BALANCE	$0				$0
b	CASH RECEIPTS	0		—		0
c	CASH DISBURSEMENTS	0		—		0
b - c = d	CASH FLOW FROM OPERATIONS	0				0
e	PP&E PURCHASE	0		—		0
f	NET BORROWINGS	0		—		0
g	INCOME TAXES PAID	0		—		0
h	SALE OF CAPITAL STOCK	50,000	[1]	1,500,000		1,550,000
a + d - e + f - g + h = i	ENDING CASH BALANCES	$50,000		1,500,000		$1,550,000

CF Transaction Sum

Balance Sheet

as of this Transaction 1		prior	+	transaction	=	sum
A	CASH	$50,000	[2]	1,500,000		$1,550,000
B	ACCOUNTS RECEIVABLE	0		—		0
C	INVENTORIES	0		—		0
D	PREPAID EXPENSES	0		—		0
A + B + C + D = E	CURRENT ASSETS	50,000				1,550,000
F	OTHER ASSETS	0		—		0
G	FIXED ASSETS @ COST	0		—		0
H	ACCUMULATED DEPRECIATION	0		—		0
G - H = I	NET FIXED ASSETS	0				0
E + F + I = J	TOTAL ASSETS	$50,000		1,500,000		$1,550,000

Assets Sum

		prior	+	transaction	=	sum
K	ACCOUNTS PAYABLE	$0		—		0
L	ACCRUED EXPENSES	0		—		0
M	CURRENT PORTION OF DEBT	0		—		0
N	INCOME TAXES PAYABLE	0		—		0
K + L + M + N = O	CURRENT LIABILITIES	0				0
P	LONG-TERM DEBT	0		—		0
Q	CAPITAL STOCK	50,000	[3]	1,500,000		1,550,000
R	RETAINED EARNINGS	0		—		0
Q + R = S	SHAREHOLDERS' EQUITY	50,000				1,550,000
O + P + S = T	TOTAL LIABILITIES & EQUITY	$50,000		1,500,000		$1,550,000

Liabilities & Equity Sum

T1. Sell 150,000 shares of AppleSeed's common stock ($1 par value) for $10 per share.

Shares of stock represent *ownership* in a corporation. A corporation can issue a single class or multiple classes of stock, each with different rights and privileges.

Common stock has the lowest preference to receive assets if the corporation is liquidated. Common stockholders vote for the board of directors.

Preferred stock has a preference over common stock when the corporation pays a dividend or distributes assets in liquidation. Usually, preferred stockholders do not have the right to vote for directors.

Note that claims of both the common and preferred stockholders are junior to claims of bondholders or other creditors of the company.

Par value is the dollar amount that is assigned to shares by the company's charter. Par value has little significance other than to keep track of stock splits.

There is no connection between the stated par value and any *underlying worth* of the stock or the enterprise.

Transaction: A group of investors is willing to exchange their $1.5 million in cash for stock certificates representing 150,000 common shares of AppleSeed Enterprises, Inc.

Note: When you formed the company you bought 50,000 shares of "founder's stock" at $1 per share for a total investment of $50,000 in cash. Thus after this sale to the investor group there will be 200,000 shares outstanding. They will own 75% of AppleSeed and you will own the rest.

1 Take the money, issue the investors common stock certificates and run to the bank to deposit the check in AppleSeed's checking account. The company has received cash, so on the *Cash Flow Statement* record the $1.5 million as SALE OF STOCK.

2 This $1.5 million in cash is a new asset for the corporation, so increase CASH in the *Balance Sheet* by the amount received from the investors.

3 Each new asset must create a corresponding liability (or an offsetting asset) or else the *Balance Sheet* will be out of balance. Issuing stock creates a liability for the company. In effect, AppleSeed "owes" the new stockholders a portions of its assets. So, increase the liability CAPITAL STOCK on the *Balance Sheet* by $1.5 million.

Income Statement

for the period including Transactions 1 through 2

		prior	+	transaction	=	sum
1	NET SALES	$0		—		$0
2	COST OF GOODS SOLD	0		—		0
1 - 2 = 3	GROSS MARGIN	0				0
4	SALES & MARKETING	0		—		0
5	RESEARCH & DEVELOPMENT	0		—		0
6	GENERAL & ADMINISTRATIVE	0	1A	6,230		6,230
4 + 5 + 6 = 7	OPERATING EXPENSE	0				6,230
3 - 7 = 8	INCOME FROM OPERATIONS	0				(6,230)
9	NET INTEREST INCOME	0		—		0
10	INCOME TAXES	0		—		0
8 + 9 - 10 = 11	NET INCOME	$0		(6,230)		($6,230)

IS Transaction Sum

Cash Flow Statement

for the period including Transactions 1 through 2

		prior	+	transaction	=	sum
a	BEGINNING CASH BALANCE	$0				$0
b	CASH RECEIPTS	0		—		0
c	CASH DISBURSEMENTS	0	2A	3,370		3,370
b - c = d	CASH FLOW FROM OPERATIONS	0				(3,370)
e	PP&E PURCHASE	0		—		0
f	NET BORROWINGS	0		—		0
g	INCOME TAXES PAID	0		—		0
h	SALE OF CAPITAL STOCK	1,550,000		—		1,550,000
a + d - e + f - g + h = i	ENDING CASH BALANCES	$1,550,000		(3,370)		$1,546,630

CF Transaction Sum

Balance Sheet

as of this Transaction 2

		prior	+	transaction	=	sum
A	CASH	$1,550,000	2B	(3,370)		$1,546,630
B	ACCOUNTS RECEIVABLE	0		—		0
C	INVENTORIES	0		—		0
D	PREPAID EXPENSES	0		—		0
A + B + C + D = E	CURRENT ASSETS	1,550,000				1,546,630
F	OTHER ASSETS	0		—		0
G	FIXED ASSETS @ COST	0		—		0
H	ACCUMULATED DEPRECIATION	0		—		0
G - H = I	NET FIXED ASSETS	0				0
E + F + I = J	TOTAL ASSETS	$1,550,000		(3,370)		$1,546,630
				Assets Sum		
K	ACCOUNTS PAYABLE	$0				0
L	ACCRUED EXPENSES	0	3	2,860		2,860
M	CURRENT PORTION OF DEBT	0		—		0
N	INCOME TAXES PAYABLE	0		—		0
K + L + M + N = O	CURRENT LIABILITIES	0				2,860
P	LONG-TERM DEBT	0		—		0
Q	CAPITAL STOCK	1,550,000		—		1,550,000
R	RETAINED EARNINGS	0	1B	(6,230)		(6,230)
Q + R = S	SHAREHOLDERS' EQUITY	1,550,000				1,543,770
O + P + S = T	TOTAL LIABILITIES & EQUITY	$1,550,000		(3,370)		$1,546,630

Liabilities & Equity Sum

T2. Pay yourself a month's salary. Book payroll-associated fringe benefits and taxes.

Congratulations! The board of directors of AppleSeed Enterprises, Inc., has hired you to manage the company at the grand salary of $5,000 per month.

Before you spend all your newfound wealth, let's calculate: (1) your actual take-home pay; (2) the cut for taxes; and (3) the total expense to the company for fringe benefits and payroll taxes.

See the table at right. It costs Apple-Seed a total of $6,230 to pay your $5,000 in salary, even though you only receive $3,370 in your paycheck.

Salary & Employment Expenses

	PAY TO EMPLOYEES	PAY TO OTHERS
MONTHLY SALARY	$5,000	
EMPLOYEE'S FICA	$(380)	$380
FEDERAL/STATE WITHHOLDING	$(1,250)	$1,250
EMPLOYER'S FICA		$380
WORKMEN'S COMPENSATION		$100
UNEMPLOYMENT INSURANCE		$250
HEALTH & LIFE INSURANCE		$500
TOTALS PER MONTH	$3,370	$2,860
TOTALS PAID TO EMPLOYEES & TO OTHERS		$6,230

Transaction: Book all payroll-associated company expenses totaling $6,230 including salary, employer's contribution to FICA (Social Security) and various insurance expenses. Issue yourself a payroll check for $3,370 (your $5,000 monthly salary minus $1,250 in federal and state withholding tax and $380 for your own contribution to FICA).

1 (1A) Salary and fringes are expenses that decrease income. Add the total monthly payroll expense of $6,230 to GENERAL & ADMINISTRATIVE expenses in the *Income Statement*. (1B) Also decrease RETAINED EARNINGS in the *Balance Sheet* by the same amount.

2 (2A) So far your payroll check is the only cash that has left the company. List the $3,370 check under CASH DISBURSEMENTS in the *Cash Flow Statement*. (2B) Also decrease CASH in the *Balance Sheet* by the same amount.

3 The remaining $2,860 in expenses—due to the government and to various insurance companies—is an obligation of the company not yet discharged (that is, owed but not yet paid). Enter this amount as an ACCRUED EXPENSE in the liability section of the *Balance Sheet*.

~

Financial Statements

Income Statement

for the period including Transactions 1 through 3

		prior	+	transaction	=	sum
1	NET SALES	$0	—			$0
2	COST OF GOODS SOLD	0	—			0
1 - 2 = 3	GROSS MARGIN	0				0
4	SALES & MARKETING	0	—			0
5	RESEARCH & DEVELOPMENT	0	—			0
6	GENERAL & ADMINISTRATIVE	6,230	—			6,230
4 + 5 + 6 = 7	OPERATING EXPENSE	6,230				6,230
3 - 7 = 8	INCOME FROM OPERATIONS	(6,230)				(6,230)
9	NET INTEREST INCOME	0	—			0
10	INCOME TAXES	0	—			0
8 + 9 - 10 = 11	NET INCOME	($6,230)		0		($6,230)

IS Transaction Sum

Cash Flow Statement

for the period including Transactions 1 through 3

		prior	+	transaction	=	sum
a	BEGINNING CASH BALANCE	$0				$0
b	CASH RECEIPTS	0	—			0
c	CASH DISBURSEMENTS	3,370	—			3,370
b - c = d	CASH FLOW FROM OPERATIONS	(3,370)				(3,370)
e	PP&E PURCHASE	0	—			0
f	NET BORROWINGS	0	1A	1,000,000		1,000,000
g	INCOME TAXES PAID	0	—			0
h	SALE OF CAPITAL STOCK	1,550,000	—			1,550,000
a + d - e + f - g + h = i	ENDING CASH BALANCES	$1,546,630		1,000,000		$2,546,630

CF Transaction Sum

Balance Sheet

as of this Transaction 3

		prior	+	transaction	=	sum
A	CASH	$1,546,630	1B	1,000,000		$2,546,630
B	ACCOUNTS RECEIVABLE	0	—			0
C	INVENTORIES	0	—			0
D	PREPAID EXPENSES	0	—			0
A + B + C + D = E	CURRENT ASSETS	1,546,630				2,546,630
F	OTHER ASSETS	0	—			0
G	FIXED ASSETS @ COST	0	—			0
H	ACCUMULATED DEPRECIATION	0	—			0
G - H = I	NET FIXED ASSETS	0				0
E + F + I = J	TOTAL ASSETS	$1,546,630		1,000,000		$2,546,630

Assets Sum

		prior	+	transaction	=	sum
K	ACCOUNTS PAYABLE	$0	—			0
L	ACCRUED EXPENSES	2,860	—			2,860
M	CURRENT PORTION OF DEBT	0	2	100,000		100,000
N	INCOME TAXES PAYABLE	0	—			0
K + L + M + N = O	CURRENT LIABILITIES	2,860				102,860
P	LONG-TERM DEBT	0	3	900,000		900,000
Q	CAPITAL STOCK	1,550,000	—			1,550,000
R	RETAINED EARNINGS	(6,230)	—			(6,230)
Q + R = S	SHAREHOLDERS' EQUITY	1,543,770				1,543,770
O + P + S = T	TOTAL LIABILITIES & EQUITY	$1,546,630		1,000,000		$2,546,630

Liabilities & Equity Sum

T3. Borrow $1 million to buy a building. Terms for the 10-year mortgage are 10% per annum.

Go to the bank and apply for a loan to buy a building to (1) manufacture and warehouse applesauce, and (2) house the administrative and sales activities of the company.

The friendly loan officer agrees that AppleSeed has a strong equity capital base and good prospects. She agrees to lend you a cool million to buy the building but demands that you pledge all the assets of the company to collateralize the loan.

She also asks for your personal guarantee to repay the loan if the company can not. What do you say? The correct answer is no. If the business fails you don't want to lose your home too.

You and your friendly banker agree on a 10-year loan amortization (that is, payback) schedule shown on the right.

Loan Amortization Schedule

YEAR	INTEREST PAYMENTS	PRINCIPAL PAYMENTS	OUTSTANDING PRINCIPAL
1	$100,000	$100,000	$900,000
2	$90,000	$100,000	$800,000
3	$80,000	$100,000	$700,000
4	$70,000	$100,000	$600,000
5	$60,000	$100,000	$500,000
6	$50,000	$100,000	$400,000
7	$40,000	$100,000	$300,000
8	$30,000	$100,000	$200,000
9	$20,000	$100,000	$100,000
10	$10,000	$100,000	$0.00
TOTAL	$550,000	$1,000,000	

Transaction: Borrow $1 million to purchase an all-purpose building. This term note will run for 10 years, calling for yearly principal payments of $100,000 plus interest at a rate of 10% per annum.

1 (1A) At the loan closing the friendly banker deposits $1 million in your checking account, thus increasing NET BORROWINGS in the *Cash Flow Statement*. (1B) Remember also, CASH increases by $1 million in the assets section of the *Balance Sheet*.

2 The current portion of debt (that is, the amount that will be repaid this year) is $100,000 and is listed in the current liabilities section of the *Balance Sheet*.

3 The remaining debt of $900,000 will be repaid more than one year in the future and thus is listed as LONG-TERM DEBT in the *Balance Sheet*.

~

Income Statement

for the period including Transactions 1 through 4	*prior*	+	*transaction*	=	*sum*
1 NET SALES	$0		—		$0
2 COST OF GOODS SOLD	0		—		0
1 - 2 = 3 GROSS MARGIN	0				0
4 SALES & MARKETING	0		—		0
5 RESEARCH & DEVELOPMENT	0		—		0
6 GENERAL & ADMINISTRATIVE	6,230		—		6,230
4 + 5 + 6 = 7 OPERATING EXPENSE	6,230				6,230
3 - 7 = 8 INCOME FROM OPERATIONS	(6,230)				(6,230)
9 NET INTEREST INCOME	0		—		0
10 INCOME TAXES	0		—		0
8 + 9 - 10 = 11 NET INCOME	($6,230)		0		($6,230)

IS Transaction Sum

Cash Flow Statement

for the period including Transactions 1 through 4	*prior*	+	*transaction*	=	*sum*
a BEGINNING CASH BALANCE	$0				$0
b CASH RECEIPTS	0		—		0
c CASH DISBURSEMENTS	3,370		—		3,370
b - c = d CASH FLOW FROM OPERATIONS	(3,370)				(3,370)
e PP&E PURCHASE	0		**1** 1,500,000		1,500,000
f NET BORROWINGS	1,000,000		—		1,000,000
g INCOME TAXES PAID	0		—		0
h SALE OF CAPITAL STOCK	1,550,000		—		1,550,000
a + d - e + f - g + h = i ENDING CASH BALANCES	$2,546,630		(1,500,000)		$1,046,630

CF Transaction Sum

Balance Sheet

as of this Transaction 4	*prior*	+	*transaction*	=	*sum*
A CASH	$2,546,630		**2** (1,500,000)		$1,046,630
B ACCOUNTS RECEIVABLE	0		—		0
C INVENTORIES	0		—		0
D PREPAID EXPENSES	0		—		0
A + B + C + D = E CURRENT ASSETS	2,546,630				1,046,630
F OTHER ASSETS	0		—		0
G FIXED ASSETS @ COST	0		**3** 1,500,000		1,500,000
H ACCUMULATED DEPRECIATION	0		—		0
G - H = I NET FIXED ASSETS	0				1,500,000
E + F + I = J TOTAL ASSETS	$2,546,630		0		$2,546,630

Assets Sum

	prior	+	*transaction*	=	*sum*
K ACCOUNTS PAYABLE	$0		—		0
L ACCRUED EXPENSES	2,860		—		2,860
M CURRENT PORTION OF DEBT	100,000		—		100,000
N INCOME TAXES PAYABLE	0		—		0
K + L + M + N = O CURRENT LIABILITIES	102,860				102,860
P LONG-TERM DEBT	900,000		—		900,000
Q CAPITAL STOCK	1,550,000		—		1,550,000
R RETAINED EARNINGS	(6,230)		—		(6,230)
Q + R = S SHAREHOLDERS' EQUITY	1,543,770				1,543,770
O + P + S = T TOTAL LIABILITIES & EQUITY	$2,546,630		0		$2,546,630

Liabilities & Equity Sum

T4. Pay $1.5 million for a building to be used for office, manufacturing and warehouse space. Set up a depreciation schedule.

You have found just the perfect building for AppleSeed Enterprises. The 100,000 square foot building is appraised at $1.1 million and the land at $550,000. The building is nicely laid out with 90,000 square feet of manufacturing and warehouse space and 10,000 square feet for offices.

You negotiate well and drive a hard bargain. You and the seller agree on a sales price for building and land of $1.5 million, a good deal for AppleSeed.

In this transaction we will buy the building, AppleSeed Enterprise's first *fixed asset*. Fixed assets (also called *Property, Plant & Equipment* or *"PP&E"*) are long-lived productive assets such as

buildings, machinery and fixtures, that are used to make, store, ship and sell product. Fixed assets are also sometimes called *capital equipment*. When you acquire a fixed asset, you add its value to the Balance Sheet as an asset.

Accounting convention and IRS regulations do not allow you to immediately "expense" the cost of acquiring a fixed asset. Because fixed assets have a long productive life, you can expense only a portion of their purchase price each year as you use them. **This yearly expense is called depreciation.**

We will deal with the depreciation concept in much more detail in later transactions.

Transaction: Purchase 100,000 square foot building and land for $1.5 million in cash. This facility will serve as AppleSeed Enterprises' headquarters, manufacturing facility and warehouse.

1 Write a check for $1.5 million to the seller of the building. Record this cash transaction under **PP&E PURCHASE** in the *Cash Flow Statement*.

2 Then, lower **CASH** in the *Balance Sheet* by the $1.5 million check that you wrote to buy the building.

3 Now you must make another entry to bring the *Balance Sheet* back into balance. Increase **FIXED ASSETS @ COST** on the *Balance Sheet* by the $1.5 million purchase price of the building. Note that this asset is recorded at actual cost, not at the appraised or any other valuation.

~

Financial Statements

Income Statement

for the period including Transactions 1 through 5

		prior	+	transaction	=	sum
1	NET SALES	$0		—		$0
2	COST OF GOODS SOLD	0		—		0
1 - 2 = 3	GROSS MARGIN	0				0
4	SALES & MARKETING	0	**1A**	7,680		7,680
5	RESEARCH & DEVELOPMENT	0		—		0
6	GENERAL & ADMINISTRATIVE	6,230	**1B**	7,110		13,340
4 + 5 + 6 = 7	OPERATING EXPENSE	6,230				21,020
3 - 7 = 8	INCOME FROM OPERATIONS	(6,230)				(21,020)
9	NET INTEREST INCOME	0		—		0
10	INCOME TAXES	0		—		0
8 + 9 - 10 = 11	NET INCOME	($6,230)		(14,790)		($21,020)

IS Transaction Sum

Cash Flow Statement

for the period including Transactions 1 through 5

		prior	+	transaction	=	sum
a	BEGINNING CASH BALANCE	$0				$0
b	CASH RECEIPTS	0		—		0
c	CASH DISBURSEMENTS	3,370	**3A**	7,960		11,330
b - c = d	CASH FLOW FROM OPERATIONS	(3,370)				(11,330)
e	PP&E PURCHASE	1,500,000		—		1,500,000
f	NET BORROWINGS	1,000,000		—		1,000,000
g	INCOME TAXES PAID	0		—		0
h	SALE OF CAPITAL STOCK	1,550,000		—		1,550,000
a + d - e + f - g + h = i	ENDING CASH BALANCES	$1,046,630		(7,960)		$1,038,670

CF Transaction Sum

Balance Sheet

as of this Transaction 5

		prior	+	transaction	=	sum
A	CASH	$1,046,630	**3B**	(7,960)		$1,038,670
B	ACCOUNTS RECEIVABLE	0		—		0
C	INVENTORIES	0		—		0
D	PREPAID EXPENSES	0		—		0
A + B + C + D = E	CURRENT ASSETS	1,046,630				1,038,670
F	OTHER ASSETS	0		—		0
G	FIXED ASSETS @ COST	1,500,000		—		1,500,000
H	ACCUMULATED DEPRECIATION	0		—		0
G - H = I	NET FIXED ASSETS	1,500,000				1,500,000
E + F + I = J	TOTAL ASSETS	$2,546,630		(7,960)		$2,538,670

Assets Sum

		prior	+	transaction	=	sum
K	ACCOUNTS PAYABLE	$0		—		0
L	ACCRUED EXPENSES	2,860	**4**	6,830		9,690
M	CURRENT PORTION OF DEBT	100,000		—		100,000
N	INCOME TAXES PAYABLE	0		—		0
K + L + M + N = O	CURRENT LIABILITIES	102,860				109,690
P	LONG-TERM DEBT	900,000		—		900,000
Q	CAPITAL STOCK	1,550,000		—		1,550,000
R	RETAINED EARNINGS	(6,230)	**2**	(14,790)		(21,020)
Q + R = S	SHAREHOLDERS' EQUITY	1,543,770				1,528,980
O + P + S = T	TOTAL LIABILITIES & EQUITY	$2,546,630		(7,960)		$2,538,670

Liabilities & Equity Sum

T5. Hire administrative and sales staff. Pay first-month salaries and book all fringe benefits and taxes.

AppleSeed will soon be in production; you had better figure out how to sell applesauce! You will also need help with administrative tasks.

Hire some SG&A employees. SG&A stands for "sales, general and administrative." SG&A is a catchall for all expenses not involved in manufacturing; that is, not added to inventory. More on this topic later.

Add to AppleSeed's SG&A payroll a secretary at the wage of $13 per hour ($2,250 per month), a bookkeeper at a salary of $3,000 per month, salesperson at $4,000 per month and a salesclerk at $10 per hour ($1,750 per month).

The table below computes SG&A take-home pay and fringe benefit costs.

SG&A Payroll Related Expenses

	PAY TO EMPLOYEES	PAY TO OTHERS
MONTHLY SALARY	$11,000	
EMPLOYEE'S FICA	$(840)	$840
FEDERAL/STATE WITHHOLDING	$(2,200)	$2,200
EMPLOYER'S FICA		$840
WORKMEN'S COMPENSATION		$400
UNEMPLOYMENT INSURANCE		$550
HEALTH & LIFE INSURANCE		$2,000
TOTALS PER MONTH	$7,960	$6,830
TOTAL PAID TO EMPLOYEES & TO OTHERS		$14,790

Transaction: Book this month's payroll-associated expenses of $14,790, (that is, $7,680 for Sales & Marketing and $7,110 for G&A). These expenses include salaries, wages, insurance and other fringe benefits. Issue payroll checks totaling $7,960 to SG&A employees.

1	(1A) On the *Income Statement* add total monthly payroll expense of $7,680 for the salesperson and clerk to SALES & MARKETING EXPENSE. (1B) Also add the payroll expense of $7,110 for the secretary and the bookkeeper to GENERAL & ADMINISTRATIVE EXPENSES.
2	Decrease RETAINED EARNINGS in the *Balance Sheet* by the total SG&A payroll of $14,790.
3	(3A) Issue payroll checks totaling $7,960 and list under CASH DISBURSEMENTS in the Cash Flow Statement. (3B) Decrease cash in the *Balance Sheet* by the same amount.
4	The $6,830 due to others is owed, but not yet paid. Place this amount as ACCRUED EXPENSE in the liability section of the *Balance Sheet*.

Financial Statements

Income Statement

	for the period including Transactions 1 through 6	prior	+	transaction	=	sum
1	NET SALES	$0		—		$0
2	COST OF GOODS SOLD	0		—		0
1 - 2 = 3	GROSS MARGIN	0				0
4	SALES & MARKETING	7,680		—		7,680
5	RESEARCH & DEVELOPMENT	0		—		0
6	GENERAL & ADMINISTRATIVE	13,340		—		13,340
4 + 5 + 6 = 7	OPERATING EXPENSE	21,020				21,020
3 - 7 = 8	INCOME FROM OPERATIONS	(21,020)				(21,020)
9	NET INTEREST INCOME	0		—		0
10	INCOME TAXES	0		—		0
8 + 9 - 10 = 11	NET INCOME	($21,020)		0		($21,020)

IS Transaction Sum

Cash Flow Statement

	for the period including Transactions 1 through 6	prior	+	transaction	=	sum
a	BEGINNING CASH BALANCE	$0				$0
b	CASH RECEIPTS	0		—		0
c	CASH DISBURSEMENTS	11,330	1	9,690		21,020
b - c = d	CASH FLOW FROM OPERATIONS	(11,330)				(21,020)
e	PP&E PURCHASE	1,500,000		—		1,500,000
f	NET BORROWINGS	1,000,000		—		1,000,000
g	INCOME TAXES PAID	0		—		0
h	SALE OF CAPITAL STOCK	1,550,000		—		1,550,000
a + d - e + f - g + h = i	ENDING CASH BALANCES	$1,038,670		(9,690)		$1,028,980

CF Transaction Sum

Balance Sheet

	as of this Transaction 6	prior	+	transaction	=	sum
A	CASH	$1,038,670	2	(9,690)		$1,028,980
B	ACCOUNTS RECEIVABLE	0		—		0
C	INVENTORIES	0		—		0
D	PREPAID EXPENSES	0		—		0
A + B + C + D = E	CURRENT ASSETS	1,038,670				1,028,980
F	OTHER ASSETS	0		—		0
G	FIXED ASSETS @ COST	1,500,000		—		1,500,000
H	ACCUMULATED DEPRECIATION	0		—		0
G - H = I	NET FIXED ASSETS	1,500,000				1,500,000
E + F + I = J	TOTAL ASSETS	$2,538,670		(9,690)		$2,528,980
				Assets Sum		
K	ACCOUNTS PAYABLE	$0		—		0
L	ACCRUED EXPENSES	9,690	3	(9,690)		0
M	CURRENT PORTION OF DEBT	100,000		—		100,000
N	INCOME TAXES PAYABLE	0		—		0
K + L + M + N = O	CURRENT LIABILITIES	109,690				100,000
P	LONG-TERM DEBT	900,000		—		900,000
Q	CAPITAL STOCK	1,550,000		—		1,550,000
R	RETAINED EARNINGS	(21,020)		—		(21,020)
Q + R = S	SHAREHOLDERS' EQUITY	1,528,980				1,528,980
O + P + S = T	TOTAL LIABILITIES & EQUITY	$2,538,670		(9,690)		$2,528,980

Liabilities & Equity Sum

T6. Pay employee health, life and disability insurance premiums and also pay unemployment, FICA and withholding taxes.

When you put yourself on AppleSeed's payroll in **Transaction 2** and then hired an SG&A staff in **Transaction 5**, you issued payroll checks to all new Apple-Seed employees.

However, you did not at that time pay all the payroll-associated expenses for fringe benefits such as health and life insurance or the withholding taxes and the FICA that you deducted from each employees' paychecks.

These expenses were booked in the *Income Statement* at the time they were incurred, but since they were not at that time actually paid, they became accrued expenses.

If an expense is booked in the *Income Statement* but you do not "satisfy the obligation" by paying it immediately, then you must record the expense as "accrued" on the Balance Sheet.

Transaction: Pay all the payroll-associated expenses that were accrued in **Transaction 2** and **Transaction 5**, including FICA, withholding tax and unemployment insurance due the government. Also pay to private insurance companies the workmen's compensation and health and life insurance premiums.

| 1 | Write checks totaling $9,690—$2,860 from **Transaction 2** plus $6,830 from **Transaction 5** for these accrued expenses. Show payments as a CASH DISBURSEMENT in the *Cash Flow Statement*. |

| 2 | Lower CASH in the asset section of the *Balance Sheet* by the same amount paid above. |

| 3 | Lower ACCRUED EXPENSES in the liabilities section of the *Balance Sheet* by the $9,690 paid above. Payment of these expenses had been deferred (accrued). Now that you have paid them you can, in effect, reverse the original deferring entry. |

Note: Actually paying these accrued expenses does not affect the *Income Statement* now. The *Income Statement* was already charged when the expenses were incurred.

~

Chapter 7. Staffing and Equipping Facility; Planning for Manufacturing

Now begins the fun stuff. In a few short weeks we will be producing thousands of cases of the best applesauce you have ever tasted.

In anticipation of beginning applesauce production, we will design our production techniques, determine raw material requirements and also our labor needs, figure our costs and establish methods to keep track of our inventories.

Finally, we will order our first raw materials and get everything ready to begin trial production in our new manufacturing plant.

~

Transaction 7. Order $250,000 worth of manufacturing machinery. Pay one-half down now.

Transaction 8. Receive and install manufacturing machinery. Pay remaining $125,000 due.

Transaction 9. Hire production workers; expense first month's salaries and wages.

- Prepare bill of materials and establish labor requirements.

- Set up plant and machinery depreciation schedules.

- Plan monthly production schedule and set standard costs.

Transaction 10. Place standing orders for raw materials with suppliers. Receive 1 million jar labels.

Income Statement

for the period including Transactions 1 through 7		prior	+	transaction	=	sum
1	NET SALES	$0	—			$0
2	COST OF GOODS SOLD	0	—			0
1 - 2 = 3	GROSS MARGIN	0				0
4	SALES & MARKETING	7,680	—			7,680
5	RESEARCH & DEVELOPMENT	0	—			0
6	GENERAL & ADMINISTRATIVE	13,340	—			13,340
4 + 5 + 6 = 7	OPERATING EXPENSE	21,020				21,020
3 - 7 = 8	INCOME FROM OPERATIONS	(21,020)				(21,020)
9	NET INTEREST INCOME	0	—			0
10	INCOME TAXES	0	—			0
8 + 9 - 10 = 11	NET INCOME	($21,020)		0		($21,020)

IS Transaction Sum

Cash Flow Statement

for the period including Transactions 1 through 7		prior	+	transaction	=	sum
a	BEGINNING CASH BALANCE	$0				$0
b	CASH RECEIPTS	0	—			0
c	CASH DISBURSEMENTS	21,020	—			21,020
b - c = d	CASH FLOW FROM OPERATIONS	(21,020)				(21,020)
e	PP&E PURCHASE	1,500,000	1	125,000		1,625,000
f	NET BORROWINGS	1,000,000	—			1,000,000
g	INCOME TAXES PAID	0	—			0
h	SALE OF CAPITAL STOCK	1,550,000	—			1,550,000
a + d - e + f - g + h = i	ENDING CASH BALANCES	$1,028,980		(125,000)		$903,980

CF Transaction Sum

Balance Sheet

as of this Transaction 7		prior	+	transaction	=	sum
A	CASH	$1,028,980	2	(125,000)		$903,980
B	ACCOUNTS RECEIVABLE	0	—			0
C	INVENTORIES	0	—			0
D	PREPAID EXPENSES	0	—			0
A + B + C + D = E	CURRENT ASSETS	1,028,980				903,980
F	OTHER ASSETS	0	3	125,000		125,000
G	FIXED ASSETS @ COST	1,500,000	—			1,500,000
H	ACCUMULATED DEPRECIATION	0	—			0
G - H = I	NET FIXED ASSETS	1,500,000				1,500,000
E + F + I = J	TOTAL ASSETS	$2,528,980		0		$2,528,980

Assets Sum

K	ACCOUNTS PAYABLE	$0	—			0
L	ACCRUED EXPENSES	0	—			0
M	CURRENT PORTION OF DEBT	100,000	—			100,000
N	INCOME TAXES PAYABLE	0	—			0
K + L + M + N = O	CURRENT LIABILITIES	100,000				100,000
P	LONG-TERM DEBT	900,000	—			900,000
Q	CAPITAL STOCK	1,550,000	—			1,550,000
R	RETAINED EARNINGS	(21,020)	—			(21,020)
Q + R = S	SHAREHOLDERS' EQUITY	1,528,980				1,528,980
O + P + S = T	TOTAL LIABILITIES & EQUITY	$2,528,980		0		$2,528,980

Liabilities & Equity Sum

T7. Place order for $250,000 worth of specialty applesause-making machinery. Pay a $125,000 deposit with remainder due on delivery.

We will need a lot of specialized machinery to make our special applesauce: apple presses, many large stainless-steel holding tanks, bottling machines, a labeling machine and so forth.

We contract with ABC AppleCrushing Machinery Inc. (ABCAM Inc. for short) to construct and install our equipment at a total cost to AppleSeed of $250,000, including delivery charges.

Before beginning all its important work, ABCAM demands a prepayment of $125,000 in cash. The remaining payment of $125,000 will be due upon the completion of installation and qualification of the equipment.

Transaction: Place an order for $250,000 worth of applesauce-making machinery. Make a prepayment of $125,000 with the balance due upon successful installation.

| 1 | Enclose a check for $125,000 with the purchase order to the machinery contractor. Show this prepayment as a **PROPERTY, PLANT & EQUIPMENT** purchase on the *Cash Flow Statement*. |

| 2 | Lower cash in the assets section of the *Balance Sheet* by the $125,000 contractor prepayment. |

| 3 | This prepayment is an asset that AppleSeed "owns." It can be viewed as a "right" to receive in the future $250,000 of equipment and only have to issue another $125,000 check to the equipment builder. Since this asset does not fit into any of the other asset categories, increase **OTHER ASSETS** by the $125,000 machinery prepayment. |

~

Income Statement

		prior	+	transaction	=	sum
1	NET SALES	$0		—		$0
2	COST OF GOODS SOLD	0		—		0
1 - 2 = 3	GROSS MARGIN	0				0
4	SALES & MARKETING	7,680		—		7,680
5	RESEARCH & DEVELOPMENT	0		—		0
6	GENERAL & ADMINISTRATIVE	13,340		—		13,340
4 + 5 + 6 = 7	OPERATING EXPENSE	21,020				21,020
3 - 7 = 8	INCOME FROM OPERATIONS	(21,020)				(21,020)
9	NET INTEREST INCOME	0		—		0
10	INCOME TAXES	0		—		0
8 + 9 - 10 = 11	NET INCOME	($21,020)		0		($21,020)

IS Transaction Sum

Cash Flow Statement

for the period including Transactions 1 through 8

		prior	+	transaction	=	sum
a	BEGINNING CASH BALANCE	$0				$0
b	CASH RECEIPTS	0		—		0
c	CASH DISBURSEMENTS	21,020		—		21,020
b - c = d	CASH FLOW FROM OPERATIONS	(21,020)				(21,020)
e	PP&E PURCHASE	1,625,000	[1]	125,000		1,750,000
f	NET BORROWINGS	1,000,000		—		1,000,000
g	INCOME TAXES PAID	0		—		0
h	SALE OF CAPITAL STOCK	1,550,000		—		1,550,000
a + d - e + f - g + h = i	ENDING CASH BALANCES	$903,980		(125,000)		$778,980

CF Transaction Sum

Balance Sheet

as of this Transaction 8

		prior	+	transaction	=	sum
A	CASH	$903,980	[2]	(125,000)		$778,980
B	ACCOUNTS RECEIVABLE	0		—		0
C	INVENTORIES	0		—		0
D	PREPAID EXPENSES	0		—		0
A + B + C + D = E	CURRENT ASSETS	903,980				778,980
F	OTHER ASSETS	125,000	[3]	(125,000)		0
G	FIXED ASSETS @ COST	1,500,000	[4]	250,000		1,750,000
H	ACCUMULATED DEPRECIATION	0		—		0
G - H = I	NET FIXED ASSETS	1,500,000				1,750,000
E + F + I = J	TOTAL ASSETS	$2,528,980		0		$2,528,980

Assets Sum

		prior	+	transaction	=	sum
K	ACCOUNTS PAYABLE	$0		—		0
L	ACCRUED EXPENSES	0		—		0
M	CURRENT PORTION OF DEBT	100,000		—		100,000
N	INCOME TAXES PAYABLE	0		—		0
K + L + M + N = O	CURRENT LIABILITIES	100,000				100,000
P	LONG-TERM DEBT	900,000		—		900,000
Q	CAPITAL STOCK	1,550,000		—		1,550,000
R	RETAINED EARNINGS	(21,020)		—		(21,020)
Q + R = S	SHAREHOLDERS' EQUITY	1,528,980				1,528,980
O + P + S = T	TOTAL LIABILITIES & EQUITY	$2,528,980		0		$2,528,980

Liabilities & Equity Sum

T8. Receive and install applesauce-making machinery. Pay the $125,000 balance due.

ABCAM does a super job—on time and within budget. They submit an invoice for their work and you are happy to pay. The applesauce machinery is installed and ready for operation.

These new machines are a *productive asset*...so-called because they will be used to produce our product and make a profit for AppleSeed.

Note that when you paid for these machines you just shifted money from one asset category on the *Balance Sheet* into another...from CASH to FIXED ASSETS. The *Income Statement* was not affected. When you use and then depreciate these assets, the *Income Statement* will take a hit. More later.

Transaction: Make final payment of $125,000, the balance due on the applesauce-making machinery.

1 Everything is working well. Accept delivery on the machinery and write a check for the $125,000 balance due. Show this payment as a PROPERTY, PLANT & EQUIPMENT purchase in the *Cash Flow Statement*.

2 Lower CASH in the assets section of the *Balance Sheet* by the $125,000 paid to the contractor.

3 Lower OTHER ASSETS by the $125,000 prepayment that now will be converted (below) to a fixed asset.

4 Increase FIXED ASSETS @ COST by the total $250,000 cost of the machinery. Half of this amount comes from this transaction (payment of the $125,000 balance due) and half from reversing the OTHER ASSET account (prepayment of $125,000 in Transaction 7) now that we have received the machinery.

～

Income Statement

for the period including Transactions 1 through 9		prior	+	transaction	=	sum
1	NET SALES	$0		—		$0
2	COST OF GOODS SOLD	0		—		0
1 - 2 = 3	GROSS MARGIN	0				0
4	SALES & MARKETING	7,680		—		7,680
5	RESEARCH & DEVELOPMENT	0		—		0
6	GENERAL & ADMINISTRATIVE	13,340	1A	4,880		18,220
4 + 5 + 6 = 7	OPERATING EXPENSE	21,020				25,900
3 - 7 = 8	INCOME FROM OPERATIONS	(21,020)				(25,900)
9	NET INTEREST INCOME	0		—		0
10	INCOME TAXES	0		—		0
8 + 9 - 10 = 11	NET INCOME	($21,020)		(4,880)		($25,900)

IS Transaction Sum

Cash Flow Statement

for the period including Transactions 1 through 9		prior	+	transaction	=	sum
a	BEGINNING CASH BALANCE	$0				$0
b	CASH RECEIPTS	0		—		0
c	CASH DISBURSEMENTS	21,020	2A	2,720		23,740
b - c = d	CASH FLOW FROM OPERATIONS	(21,020)				(23,740)
e	PP&E PURCHASE	1,750,000		—		1,750,000
f	NET BORROWINGS	1,000,000		—		1,000,000
g	INCOME TAXES PAID	0		—		0
h	SALE OF CAPITAL STOCK	1,550,000		—		1,550,000
a + d - e + f - g + h = i	ENDING CASH BALANCES	$778,980		(2,720)		$776,260

CF Transaction Sum

Balance Sheet

as of this Transaction 9		prior	+	transaction	=	sum
A	CASH	$778,980	2B	(2,720)		$776,260
B	ACCOUNTS RECEIVABLE	0		—		0
C	INVENTORIES	0		—		0
D	PREPAID EXPENSES	0		—		0
A + B + C + D = E	CURRENT ASSETS	778,980				776,260
F	OTHER ASSETS	0		—		0
G	FIXED ASSETS @ COST	1,750,000		—		1,750,000
H	ACCUMULATED DEPRECIATION	0		—		0
G - H = I	NET FIXED ASSETS	1,750,000				1,750,000
E + F + I = J	TOTAL ASSETS	$2,528,980		(2,720)		$2,526,260

Assets Sum

		prior	+	transaction	=	sum
K	ACCOUNTS PAYABLE	$0				0
L	ACCRUED EXPENSES	0	3	2,160		2,160
M	CURRENT PORTION OF DEBT	100,000		—		100,000
N	INCOME TAXES PAYABLE	0		—		0
K + L + M + N = O	CURRENT LIABILITIES	100,000				102,160
P	LONG-TERM DEBT	900,000				900,000
Q	CAPITAL STOCK	1,550,000		—		1,550,000
R	RETAINED EARNINGS	(21,020)	1B	(4,880)		(25,900)
Q + R = S	SHAREHOLDERS' EQUITY	1,528,980				1,524,100
O + P + S = T	TOTAL LIABILITIES & EQUITY	$2,528,980		(2,720)		$2,526,260

Liabilities & Equity Sum

T9. Hire production workers. Expense first month's salary and wages.

The plant is shaping up and we need manufacturing workers and a supervisor to guide them along.

Hire the supervisor at a salary of $3,750 per month and have her start immediately. Using similar calculations to those in the table for **Transaction 5**, the supervisor will receive $2,720 per month in take-home pay. The company will also pay $2,160 in fringes and various taxes to the government. Salary, fringes and taxes for the supervisor total $4,880 per month.

We will begin paying the supervisor right away. But, since we have not yet started production, we will charge this month's salary to G&A as a start-up expense. Normally the manufacturing salary and wage expense is charged to inventory. More later.

The supervisor starts interviewing hourly production workers. Wages will be $12.50 per hour plus fringes with an expected 40 hour week. Hire five workers and tell them to report next month when we expect to start production.

AppleSeed's manufacturing payroll now totals $17,180 per month: $4,880 for the supervisor and $12,300 for the five hourly workers.

Production Labor Costs	TAKE-HOME PAY TO EMPLOYEES	FRINGE BENEFITS AND TAXES	TOTALS
SUPERVISOR	$2,720	$2,160	$4,880
HOURLY WORKERS	$6,300	$6,000	$12,300
MANUFACTURING	$9,020	$8,160	$17,180

Transaction: Book supervisor's salary and associated payroll expenses as a General & Administrative expense since we have not yet started production. Issue first month's salary check. Make no entries for hourly workers since they have not yet reported for work.

1 (1A) On the *Income Statement* add $4,880 (the total salary and payroll costs for the supervisor) to GENERAL & ADMINISTRATIVE EXPENSE. (1B) Decrease RETAINED EARNINGS in the liabilities section of the *Balance Sheet* by the same amount.

2 (2A) Issue a payroll check totaling $2,720 and list under CASH DISBURSEMENT in the *Cash Flow Statement*. (2B) Decrease CASH in the *Balance Sheet* by the same amount.

3 The remaining $2,160 in benefits and taxes is owed but not yet paid. Place this amount as an ACCRUED EXPENSE on the *Balance Sheet*.

Manufacturing Costing

How much will it cost to make our fine applesauce? How should we account for manufacturing costs? How will we correctly value our inventory? These are essential questions for managing the books of our business

~

Manufacturing businesses such as AppleSeed Enterprises Inc., compute product cost by determining and then adding three separate cost elements. The three common cost elements are: (1) raw material costs; (2) direct labor costs; and (3) overhead costs.

Overhead costs is a catchall category for costs that cannot be assigned to a specific product, but rather are ongoing costs required just to keep the plant open. Examples of overhead costs include costs for plant space, heat, light, power, supervisory labor, depreciation and so forth.

We will discuss so-called *direct costs* first and then overhead costs. Direct costs (basically materials and labor) are simple and easy to understand.

After discussing each element of manufacturing cost separately, we will then summarize them into a product "standard" cost for use in (1) inventory valuation on the Balance Sheet, and (2) computing the cost of product sold for entry on the Income Statement.

Cost of Raw Materials. See Apple-Seed's applesauce "Bill of Materials" below. This table lists all of the materials that go into our product and the unit cost of these materials in normal commercial purchase quantities. Also shown is the amount and cost of materials that go into a single shipping "unit" of our product, in this instance a case containing 12 jars of applesauce.

From the Bill of Materials below we see that we buy apples in ton quantities at a price of $120 per ton delivered to our plant. Also, each 12-jar case of our applesauce takes 33 lbs. of apples to produce. Because 2,000 lbs. of apples costs us $120, we will pay $1.98 for the 33 lbs. of apples that will go into a case of applesauce.

AppleSeed Enterprises Applesauce Bill of Materials

	PRICE PER UNIT OF RAW MATERIAL	UNIT OF MEASURE FOR RAW MATERIAL	QUANTITY REQUIRED PER CASE OF 12 JARS	EXTENDED COST PER CASE OF 12
APPLES	$120	ton	33.00 lbs.	$1.98
SUGAR	$140	1000 lbs.	2.30 lbs.	$0.32
CINNAMON	$280	100 lbs.	0.35 oz.	$0.06
GLASS JAR	$55	gross	12	$4.60
JAR CAP	$10	gross	12	$0.83
JAR LABEL	$200	10,000	12	$0.24
LARGE BOX	$75	gross	1	$0.52
			COST PER CASE	$8.55

Using a similar calculation for all the other raw materials in our product yields a total materials cost of $8.55 per 12-jar case of applesauce.

Cost of Direct Labor. We have designed our plant to manufacture up to 20,000 cases of applesauce each month. Because the plant is highly automated, we will need only five hourly workers to achieve this production level.

Our total hourly labor payroll for a single month is $12,300 (as computed in **Transaction 9**). Divide this labor cost by the 20,000 cases we plan to produce each month. We compute a direct labor cost of $0.62 for each case of applesauce made.

Manufacturing Labor Per Case

Hourly payroll per month	$12,300.00
÷ Cases produced	20,000
= Hourly payroll per case	$0.62

We have just estimated the first two elements of product cost—materials and direct labor. They were easy compared to what follows: overhead and depreciation.

Overhead

It is not difficult to see how material cost should be added as a part of product costs. Same for direct labor. But "overhead" is not so simple.

It takes more than just materials and labor to make a product. It takes a manufacturing building; it takes machinery; it takes heat, light and power; and it takes supervisors to make things run properly. These costs don't go "directly" into the product as do materials and labor, but they are costs to make the product nonetheless.

～

On the next pages we will study depreciation charges for AppleSeed and then come back to compute total overhead costs and total manufacturing costs for making our applesauce.

Depreciation

A major cost for AppleSeed is the *depreciation* of machinery and buildings used to make our product. Basically, depreciation is a way of charging to *current activities* a pro-rata *portion of the original purchase price* of long-lived assets.

For example, suppose we purchase a $100,000 machine. Over its useful life it will make 500,000 jars of applesauce. Therefore, each jar should be charged a $0.20 cost for its pro-rata use of that machine. Thus we would add $0.20 to the cost of each jar as a *depreciation charge*.

To simplify, both accounting practice and tax laws say that fixed assets such as buildings and machinery can be "written off" or "depreciated" each year by a certain specified portion of their value. Some assets are written off over a longer useful life (buildings over 20 to 30 years) or a shorter useful life (automobiles over 5 years).

Depreciation Schedule. Look at AppleSeed Enterprises' fixed asset depreciation schedule on the facing page. Listed in the left-most column are AppleSeed's fixed assets. Note that the total amount under "original purchase price" is the same amount shown on AppleSeed's Balance Sheet for *Fixed Assets @ Cost.*

Depreciation is just a method of dribbling the costs of fixed assets through the Income Statement over time ... as you use the assets.

AppleSeed Enterprises Fixed Asset Depreciation Schedule

	ORIGINAL PURCHASE PRICE	YEARS OF USEFUL	DEPRECIATION CHARGE EACH YEAR	BOOK VALUE AT END OF YEAR 1	BOOK VALUE AT END OF YEAR 2	BOOK VALUE AT END OF YEAR 3
BUILDING	$1,000,000	20	$50,000	$950,000	$900,000	$850,000
LAND	$500,000	forever	$0	$500,000	$500,000	$500,000
MACHINERY	$250,000	7	$35,714	$214,286	$178,572	$142,858
TOTALS	$1,750,000		$85,714	$1,664,286	$1,578,572	$1,492,858

The next column lists the useful life that AppleSeed will use to compute depreciation for each asset class. In the next column we list the actual yearly depreciation amount when using the "straight-line" method to compute depreciation. Straight-line yearly depreciation equals original cost divided by years of useful life.

Note that with straight-line depreciation, the same amount of depreciation is taken for each year of useful life. "Accelerated" depreciation methods allow you to depreciate more in early years.

Book Value. The remaining three columns show the "book value" of AppleSeed's fixed assets at the end of each of the next three years. Book value is just the original purchase price of a fixed asset less all the depreciation charges taken over the years—the so-called "accumulated depreciation." The book value of the fixed assets is shown on the Balance Sheet as *Net Fixed Assets*.

Note that book value is an accounting definition of "value." It does not necessarily correspond to any actual resale value or replacement value.

Effect on Income. Each year Apple-Seed will add $85,714 (or $7,143 per month) to its costs to account for its use of fixed assets throughout the year. This charge will hit the Income Statement as an element of product costs shown in *Cost of Goods Sold*. More later.

Effect on Cash. Unlike most other expenses, you don't pay a depreciation charge with cash. That is to say, cash balance and cash flow are not affected as you depreciate a fixed asset. Why is this so? Sounds like a free lunch?

Depreciation is not free. When you originally purchased the fixed asset you paid its total cost with cash. The Cash Flow Statement showed the payment at full purchase price. But this purchase price did not go through Income Statement as an expense *at that time*. We depreciate the full cost of a long-lived asset over time in the Income Statement.

Depreciation is just a method of dribbling the costs of fixed assets through the Income Statement over time, as you use the assets.

Overhead Continued

AppleSeed Enterprises' manufacturing overhead is made up of the supervisor's salary, depreciation charges and other odds and ends such as heat, light and power, and general supplies. Most of these costs must be paid regardless of the production volume. That is, these costs are generally the same whether we produce a lot or a little applesauce.

Let's compute AppleSeed's manufacturing overhead. From **Transaction 9** we see that the supervisor's total payroll cost is $4,880 per month. From the computations on the prior page we see that

Product Cost @ Three Different Production Levels

	COSTS PER CASE	COSTS PER MONTH	TOTAL COSTS FOR 10,000 CASES PER MONTH	TOTAL COSTS FOR 20,000 CASES PER MONTH	TOTAL COSTS FOR 30,000 CASES PER MONTH
RAW MATERIALS	$8.55		$85,500	$171,000	$256,500
DIRECT LABOR	$0.62		$6,150	$12,300	$18,450
OVERHEAD— SUPERVISOR		$4,880	$4,880	$4,880	$4,880
DEPRECIATION		$7,143	$7,143	$7,143	$7,143
ALL OTHER		$8,677	$8,677	$8,677	$8,677
TOTAL MANUFACTURING $ COST IN MONTH			$112,350	$204,000	$295,650
CASES MANUFACTURED IN MONTH			10,000	20,000	30,000
$ MANUFACTURING COST PER CASE			$11.24	$10.20	$9.86

depreciation is $7,143 per month. Let's assume that all other elements of overhead (heat, power, etc.) will cost $8,677 per month. Thus AppleSeed's total manufacturing overhead is $20,700 each and every month as shown below:

Supervisory payroll	$4,880
Depreciation	7,143
all other costs	8,677
Total monthly overhead	$20,700

But note that it all does not go out as cash each month. Remember, depreciation is a non-cash expense...just a bookkeeping entry. The actual cash outlay for overhead is only the supervisor's salary and the "all other" expense that totals together $13,577 each month.

Fixed and Variable Costs

Some of AppleSeed's manufacturing costs get larger (in total) with each additional case the company makes. For example, with more cases produced, more raw material is consumed. Ten cases require $85.50 worth of raw materials; 100 cases require $855 worth of raw materials. This type of cost, one that varies directly and proportionally with production volume, is called a *variable cost.* Direct labor is another example of a variable cost.

A cost that does not normally change with the volume level of production is called a *fixed cost.* Examples of AppleSeed fixed costs are supervisory labor costs and depreciation. Generally the elements of overhead are fixed costs.

What is important about the concept of fixed and variable costs? Costs to produce a manufactured product can vary greatly depending on production volume and proportion of fixed versus variable costs elements in product cost.

Thus, when we talk about the cost of an individual case of applesauce to manufacture, we must also state a production volume. Then the total fixed manufacturing costs can be "allocated" proportionally to each individual unit of production. Thus we can establish a cost for inventory valuation and cost of goods sold computation.

See the table above. It shows different product costs at different production volumes. Actual costs to produce a case of applesauce vary between $11.24 and $9.86 depending on whether we produce 10,000 or up to 30,000 cases. The lower case cost is at the higher volume. When we talk about what an individual case of applesauce costs us to make, we must also state a production volume.

Now we are ready to compute Apple-Seed's product costs and determine how to value our inventory.

Standard Cost System

Okay, let's pull all the manufacturing costs together and compute what a case of applesauce costs to make. But remember, we cannot compute the unit cost of a case of applesauce until we set a monthly level of production.

In the production costing chart shown on the previous page, we have computed the total monthly costs to produce applesauce at three different production volumes: 10,000, 20,000 or 30,000 cases per month. We have also computed for these production volumes AppleSeed's cost per case. Depending on our monthly production volume, a single case of applesauce can cost between $11.24 (at 10,000 cases per month) and $9.86 (at 30,000 cases per month) ... quite a significant difference!

The so-called *standard cost* is an estimate of product unit cost assuming a certain production volume. Accountants use standard cost as a good estimate of real costs to simplify day-to-day accounting transactions.

Establishing a standard cost will be useful for maintaining AppleSeed Enterprises' books. We will use this standard cost to value *Inventory* and to establish *Cost of Goods Sold* (COGS) when we sell our product.

AppleSeed's planned production is 20,000 cases per month. From the table on the previous page, we expect our actual costs will be $10.20 per case of applesauce we manufacture The table shows this standard cost broken down by element of cost. We will be using this breakdown in later transactions.

Variances. What happens if at the end of a period we find that we manufactured either more (or less) than 20,000 cases per month? Won't the "costs" then change? Yes, costs will change. We will account for this overestimate or underestimate of costs by making manufacturing variance adjustments to the books. More on this topic later.

AppleSeed Enterprises Standard Cost Calculations by Cost Element @ 20,000 Cases per Month Production Level

	TOTAL COST PER MONTH AT 20,000 CASE PRODUCTION	COST PER CASE	TO EMPLOYEES	FRINGES AND TAXES	TO SUPPLIERS	DEPRECIATION CHARGE
RAW MATERIALS	$171,000	$8.55			$8.55	
DIRECT LABOR	$12,300	$0.62	$0.32	$0.30		
OVERHEAD: SUPERVISOR	$4,880	$0.24	$0.14	$0.10		
DEPRECIATION	$7,143	$0.36				$0.36
ALL OTHER	$8,677	$0.43			$0.43	
	$204,000	$10.20	$.46	$0.40	$8.98	$0.36
TOTALS PER MONTH			$9,020	$8,160	$179,677	$7,143

Income Statement

for the period including Transactions 1 through 10		*prior*	+	*transaction*	=	*sum*
1	NET SALES	$0	—			$0
2	COST OF GOODS SOLD	0	—			0
1 - 2 = 3	GROSS MARGIN	0				0
4	SALES & MARKETING	7,680	—			7,680
5	RESEARCH & DEVELOPMENT	0	—			0
6	GENERAL & ADMINISTRATIVE	18,220	—			18,220
4 + 5 + 6 = 7	OPERATING EXPENSE	25,900				25,900
3 - 7 = 8	INCOME FROM OPERATIONS	(25,900)				(25,900)
9	NET INTEREST INCOME	0	—			0
10	INCOME TAXES	0	—			0
8 + 9 - 10 = 11	NET INCOME	($25,900)		0		($25,900)

IS Transaction Sum

Cash Flow Statement

for the period including Transactions 1 through 10		*prior*	+	*transaction*	=	*sum*
a	BEGINNING CASH BALANCE	$0				$0
b	CASH RECEIPTS	0	—			0
c	CASH DISBURSEMENTS	23,740	—			23,740
b - c = d	CASH FLOW FROM OPERATIONS	(23,740)				(23,740)
e	PP&E PURCHASE	1,750,000	—			1,750,000
f	NET BORROWINGS	1,000,000	—			1,000,000
g	INCOME TAXES PAID	0	—			0
h	SALE OF CAPITAL STOCK	1,550,000	—			1,550,000
a + d - e + f - g + h = i	ENDING CASH BALANCES	$776,260		0		$776,260

CF Transaction Sum

Balance Sheet

as of this Transaction 10		*prior*	+	*transaction*	=	*sum*
A	CASH	$776,260	—			$776,260
B	ACCOUNTS RECEIVABLE	0	—			0
C	INVENTORIES	0	[1]	20,000		20,000
D	PREPAID EXPENSES	0	—			0
A + B + C + D = E	CURRENT ASSETS	776,260				796,260
F	OTHER ASSETS	0	—			0
G	FIXED ASSETS @ COST	1,750,000	—			1,750,000
H	ACCUMULATED DEPRECIATION	0	—			0
G - H = I	NET FIXED ASSETS	1,750,000				1,750,000
E + F + I = J	TOTAL ASSETS	$2,526,260		20,000		$2,546,260

Assets Sum

		prior	+	*transaction*	=	*sum*
K	ACCOUNTS PAYABLE	$0	[2]	20,000		20,000
L	ACCRUED EXPENSES	2,160	—			2,160
M	CURRENT PORTION OF DEBT	100,000	—			100,000
N	INCOME TAXES PAYABLE	0	—			0
K + L + M + N = O	CURRENT LIABILITIES	102,160				122,160
P	LONG-TERM DEBT	900,000	—			900,000
Q	CAPITAL STOCK	1,550,000	—			1,550,000
R	RETAINED EARNINGS	(25,900)	—			(25,900)
Q + R = S	SHAREHOLDERS' EQUITY	1,524,100				1,524,100
O + P + S = T	TOTAL LIABILITIES & EQUITY	$2,526,260		20,000		$2,546,260

Liabilities & Equity Sum

T10. Place an order for raw materials (apples, spices, packaging materials). Receive 1 million specially printed jar labels at $0.02 each.

We must order and receive raw materials before AppleSeed Enterprises can start its production. The table below shows the quantities of various materials required for our monthly planned production level of 20,000 cases. Place a standing order with your suppliers for delivery of these quantities of raw materials each month.

To get a good price on very special four-color labels, the printer demands a press run of 1 million labels at $0.02 each. Place the label order and receive the labels from the printer.

Raw Material Costs and Monthly Production Requirements

	QUANTITY PER CARTON	COST PER CARTON	QUANTITY NEEDED FOR 20,000 CARTONS	EXTENDED COST FOR 20,000 CARTONS
APPLES	33.00 lbs.	$1.98	330 tons	$39,600
SUGAR	2.30 lbs.	$0.32	52 tons	$6,400
CINNAMON	0.35 oz.	$0.06	438 lbs.	$1,200
GLASS JAR	12	$4.60	1,667 gross	$92,000
JAR CAP	12	$0.83	1,667 gross	$16,600
JAR LABEL	12	$0.24	1,667 gross	$4,800
LARGE BOX	1	$0.52	139 gross	$10,400
TOTALS		$8.55		$171,000

Transaction: Order and receive 1 million applesauce jar labels at a cost of $0.02 each for a total of $20,000 to be paid 30 days after delivery.

1 Place the labels in raw material inventory for use when we start production. Increase INVENTORY by $20,000 in the assets section of the *Balance Sheet*.

2 We owe our printer for the labels, but we will pay the bill later. Increase ACCOUNTS PAYABLE by $20,000 in the liabilities section of the *Balance Sheet*.

Note: Simply placing an order for raw materials has no effect on any of the three financial statements. However, when you do receive materials, the *Balance Sheet* is modified to account for these new assets and the balancing new liabilities—what you own for the materials is listed as an ACCOUNTS PAYABLE.

Chapter 8.
Manufacturing Operations Startup

We are ready to start producing applesauce. The machinery is up and running, the workers are hired and we are about to receive a supply of raw materials.

While manufacturing goes fairly smoothly, we do botch a half-day's production and have to scrap it. We will learn how to value our inventory "at standard" and book our first manufacturing variance. Raw materials keep rolling in.

~

Transaction 11. Receive two months' supply of raw materials.

Transaction 12. Start up production. Pay workers and supervisor for the month.

Transaction 13. Book depreciation and other manufacturing overhead costs for the month.

Transaction 14. Pay for labels received in Transaction 10.

Transaction 15. Finish manufacturing 19,500 cases and move them into "finished goods."

Transaction 16. Scrap 500 cases of work-in-process inventory.

- Manufacturing variances: what can go wrong; what can go right.

Transaction 17. Pay for the two months' supply of raw materials received in Transaction 11.

Transaction 18. Manufacture another month's supply of applesauce.

Income Statement

for the period including Transactions 1 through 11		prior	+	transaction	=	sum
1	NET SALES	$0	—			$0
2	COST OF GOODS SOLD	0	—			0
1 - 2 = 3	GROSS MARGIN	0				0
4	SALES & MARKETING	7,680	—			7,680
5	RESEARCH & DEVELOPMENT	0	—			0
6	GENERAL & ADMINISTRATIVE	18,220	—			18,220
4 + 5 + 6 = 7	OPERATING EXPENSE	25,900				25,900
3 - 7 = 8	INCOME FROM OPERATIONS	(25,900)				(25,900)
9	NET INTEREST INCOME	0	—			0
10	INCOME TAXES	0	—			0
8 + 9 - 10 = 11	NET INCOME	($25,900)		0		($25,900)

IS Transaction Sum

Cash Flow Statement

for the period including Transactions 1 through 11		prior	+	transaction	=	sum
a	BEGINNING CASH BALANCE	$0				$0
b	CASH RECEIPTS	0	—			0
c	CASH DISBURSEMENTS	23,740	—			23,740
b - c = d	CASH FLOW FROM OPERATIONS	(23,740)				(23,740)
e	PP&E PURCHASE	1,750,000	—			1,750,000
f	NET BORROWINGS	1,000,000	—			1,000,000
g	INCOME TAXES PAID	0	—			0
h	SALE OF CAPITAL STOCK	1,550,000	—			1,550,000
a + d - e + f - g + h = i	ENDING CASH BALANCES	$776,260		0		$776,260

CF Transaction Sum

Balance Sheet

as of this Transaction 11		prior	+	transaction	=	sum
A	CASH	$776,260	—			$776,260
B	ACCOUNTS RECEIVABLE	0	—			0
C	INVENTORIES	20,000	[1]	332,400		352,400
D	PREPAID EXPENSES	0	—			0
A + B + C + D = E	CURRENT ASSETS	796,260				1,128,660
F	OTHER ASSETS	0	—			0
G	FIXED ASSETS @ COST	1,750,000	—			1,750,000
H	ACCUMULATED DEPRECIATION	0	—			0
G - H = I	NET FIXED ASSETS	1,750,000				1,750,000
E + F + I = J	TOTAL ASSETS	$2,546,260		332,400		$2,878,660

Assets Sum

K	ACCOUNTS PAYABLE	$20,000	[2]	332,400		352,400
L	ACCRUED EXPENSES	2,160	—			2,160
M	CURRENT PORTION OF DEBT	100,000	—			100,000
N	INCOME TAXES PAYABLE	0	—			0
K + L + M + N = O	CURRENT LIABILITIES	122,160				454,560
P	LONG-TERM DEBT	900,000	—			900,000
Q	CAPITAL STOCK	1,550,000	—			1,550,000
R	RETAINED EARNINGS	(25,900)	—			(25,900)
Q + R = S	SHAREHOLDERS' EQUITY	1,524,100				1,524,100
O + P + S = T	TOTAL LIABILITIES & EQUITY	$2,546,260		332,400		$2,878,660

Liabilities & Equity Sum

T11. Receive a two months' supply of raw materials.

Receive two months' supply of the rest of the raw materials necessary to manufacture our splendid applesauce. We will buy them on credit. Our suppliers will ship the materials to us now and not expect payment for a little while.

> Now is the time for AppleSeed to set up an *Inventory Valuation Worksheet*. (See table below.) This worksheet will help us compute the value of our inventory as we make and sell applesauce.
>
> The worksheet will list the effects of all transactions that change inventory values. The "Total Inventory" value at the bottom of the worksheet will always equal the INVENTORY value shown on our *Balance Sheet*.

Our inventory will be divided into three groups depending on where it is in the manufacturing process. These categories will not show up on the *Balance Sheet*. The *Balance Sheet* lists only the total inventory figure. You'll see in future transactions how useful it is to account for inventory valuation using these three classifications:

Raw Material Inventory is just that, "raw" purchased goods unmodified by us and waiting to be processed.

Work-In-Process ("WIP") refers to materials that are being processed by our machines and by our labor force. Work-in-process has added value because of our processing. More on this concept later.

Finished Goods Inventory product finished and ready to ship. For inventory valuation purposes we will use the "standard cost" we computed earlier to value our finished goods.

Transaction: Receive a two months' supply of all raw materials (apples, sugar, cinnamon, jars, caps, boxes) worth $332,400 in total. (That is, $8.55 total materials per case less $0.24 for the already received labels times 40,000 cases.)

1 Increase INVENTORIES account on the *Balance Sheet* by the $332,400 cost of these materials.

2 Increase ACCOUNTS PAYABLE on the *Balance Sheet* by the value of the materials received.

Inventory Valuation Worksheet	RAW MATERIAL	WORK IN PROCESS	FINISHED GOODS
INVENTORY VALUES AT STARTUP (PRIOR TO T10)	$0.00	$0	$0
A. Receive labels (**T10**)	$20,000	$0	$0
B. Receive 2 months' supply of other raw materials (**T11**)	$332,400	$0	$0
SUBTOTALS (AS OF THIS TRANSACTION)	$352,400	$0	$0
TOTAL INVENTORY			$352,400

Income Statement

for the period including Transactions 1 through 12	prior	+	transaction	=	sum
1 NET SALES	$0		—		$0
2 COST OF GOODS SOLD	0		—		0
1 - 2 = 3 GROSS MARGIN	0				0
4 SALES & MARKETING	7,680		—		7,680
5 RESEARCH & DEVELOPMENT	0		—		0
6 GENERAL & ADMINISTRATIVE	18,220		—		18,220
4 + 5 + 6 = 7 OPERATING EXPENSE	25,900				25,900
3 - 7 = 8 INCOME FROM OPERATIONS	(25,900)				(25,900)
9 NET INTEREST INCOME	0		—		0
10 INCOME TAXES	0		—		0
8 + 9 - 10 = 11 NET INCOME	($25,900)		0		($25,900)

IS Transaction Sum

Cash Flow Statement

for the period including Transactions 1 through 12	prior	+	transaction	=	sum
a BEGINNING CASH BALANCE	$0				$0
b CASH RECEIPTS	0		—		0
c CASH DISBURSEMENTS	23,740	1A	9,020		32,760
b - c = d CASH FLOW FROM OPERATIONS	(23,740)				(32,760)
e PP&E PURCHASE	1,750,000		—		1,750,000
f NET BORROWINGS	1,000,000		—		1,000,000
g INCOME TAXES PAID	0		—		0
h SALE OF CAPITAL STOCK	1,550,000		—		1,550,000
a + d - e + f - g + h = i ENDING CASH BALANCES	$776,260		(9,020)		$767,240

CF Transaction Sum

Balance Sheet

as of this Transaction 12	prior	+	transaction	=	sum
A CASH	$776,260	1B	(9,020)		$767,240
B ACCOUNTS RECEIVABLE	0		—		0
C INVENTORIES	352,400	3	17,180		369,580
D PREPAID EXPENSES	0		—		0
A + B + C + D = E CURRENT ASSETS	1,128,660				1,136,820
F OTHER ASSETS	0		—		0
G FIXED ASSETS @ COST	1,750,000		—		1,750,000
H ACCUMULATED DEPRECIATION	0		—		0
G - H = I NET FIXED ASSETS	1,750,000				1,750,000
E + F + I = J TOTAL ASSETS	$2,878,660		8,160		$2,886,820
			Assets Sum		
K ACCOUNTS PAYABLE	$352,400		—		$352,400
L ACCRUED EXPENSES	2,160	2	8,160		10,320
M CURRENT PORTION OF DEBT	100,000		—		100,000
N INCOME TAXES PAYABLE	0		—		0
K + L + M + N = O CURRENT LIABILITIES	454,560				462,720
P LONG-TERM DEBT	900,000		—		900,000
Q CAPITAL STOCK	1,550,000		—		1,550,000
R RETAINED EARNINGS	(25,900)		—		(25,900)
Q + R = S SHAREHOLDERS' EQUITY	1,524,100				1,524,100
O + P + S = T TOTAL LIABILITIES & EQUITY	$2,878,660		8,160		$2,886,820

Liabilities & Equity Sum

T12. Start Production. Pay manufacturing employees their first month's salary. Book all the payroll associated fringe benefits and taxes.

We are finally ready to produce applesauce. The plant is ready and the workers have just shown up for work.

A month's supply of raw material ($8.55 per case times 20,000 cases equals a total of $171,000) is on its way from storage onto the plant floor to await processing. On the inventory worksheet we will "move" this raw material into work-in-process.

Also, with this transaction we will pay our workers and the supervisor a month's salary and wages. Because these salary and wages go toward producing product they are called *costs*. These manufacturing costs will be accounted for by adding them to our work-in-process inventory. Thus, our inventory will increase in value by the amount of labor that we add while we process our product.

Transaction 9 showed the detail amounts for our manufacturing payroll. Because we were not yet in production, then, we charged the *Income Statement* with the expense covering the supervisor's salary. Now that we are manufacturing product, these salary and wages are costs that increase the value of our product...and are shown as an increase in inventory.

Transaction: Pay production workers' wages and supervisor's salary for the month. Book associated fringe benefits and payroll taxes.

1 Cut checks for $9,020 for take-home salary and workers' wages. (1A) Increase CASH DISBURSEMENTS by that amount in the *Cash Flow Statement*. (1B) Lower CASH by that amount in the *Balance Sheet*.

2 Book payroll-associated fringes and taxes of $8,160 as ACCRUED EXPENSES on the *Balance Sheet*.

3 Increase INVENTORY value on the *Balance Sheet* by $17,180, that is, $9,020 in salary and wages plus $8,160 in benefits and taxes.

Inventory Valuation Worksheet	RAW MATERIAL	WORK IN PROCESS	FINISHED GOODS
INVENTORY VALUES FROM T11.	$352,400	$0	$0
C. Move material to make 20,000 cases from raw material to WIP.	($171,000)	$171,000	$0
D. Pay supervisor and workers for the month. See **T9**.	$0	$17,180	$0
SUBTOTALS (AS OF THIS TRANSACTION)	$181,400	$188,180	$0
	TOTAL INVENTORY		$369,580

Income Statement

for the period including Transactions 1 through 13		prior	+	transaction	=	sum
1	NET SALES	$0	—			$0
2	COST OF GOODS SOLD	0	—			0
1 - 2 = 3	GROSS MARGIN	0				0
4	SALES & MARKETING	7,680	—			7,680
5	RESEARCH & DEVELOPMENT	0	—			0
6	GENERAL & ADMINISTRATIVE	18,220	—			18,220
4 + 5 + 6 = 7	OPERATING EXPENSE	25,900				25,900
3 - 7 = 8	INCOME FROM OPERATIONS	(25,900)				(25,900)
9	NET INTEREST INCOME	0	—			0
10	INCOME TAXES	0	—			0
8 + 9 - 10 = 11	NET INCOME	($25,900)	0			($25,900)

IS Transaction Sum

Cash Flow Statement

for the period including Transactions 1 through 13		prior	+	transaction	=	sum
a	BEGINNING CASH BALANCE	$0				$0
b	CASH RECEIPTS	0	—			0
c	CASH DISBURSEMENTS	32,760	—			32,760
b - c = d	CASH FLOW FROM OPERATIONS	(32,760)				(32,760)
e	PP&E PURCHASE	1,750,000	—			1,750,000
f	NET BORROWINGS	1,000,000	—			1,000,000
g	INCOME TAXES PAID	0	—			0
h	SALE OF CAPITAL STOCK	1,550,000	—			1,550,000
a + d - e + f - g + h = i	ENDING CASH BALANCES	$767,240	0			$767,240

CF Transaction Sum

Balance Sheet

as of this Transaction 13		prior	+	transaction	=	sum
A	CASH	$767,240		—		$767,240
B	ACCOUNTS RECEIVABLE	0		—		0
C	INVENTORIES	369,580	3	15,820		385,400
D	PREPAID EXPENSES	0		—		0
A + B + C + D = E	CURRENT ASSETS	1,136,820				1,152,640
F	OTHER ASSETS	0		—		0
G	FIXED ASSETS @ COST	1,750,000		—		1,750,000
H	ACCUMULATED DEPRECIATION	0	2	7,143		7,143
G - H = I	NET FIXED ASSETS	1,750,000				1,742,857
E + F + I = J	TOTAL ASSETS	$2,886,820		8,677		$2,895,497

Assets Sum

K	ACCOUNTS PAYABLE	$352,400	1	8,677		$361,077
L	ACCRUED EXPENSES	10,320		—		10,320
M	CURRENT PORTION OF DEBT	100,000		—		100,000
N	INCOME TAXES PAYABLE	0		—		0
K + L + M + N = O	CURRENT LIABILITIES	462,720				471,397
P	LONG-TERM DEBT	900,000		—		900,000
Q	CAPITAL STOCK	1,550,000		—		1,550,000
R	RETAINED EARNINGS	(25,900)		—		(25,900)
Q + R = S	SHAREHOLDERS' EQUITY	1,524,100				1,524,100
O + P + S = T	TOTAL LIABILITIES & EQUITY	$2,886,820		8,677		$2,895,497

Liabilities & Equity Sum

T13. Book depreciation and all other manufacturing overhead costs for the month.

As we are busily working on applesauce-making, there are a few bean-counting details that must be performed.

We are using our new machines in our very beautifully refurbished building. Something has to pay for all this splendor. With this transaction we will depreciate our machinery and building.

This depreciation charge is a manufacturing cost ... a legitimate cost of making our applesauce. Thus, when we book this depreciation we will add it in as a cost of manufacturing by increasing the value of our work-in-process inventory. Remember, all the manufacturing costs go into inventory.

Depreciation is a "non-cash" transaction, so we will not alter cash or accounts payable when we book AppleSeed's depreciation charge. No such luck with the "all other" overhead charges. We will eventually have to pay for them. Thus, accounts payable will be increased by what we owe.

Transaction: Book this month's manufacturing depreciation of $7,143 and $8,677 covering "all other" overhead costs. Note that depreciation is not a cash expense and will not lower our cash balance. But, the "all other" overhead we will eventually have to pay with cash.

1 Increase ACCOUNTS PAYABLE on the *Balance Sheet* by $8,677 covering the "all other" manufacturing overhead.

2 Increase ACCUMULATED DEPRECIATION on the *Balance Sheet* by this month's $7,143 depreciation charge.

3 Increase INVENTORY on the *Balance Sheet* by $15,820 covering this month's depreciation of $7,143 plus the $8,677 "all other" manufacturing overhead.

~

Inventory Valuation Worksheet	RAW MATERIAL	WORK IN PROCESS	FINISHED GOODS
INVENTORY VALUES FROM T12.	$181,400	$188,180	$0
E. Book manufacturing depreciation for the month.	$0.00	$7,143	$0
F. Book all other manufacturing overhead costs.	$0.00	$8,677	$0
SUBTOTALS (AS OF THIS TRANSACTION)	$181,400	$204,000	$0
TOTAL INVENTORY			$385,400

Income Statement

		for the period including Transactions 1 through 14	prior	+	transaction	=	sum
1		NET SALES	$0	—			$0
2		COST OF GOODS SOLD	0	—			0
1 - 2 = 3		GROSS MARGIN	0				0
4		SALES & MARKETING	7,680	—			7,680
5		RESEARCH & DEVELOPMENT	0	—			0
6		GENERAL & ADMINISTRATIVE	18,220	—			18,220
4 + 5 + 6 = 7		OPERATING EXPENSE	25,900				25,900
3 - 7 = 8		INCOME FROM OPERATIONS	(25,900)				(25,900)
9		NET INTEREST INCOME	0	—			0
10		INCOME TAXES	0	—			0
8 + 9 - 10 = 11		NET INCOME	($25,900)		0		($25,900)

IS Transaction Sum

Cash Flow Statement

		for the period including Transactions 1 through 14	prior	+	transaction	=	sum
a		BEGINNING CASH BALANCE	$0				$0
b		CASH RECEIPTS	0	—			0
c		CASH DISBURSEMENTS	32,760	1	20,000		52,760
b - c = d		CASH FLOW FROM OPERATIONS	(32,760)				(52,760)
e		PP&E PURCHASE	1,750,000	—			1,750,000
f		NET BORROWINGS	1,000,000	—			1,000,000
g		INCOME TAXES PAID	0	—			0
h		SALE OF CAPITAL STOCK	1,550,000	—			1,550,000
a + d - e + f - g + h = i		ENDING CASH BALANCES	$767,240		(20,000)		$747,240

CF Transaction Sum

Balance Sheet

		as of this Transaction 14	prior	+	transaction	=	sum
A		CASH	$767,240	2	(20,000)		$747,240
B		ACCOUNTS RECEIVABLE	0	—			0
C		INVENTORIES	385,400	—			385,400
D		PREPAID EXPENSES	0	—			0
A + B + C + D = E		CURRENT ASSETS	1,152,640				1,132,640
F		OTHER ASSETS	0	—			0
G		FIXED ASSETS @ COST	1,750,000	—			1,750,000
H		ACCUMULATED DEPRECIATION	7,143	—			7,143
G - H = I		NET FIXED ASSETS	1,742,857				1,742,857
E + F + I = J		TOTAL ASSETS	$2,895,497		(20,000)		$2,875,497
					Assets Sum		
K		ACCOUNTS PAYABLE	$361,077	3	(20,000)		$341,077
L		ACCRUED EXPENSES	10,320	—			10,320
M		CURRENT PORTION OF DEBT	100,000	—			100,000
N		INCOME TAXES PAYABLE	0	—			0
K + L + M + N = O		CURRENT LIABILITIES	471,397				451,397
P		LONG-TERM DEBT	900,000	—			900,000
Q		CAPITAL STOCK	1,550,000	—			1,550,000
R		RETAINED EARNINGS	(25,900)	—			(25,900)
Q + R = S		SHAREHOLDERS' EQUITY	1,524,100				1,524,100
O + P + S = T		TOTAL LIABILITIES & EQUITY	$2,895,497		(20,000)		$2,875,497

Liabilities & Equity Sum

T14. Pay $20,000 for the labels received in Transaction 10.

We received our applesauce jar labels over a month ago and the printer is very anxious to get paid. When we received the jar labels we created an accounts payable. When we pay this vendor with cash we will "reverse" the payable at the same time we lower cash.

Note, paying for this raw material in no way affects the values in our Inventory Valuation Worksheet. The inventory was increased by the cost of the labels when we received them and created an accounts payable.

Transaction: Pay for 1 million labels received in **Transaction 10**. Issue a check to our vendor for $20,000 as payment in full.

| 1 | Cut a check for $20,000 to pay the label printer. Increase CASH DISBURSEMENTS by that amount in the *Cash Flow Statement*. |

| 2 | Lower CASH by $20,000 in the assets section of the *Balance Sheet* since we wrote the check. |

| 3 | Lower ACCOUNTS PAYABLE in the liabilities section of the *Balance Sheet* by the $20,000 that we no longer owe (since we just paid as described above). |

~

Inventory Valuation Worksheet	RAW MATERIAL	WORK IN PROCESS	FINISHED GOODS
INVENTORY VALUES FROM T13.	$181,400	$204,000	$0
G. Pay for labels received in T10.	$0	$0	$0
SUBTOTALS (AS OF THIS TRANSACTION)	$181,400	$204,000	$0
TOTAL INVENTORY			$385,400

Income Statement

for the period including Transactions 1 through 15	prior	+ transaction =	sum
1 NET SALES	0	—	$0
2 COST OF GOODS SOLD	0	—	0
1 - 2 = 3 GROSS MARGIN	0		0
4 SALES & MARKETING	7,680	—	7,680
5 RESEARCH & DEVELOPMENT	0	—	0
6 GENERAL & ADMINISTRATIVE	18,220	—	18,220
4 + 5 + 6 = 7 OPERATING EXPENSE	25,900		25,900
3 - 7 = 8 INCOME FROM OPERATIONS	(25,900)		(25,900)
9 NET INTEREST INCOME	0	—	0
10 INCOME TAXES	0	—	0
8 + 9 - 10 = 11 NET INCOME	(25,900)	0	($25,900)

IS Transaction Sum

Cash Flow Statement

for the period including Transactions 1 through 15	prior	+ transaction =	sum
a BEGINNING CASH BALANCE	0		$0
b CASH RECEIPTS	0	—	0
c CASH DISBURSEMENTS	52,760	—	52,760
b - c = d CASH FLOW FROM OPERATIONS	(52,760)		(52,760)
e PP&E PURCHASE	1,750,000	—	1,750,000
f NET BORROWINGS	1,000,000	—	1,000,000
g INCOME TAXES PAID	0	—	0
h SALE OF CAPITAL STOCK	1,550,000	—	1,550,000
a + d - e + f - g + h = i ENDING CASH BALANCES	747,240	0	$747,240

CF Transaction Sum

Balance Sheet

as of this Transaction 15	prior	+ transaction =	sum
A CASH	747,240	—	$747,240
B ACCOUNTS RECEIVABLE	0	—	0
C INVENTORIES	385,400	—	385,400
D PREPAID EXPENSES	0	—	0
A + B + C + D = E CURRENT ASSETS	1,132,640		1,132,640
F OTHER ASSETS	0	—	0
G FIXED ASSETS @ COST	1,750,000	—	1,750,000
H ACCUMULATED DEPRECIATION	7,143	—	7,143
G - H = I NET FIXED ASSETS	1,742,857		1,742,857
E + F + I = J TOTAL ASSETS	2,875,497	0	$2,875,497

Assets Sum

	prior	+ transaction =	sum
K ACCOUNTS PAYABLE	341,077	—	$341,077
L ACCRUED EXPENSES	10,320	—	10,320
M CURRENT PORTION OF DEBT	100,000	—	100,000
N INCOME TAXES PAYABLE	0	—	0
K + L + M + N = O CURRENT LIABILITIES	451,397		451,397
P LONG-TERM DEBT	900,000	—	900,000
Q CAPITAL STOCK	1,550,000	—	1,550,000
R RETAINED EARNINGS	(25,900)	—	(25,900)
Q + R = S SHAREHOLDERS' EQUITY	1,524,100		1,524,100
O + P + S = T TOTAL LIABILITIES & EQUITY	2,875,497	0	$2,875,497

Liabilities & Equity Sum

T15. Finish production of 19,500 cases of our applesauce. Move product from work-in-process ("WIP") Inventory into Finished Goods.

Manufacturing our product is a continuous flow of raw material and labor into work-in-process inventory and then on to finished goods.

When we have finally boxed our finished jars of applesauce and they are ready for shipping, we place them in our finished goods warehouse. We will value this inventory at "standard cost," ready to become a COST OF GOODS amount when we ship.

On our Inventory Valuation Worksheet we will decrease work-in-process inventory and also increase finished goods inventory by the same amount, the value of goods we moved from work-in-process to finished goods.

Remember, we started out to make 20,000 cases. But somewhere in the process we lost some product and only ended up with 19,500 cases. We will "move" these 19,500 cases into finished goods inventory. In the next transaction we will deal with what happened and how to account for the remaining 500 cases.

The inventory value of the 19,500 cases to be transferred is $198,900—a $10.20 standard cost times 19,500 cases. Note that while accounting entries (see below) are made in our Inventory Valuation Worksheet as we move work-in-process inventory into finished goods, no change is made in the company's *Income Statement, Balance Sheet* or *Cash Flow Statement.*

Inventory values will become COST OF GOODS only when we ship product to customers.

Transaction: This movement of inventory into a different class is really just an internal management control transaction as far as the financial statements are concerned. There is no effect on the three major financial statements of AppleSeed. INVENTORIES on the *Balance Sheet* remains the same. Our Inventory Valuation Worksheet, as shown below, reflects the change in inventory status.

~

Inventory Valuation Worksheet	RAW MATERIAL	WORK IN PROCESS	FINISHED GOODS
INVENTORY VALUES FROM T14.	$181,400	$204,000	$0
H Move 19,500 cases from WIP into FG @ standard cost.	$0	$(198,900)	$198,900
SUBTOTALS (AS OF THIS TRANSACTION)	$181,400	$5,100	$198,900
		TOTAL INVENTORY	$385,400

Income Statement

for the period including Transactions 1 through 16		*prior*	+	*transaction*	=	*sum*
1	NET SALES	$0		—		$0
2	COST OF GOODS SOLD	0	[2]	5,100		5,100
1 - 2 = 3	GROSS MARGIN	0				(5,100)
4	SALES & MARKETING	7,680		—		7,680
5	RESEARCH & DEVELOPMENT	0		—		0
6	GENERAL & ADMINISTRATIVE	18,220		—		18,220
4 + 5 + 6 = 7	OPERATING EXPENSE	25,900				25,900
3 - 7 = 8	INCOME FROM OPERATIONS	(25,900)				(31,000)
9	NET INTEREST INCOME	0		—		0
10	INCOME TAXES	0		—		0
8 + 9 - 10 = 11	NET INCOME	($25,900)		(5,100)		($31,000)

IS Transaction Sum

Cash Flow Statement

for the period including Transactions 1 through 16		*prior*	+	*transaction*	=	*sum*
a	BEGINNING CASH BALANCE	$0				$0
b	CASH RECEIPTS	0		—		0
c	CASH DISBURSEMENTS	52,760		—		52,760
b - c = d	CASH FLOW FROM OPERATIONS	(52,760)				(52,760)
e	PP&E PURCHASE	1,750,000		—		1,750,000
f	NET BORROWINGS	1,000,000		—		1,000,000
g	INCOME TAXES PAID	0		—		0
h	SALE OF CAPITAL STOCK	1,550,000		—		1,550,000
a + d - e + f - g + h = i	ENDING CASH BALANCES	$747,240		0		$747,240

CF Transaction Sum

Balance Sheet

as of this Transaction 16		*prior*	+	*transaction*	=	*sum*
A	CASH	$747,240		—		$747,240
B	ACCOUNTS RECEIVABLE	0		—		0
C	INVENTORIES	385,400	[1]	(5,100)		380,300
D	PREPAID EXPENSES	0		—		0
A + B + C + D = E	CURRENT ASSETS	1,132,640				1,127,540
F	OTHER ASSETS	0		—		0
G	FIXED ASSETS @ COST	1,750,000		—		1,750,000
H	ACCUMULATED DEPRECIATION	7,143		—		7,143
G - H = I	NET FIXED ASSETS	1,742,857				1,742,857
E + F + I = J	TOTAL ASSETS	$2,875,497		(5,100)		$2,870,397

Assets Sum

K	ACCOUNTS PAYABLE	$341,077		—		$341,077
L	ACCRUED EXPENSES	10,320		—		10,320
M	CURRENT PORTION OF DEBT	100,000		—		100,000
N	INCOME TAXES PAYABLE	0		—		0
K + L + M + N = O	CURRENT LIABILITIES	451,397				451,397
P	LONG-TERM DEBT	900,000		—		900,000
Q	CAPITAL STOCK	1,550,000		—		1,550,000
R	RETAINED EARNINGS	(25,900)	[3]	(5,100)		(31,000)
Q + R = S	SHAREHOLDERS' EQUITY	1,524,100				1,519,000
O + P + S = T	TOTAL LIABILITIES & EQUITY	$2,875,497		(5,100)		$2,870,397

Liabilities & Equity Sum

T16. Scrap 500 cases worth of work-in-process inventory.

After we moved all the product that we could find (19,500 cases) into finished goods, we looked around for the remaining 500 cases we had expected to make.

We started out with enough material to make 20,000 cases but seem to have produced only 19,500 cases. The material and labor expenditures for these remaining 500 cases still remain in work-in-process inventory—but where is the product?

Our production supervisor comes up with the answer. It seems that our workers had some trouble starting up some of the new machines. Everything is fixed now, but for the first month of production every 40th jar of applesauce got smashed in the innards of the conveyor belts!

Thus, our output was only 19,500 cases and we spoiled 500 cases. We still expended the labor to produce 20,000 cases and we used all the material required to produce 20,000 cases, but at the end we only produced 19,500 cases.

Oh well, no use crying over spilled applesauce. But how should we account for the loss? Scrap the value of 500 cases of applesauce. Lower the value of work-in-process inventory and take a corresponding loss on the *Income Statement*.

Transaction: Scrap the value of 500 cases of applesauce from the work-in-process inventory. Take a loss on the *Income Statement* for this amount.

1 Reduce **INVENTORIES** on the *Balance Sheet* by the $5,100 value of the inventory to be scrapped (that is 500 cases times the standard cost of $10.20 each).

2 Charge $5,100 to **COST OF GOODS** for the loss in value of the inventory due to scrapping 500 cases of work-in-process inventory.

3 Remember that the resulting loss in the *Income Statement* must be reflected as a decrease in **RETAINED EARNINGS** in the *Balance Sheet*.

~

Inventory Valuation Worksheet	RAW MATERIAL	WORK IN PROCESS	FINISHED GOODS
INVENTORY VALUES FROM T15.	$181,400	$5,100	$198,900
I. Scrap 500 cases of applesauce from WIP inventory.	$0	$(5,100)	$0
SUBTOTALS (AS OF THIS TRANSACTION)	$181,400	$0	$198,900
		TOTAL INVENTORY	$380,300

Manufacturing Variances

The most efficient type of cost accounting is one that makes use of predetermined costs—referred to as *standard* costs. This procedure consists of setting, in advance of production, what the unit cost *should* be, and upon completion of production, comparing the actual costs with these *standard costs*. Any differences (either positive or negative) are then applied to the financial statements as a "variance" in order to reflect reality.

Standard Costs

We at AppleSeed Enterprises use a *standard costing system* to value our inventory. It is a convenient and accurate way to run the books and to account for what our products cost.

But, remember, the standard cost is what we *expect* our product to cost if all goes according to plan. That is, all must go *exactly* as expected (or excess money spent in one area must be saved in another) if our *actual cost* is to equal our standard cost.

In using a standard costing system the various costs for materials, labor and overhead are booked into inventory at their *actual amounts*. But when product is placed in finished goods and then is sold, the transaction is performed "at standard."

The difference between the actual and the standard cost is then booked in the accounting records. These differences, if any, are called *manufacturing variances*.

Types of Variances For AppleSeed's product and production costs to be "at standard," that is, for no manufacturing cost variances to have occurred:

- We must produce 20,000 cases in a month—no more, no less. *Otherwise we will have a **volume variance.***

- Our raw material must cost what we have estimated— no more, no less. *Otherwise we will have a **purchase variance.***

- The amount of raw material used must be just that planned. *Otherwise we will have a **yield variance.***

- We need no more or less direct labor and no overtime to produce our 20,000 cases. *Otherwise we will have a **labor variance.***

- We don't have excess scrap produced in the production process. *Otherwise we will have a **scrap variance.***

For AppleSeed's product and production costs to be at standard, that is, for no variances to have occurred:

1. We must produce exactly 20,000 cases in a month.
2. Our raw material must cost exactly what we have estimated.
3. The amount of raw material used must be just as planned.
4. We need no more or less direct labor and no overtime to produce our 20,000 cases.
5. We don't have excess scrap produced in the production process.

Most often everything does not come out perfectly. We will then have to apply variances to our books. Remember, our production cost accounting relied upon standard cost. We used this standard cost to apply costs to inventory and to cost of goods sold. If actual costs were different and they always are, hopefully by just a little bit—we will have to adjust the books by entering variance amounts.

Note that while it does not apply to AppleSeed, there is one other kind of manufacturing variance, the *mix variance*. A multi-product company can make more (or less) of one product than planned. This production difference can result in more (or less) overhead "absorption" depending on the relative overhead contribution of the products actually produced. This "under" or "over absorption" is accounted for as a product mix variance.

In summary, volume variances occur when we make more or less product than we had planned. Thus we must spread our fixed costs and overhead over less product (resulting in a higher cost) or over more product (resulting in a lower cost).

Spending variances can occur when raw materials cost more or less than planned. Actual product cost reflects these differences.

Labor variances are very easy to understand. If it takes more man-hours to make our product than expected by the standard, then our product must cost more than planned.

If AppleSeed continuously books large manufacturing variances each month, we should modify our standard costs to make them conform more closely to reality.

Income Statement

for the period including Transactions 1 through 17		prior	+	transaction	=	sum
1	NET SALES	$0		—		$0
2	COST OF GOODS SOLD	5,100		—		5,100
1 - 2 = 3	GROSS MARGIN	(5,100)				(5,100)
4	SALES & MARKETING	7,680		—		7,680
5	RESEARCH & DEVELOPMENT	0		—		0
6	GENERAL & ADMINISTRATIVE	18,220		—		18,220
4 + 5 + 6 = 7	OPERATING EXPENSE	25,900				25,900
3 - 7 = 8	INCOME FROM OPERATIONS	(31,000)				(31,000)
9	NET INTEREST INCOME	0		—		0
10	INCOME TAXES	0		—		0
8 + 9 - 10 = 11	NET INCOME	($31,000)		0		($31,000)

IS Transaction Sum

Cash Flow Statement

for the period including Transactions 1 through 17		prior	+	transaction	=	sum
a	BEGINNING CASH BALANCE	$0				$0
b	CASH RECEIPTS	0		—		0
c	CASH DISBURSEMENTS	52,760	**1**	150,000		202,760
b - c = d	CASH FLOW FROM OPERATIONS	(52,760)				(202,760)
e	PP&E PURCHASE	1,750,000		—		1,750,000
f	NET BORROWINGS	1,000,000		—		1,000,000
g	INCOME TAXES PAID	0		—		0
h	SALE OF CAPITAL STOCK	1,550,000		—		1,550,000
a + d - e + f - g + h = i	ENDING CASH BALANCES	$747,240		(150,000)		$597,240

CF Transaction Sum

Balance Sheet

as of this Transaction 17		prior	+	transaction	=	sum
A	CASH	$747,240	**2**	(150,000)		$597,240
B	ACCOUNTS RECEIVABLE	0		—		0
C	INVENTORIES	380,300		—		380,300
D	PREPAID EXPENSES	0		—		0
A + B + C + D = E	CURRENT ASSETS	1,127,540				977,540
F	OTHER ASSETS	0		—		0
G	FIXED ASSETS @ COST	1,750,000		—		1,750,000
H	ACCUMULATED DEPRECIATION	7,143		—		7,143
G - H = I	NET FIXED ASSETS	1,742,857				1,742,857
E + F + I = J	TOTAL ASSETS	$2,870,397		(150,000)		$2,720,397

Assets Sum

K	ACCOUNTS PAYABLE	$341,077	**3**	(150,000)		$191,077
L	ACCRUED EXPENSES	10,320		—		10,320
M	CURRENT PORTION OF DEBT	100,000		—		100,000
N	INCOME TAXES PAYABLE	0		—		0
K + L + M + N = O	CURRENT LIABILITIES	451,397				301,397
P	LONG-TERM DEBT	900,000		—		900,000
Q	CAPITAL STOCK	1,550,000		—		1,550,000
R	RETAINED EARNINGS	(31,000)		—		(31,000)
Q + R = S	SHAREHOLDERS' EQUITY	1,519,000				1,519,000
O + P + S = T	TOTAL LIABILITIES & EQUITY	$2,870,397		(150,000)		$2,720,397

Liabilities & Equity Sum

T17. Pay for a portion of the raw materials received in Transaction 11.

With our first month's production successfully placed in our finished goods warehouse, we throw a company picnic in celebration.

Halfway through the first hot dog an important telephone call comes in. The president of Acme Apple and Jar Supply Incorporated, our apple and jar supplier, is on the line. He is calling to see how we are doing and when we plan to pay our bill for apples and jars. He suggests $150,000 or so would be appreciated.

Because we want to remain on good terms with this important supplier, we tell him, "The check is in the mail," and rush back to our offices to put it there.

Looking at our listing of current accounts payable, we note that we owe Acme: $79,200 for apples, $184,000 for jars, and $33,200 for jar caps—a total of $296,400 outstanding.

Take out the checkbook and write the check.

Transaction: Pay a major supplier a portion of what is due for apples and jars. Cut a check for $150,000 in partial payment.

| 1 | Cut a check for $150,000 to pay the supplier. Increase CASH DISBURSEMENTS by that amount in the *Cash Flow Statement*. |

| 2 | Lower CASH by $150,000 in the assets section of the *Balance Sheet*. |

| 3 | Lower ACCOUNTS PAYABLE in the liabilities section of the *Balance Sheet* by the $150,000 that we no longer owe ... since we just paid as described above. |

Note: Actually paying for raw materials does not affect our inventory value in any way. Inventory value increased when we received the raw material and we created an accounts payable.

~

Inventory Valuation Worksheet	RAW MATERIAL	WORK IN PROCESS	FINISHED GOODS
INVENTORY VALUES FROM T16.	$181,400	$0	$198,900
J. Pay for raw materials received in T11.	$0	$0	$0
SUBTOTALS (AS OF THIS TRANSACTION)	$181,400	$0	$198,900
	TOTAL INVENTORY		$380,300

Income Statement

for the period including Transactions 1 through 18

		prior	+	transaction	=	sum
1	NET SALES	$0		—		$0
2	COST OF GOODS SOLD	5,100	[1]	1,530		6,630
1 - 2 = 3	GROSS MARGIN	(5,100)				(6,630)
4	SALES & MARKETING	7,680		—		7,680
5	RESEARCH & DEVELOPMENT	0		—		0
6	GENERAL & ADMINISTRATIVE	18,220		—		18,220
4 + 5 + 6 = 7	OPERATING EXPENSE	25,900				25,900
3 - 7 = 8	INCOME FROM OPERATIONS	(31,000)				(32,530)
9	NET INTEREST INCOME	0		—		0
10	INCOME TAXES	0		—		0
8 + 9 - 10 = 11	NET INCOME	($31,000)		(1,530)		($32,530)

IS Transaction Sum

Cash Flow Statement

for the period including Transactions 1 through 18

		prior	+	transaction	=	sum
a	BEGINNING CASH BALANCE	$0				$0
b	CASH RECEIPTS	0		—		0
c	CASH DISBURSEMENTS	202,760	[2]	9,020		211,780
b - c = d	CASH FLOW FROM OPERATIONS	(202,760)				(211,780)
e	PP&E PURCHASE	1,750,000		—		1,750,000
f	NET BORROWINGS	1,000,000		—		1,000,000
g	INCOME TAXES PAID	0		—		0
h	SALE OF CAPITAL STOCK	1,550,000		—		1,550,000
a + d - e + f - g + h = i	ENDING CASH BALANCES	$597,240		(9,020)		$588,220

CF Transaction Sum

Balance Sheet

as of this Transaction 18

		prior	+	transaction	=	sum
A	CASH	$597,240	[3]	(9,020)		$588,220
B	ACCOUNTS RECEIVABLE	0		—		0
C	INVENTORIES	380,300	[4]	197,670		577,970
D	PREPAID EXPENSES	0		—		0
A + B + C + D = E	CURRENT ASSETS	977,540				1,166,190
F	OTHER ASSETS	0		—		0
G	FIXED ASSETS @ COST	1,750,000		—		1,750,000
H	ACCUMULATED DEPRECIATION	7,143	[5]	7,143		14,286
G - H = I	NET FIXED ASSETS	1,742,857				1,735,714
E + F + I = J	TOTAL ASSETS	$2,720,397		181,507		$2,901,904

Assets Sum

		prior	+	transaction	=	sum
K	ACCOUNTS PAYABLE	$191,077	[6]	174,877		$365,954
L	ACCRUED EXPENSES	10,320	[7]	8,160		18,480
M	CURRENT PORTION OF DEBT	100,000		—		100,000
N	INCOME TAXES PAYABLE	0		—		0
K + L + M + N = O	CURRENT LIABILITIES	301,397				484,434
P	LONG-TERM DEBT	900,000		—		900,000
Q	CAPITAL STOCK	1,550,000		—		1,550,000
R	RETAINED EARNINGS	(31,000)	[8]	(1,530)		(32,530)
Q + R = S	SHAREHOLDERS' EQUITY	1,519,000				1,517,470
O + P + S = T	TOTAL LIABILITIES & EQUITY	$2,720,397		181,507		$2,901,904

Liabilities & Equity Sum

T18. Manufacture another month's worth of our wonderful applesauce.

Things are progressing at our enterprise. With this multiple transaction we will make another month's worth of applesauce and pay a few bills. Soon we will be ready to ship applesauce to our valued customers!

Shown at the bottom of the page are the series *(K through Q)* of Inventory Valuation Worksheet entries for the rest of the month. The table below translates these actions into transactions to post to AppleSeed's financial statements.

Transactions: Make entries in the *Income Statement, Cash Flow Statement* and *Balance Sheet* as shown in the total column at below right. *Note that for each worksheet entry (K through Q below), the change in Assets equals the change in Liabilities.*

WORKSHEET ENTRY	K.	L.	M.	N.	O.	P.	Q.	TOTALS	
COST OF GOODS							$1,530	$1,530	[1]
CASH DISBURSEMENTS			$9,020					$9,020	[2]
CASH			$(9,020)					$(9,020)	[3]
INVENTORY	$166,200		$17,180	$7,143	$8,677		$(1,530)	$197,670	[4]
ACCUM. DEPRECIATION				$(7,143)				$(7,143)	[5]
CHANGE IN ASSETS	$166,200	$0	$8,160	$0	$8,677	$0	$(1,530)	$181,507	
ACCOUNTS PAYABLE	$166,200				$8,677			$174,877	[6]
ACCRUED EXPENSES			$8,160					$8,160	[7]
RETAINED EARNINGS							$(1,530)	$(1,530)	[8]
CHANGE IN LIABILITIES	$166,200	$0	$8,160	$0	$8,677	$0	$(1,530)	$181,507	

Inventory Valuation Worksheet	RAW MATERIAL	WORK IN PROCESS	FINISHED GOODS
INVENTORY VALUES FROM T17.	$181,400	$0	$198,900
K. Receive a month's raw material supply less labels. (see T10)	$166,200	$0	$0
L. Move a month's supply of raw materials into WIP. (see T12)	$(171,000)	$171,000	$0
M. Pay hourly workers/supervisor for another month. (see T12)	$0	$17,180	$0
N. Book manufacturing depreciation for the month. (see T13)	$0	$7,143	$0
O. Book "all other" mfg. overhead for another month. (see T13)	$0	$8,677	$0
P. Move 19,000 cases to finished goods @ standard cost.	$0	$(193,800)	$193,800
Q. Scrap 150 cases from WIP. (see T16)	$0	$(1,530)	$0
SUBTOTALS (AS OF THIS TRANSACTION)	$176,600	$8,670	$392,700
TOTAL INVENTORY			$577,970

Chapter 9. Marketing and Selling

A wise old consultant once said, "Really, the only thing you need to be in business is a customer."

AppleSeed Enterprises, Inc., is ready to find customers for its super new brand of applesauce. We will begin marketing our product and testing the receptiveness of the marketplace to a new supplier...us!

Next (unfortunately), we will suffer one major risk of doing business, the deadbeat customer.

~

Transaction 19. Produce advertising fliers and T-shirt giveaways.

- Product pricing and break-even analysis.

Transaction 20. A new customer orders 1,000 cases of applesauce. Ship 1,000 cases at $15.90 per case.

Transaction 21. Take an order (on credit) for 15,000 cases at $15.66 per case.

Transaction 22. Ship and invoice customer for 15,000 cases of applesauce ordered in Transaction 21.

Transaction 23. Receive payment of $234,900 for shipment made in Transaction 22 and pay the broker his due.

Transaction 24. Oops! Customer goes bankrupt. Write off cost of 1,000 cases as a bad debt.

Income Statement

for the period including Transactions 1 through 19		*prior*	+	*transaction*	=	*sum*
1	NET SALES	$0	—			$0
2	COST OF GOODS SOLD	6,630	—			6,630
1 - 2 = 3	GROSS MARGIN	(6,630)				(6,630)
4	SALES & MARKETING	7,680	[1]	103,250		110,930
5	RESEARCH & DEVELOPMENT	0	—			0
6	GENERAL & ADMINISTRATIVE	18,220	—			18,220
4 + 5 + 6 = 7	OPERATING EXPENSE	25,900				129,150
3 - 7 = 8	INCOME FROM OPERATIONS	(32,530)				(135,780)
9	NET INTEREST INCOME	0	—			0
10	INCOME TAXES	0	—			0
8 + 9 - 10 = 11	NET INCOME	($32,530)		(103,250)		($135,780)

IS Transaction Sum

Cash Flow Statement

for the period including Transactions 1 through 19		*prior*	+	*transaction*	=	*sum*
a	BEGINNING CASH BALANCE	$0				$0
b	CASH RECEIPTS	0	—			0
c	CASH DISBURSEMENTS	211,780	—			211,780
b - c = d	CASH FLOW FROM OPERATIONS	(211,780)				(211,780)
e	PP&E PURCHASE	1,750,000	—			1,750,000
f	NET BORROWINGS	1,000,000	—			1,000,000
g	INCOME TAXES PAID	0	—			0
h	SALE OF CAPITAL STOCK	1,550,000	—			1,550,000
a + d - e + f - g + h = i	ENDING CASH BALANCES	$588,220		0		$588,220

CF Transaction Sum

Balance Sheet

as of this Transaction 19		*prior*	+	*transaction*	=	*sum*
A	CASH	$588,220	—			$588,220
B	ACCOUNTS RECEIVABLE	0	—			0
C	INVENTORIES	577,970	—			577,970
D	PREPAID EXPENSES	0	—			0
A + B + C + D = E	CURRENT ASSETS	1,166,190				1,166,190
F	OTHER ASSETS	0	—			0
G	FIXED ASSETS @ COST	1,750,000	—			1,750,000
H	ACCUMULATED DEPRECIATION	14,286	—			14,286
G - H = I	NET FIXED ASSETS	1,735,714				1,735,714
E + F + I = J	TOTAL ASSETS	$2,901,904		0		$2,901,904

Assets Sum

		prior	+	*transaction*	=	*sum*
K	ACCOUNTS PAYABLE	$365,954	[3]	103,250		$469,204
L	ACCRUED EXPENSES	18,480	—			18,480
M	CURRENT PORTION OF DEBT	100,000	—			100,000
N	INCOME TAXES PAYABLE	0	—			0
K + L + M + N = O	CURRENT LIABILITIES	484,434				587,684
P	LONG-TERM DEBT	900,000	—			900,000
Q	CAPITAL STOCK	1,550,000	—			1,550,000
R	RETAINED EARNINGS	(32,530)	[2]	(103,250)		(135,780)
Q + R = S	SHAREHOLDERS' EQUITY	1,517,470				1,414,220
O + P + S = T	TOTAL LIABILITIES & EQUITY	$2,901,904		0		$2,901,904

Liabilities & Equity Sum

T19. Produce product advertising fliers and T-shirt giveaways.

The usual method of selling our type of product is through a food broker to a retail store and then ultimately to the consumer. Food brokers serve the purpose of manufacturers' representatives, convincing retailers to stock various brands of product. For their efforts, these brokers receive a commission of about 2% of sales. They do not take title to the goods, they just smooth the way.

AppleSeed engages topflight manufacturers' representative, SlickSales and Associates, to market its products. SlickSales and AppleSeed negotiate a sales commission of 2% of gross revenue to be paid SlickSales for placing AppleSeed's applesauce.

SlickSales requests that AppleSeed prepare and then supply them with sales literature to be given prospective customers. Everybody agrees that a direct mail promotion would be a good idea too.

We hire an advertising agency to design, print and mail a very fancy brochure to promote AppleSeed's applesauce products.

The agency also produces 10,000 AppleSeed Applesauce T-shirts to ship to supermarkets for use as a promotional giveaway.

Transaction: Our advertising agency submits a bill for designing, printing and mailing 4,500 very fancy brochures for a $38,250 total cost. The T-shirts cost $6.50 each for a total of $65,000 for 10,000 shirts. Book these amounts as an AppleSeed Enterprises marketing and selling expense.

| 1 | Book brochure and T-shirt expenses totaling $103,250 under SALES & MARKETING expense in the *Income Statement*. |

| 2 | Lower RETAINED EARNINGS in the liabilities section of the *Balance Sheet* by this $103,250 marketing expense. |

| 3 | Increase ACCOUNTS PAYABLE in the liabilities section of the *Balance Sheet* by the same amount for the bill we owe the advertising agency. |

~

Product Pricing

What should we charge for our delicious applesauce? How should we price our product?

Marketing textbooks say that pricing decisions are best made in the marketplace. Price-setting should be based on a competitive understanding and on our competitive goals. Manufacturing costs should have little bearing on pricing decisions.

After we have set a competitive price we should then look at our costs to see that an adequate profit can be made. If we can't make our desired profit selling our applesauce at a competitive price then we have just two options: lower costs or exit the business.

Market Pricing

Who are AppleSeed's competitors? How does our product compare with their offerings? What do they all charge for applesauce? What should *we* charge?

The chart below shows the wholesale and retail pricing structure for several brands of applesauce sold in our market. The chart translates the various mark-ups (manufacturer's, wholesaler's and retailer's markups) into selling and cost prices at each level of distribution. Remember that a low-level distributor's price is the next upper-level distributor's cost.

We decide to position AppleSeed's applesauce as a mid-priced brand of very high quality. We think that at a retail price of $1.905 a jar (or $22.86 for a case of 12 jars), we offer good value. But can we make a profit at this selling price? A break-even analysis will help us answer this important question.

Review the volume and costs analysis on the facing page. Then look at the break-even chart on page 150.

Comparative Applesauce Prices

	MFG'S SELLING PRICE	WHOLESALER'S SELLING PRICE	RETAILER'S SELLING PRICE
	Base Price	Plus 15%	Plus 25%
% OF MFG'S SELLING PRICE	100%	115%	143%
% OF RETAILER'S SELLING PRICE	70%	80%	100%
BRAND A	$15.21	$17.49	$21.86
BRAND B	$15.40	$17.71	$22,14
BRAND C	$16.58	$19.07	$23.84
APPLESEED BRAND	$15.90	$18.29	$22.86

AppleSeed Enterprises Annual Manufacturing Expenditures
at Various Sales and Production Volumes

	VARIABLE COST PER CASE	TOTAL FIXED COST PER YEAR	ANNUAL TOTALS @ ZERO CASES PER MONTH	ANNUAL TOTALS @ 5,000 CASES PER MONTH	ANNUAL TOTALS @10,000 CASES PER MONTH	ANNUAL TOTALS @ 15,000 CASES PER MONTH	ANNUAL TOTALS @ 20,000 CASES PER MONTH
Total Annual Variable Costs at Several Production Volumes							
MATERIAL COSTS	$8.550	—	$0	$513,000	$1,026,000	$1,539,000	$2,052,000
DIRECT LABOR	$0.615	—	$0	$36,900	$73,800	$110,700	$147,600
BROKER	$0.318	—	$0	$19,080	$38,160	$57,240	$76,320
TOTAL ANNUAL VARIABLE COSTS	$9.483	—	$0	$568,980	$1,137,960	$1,706,940	$2,275,920

Total Annual Fixed Costs (No Change with Increasing Production Volume)

MANUFACTURING SUPERVISOR	—	$58,650					
DEPRECIATION	—	$85,714					
ALL OTHER MFG. EXPENSE	—	$104,124	*TOTAL FIXED COSTS ARE CONSTANT AT ALL PRODUCTION VOLUME LEVELS*				
SG&A SALARIES	—	$251,160					
INTEREST EXPENSE	—	$100,000					
MARKETING & OTHER EXPENSES	—	$223,250					
TOTAL ANNUAL FIXED COSTS	—	$822,898	$822,898	$822,898	$822,898	$822,898	$822,898

Profit & Loss Statements at Several Production Volumes

	ANNUAL REVENUE @ $15.90 PER CASE	$0	$954,000	$1,908,000	$2,862,000	$3,816,000
LESS	TOTAL ANNUAL VARIABLE COSTS	$0	$568,980	$1,137,960	$1,706,940	$2,275,920
LESS	TOTAL ANNUAL FIXED COSTS	$822,898	$822,898	$822,898	$822,898	$822,898
EQUALS	TOTAL ANNUAL PROFIT (LOSS)	$(822,898)	$(437,878)	$(52,858)	$332,162	$717,182

Break-even Analysis

Financial types (such as AppleSeed's bankers) will ask the question, "How much will you have to sell to make a profit?"

This revenue value, where increasing volume turns losses into profits, is called the company's *break-even point*.

> **The break-even point is that sales volume where revenues are exactly equal to costs plus expenses and, thus, the company neither makes a profit nor suffers a loss.**

Your banker is sizing the company's operations and gauging whether a profitable sales volume will be easy or difficult to achieve. A break-even analysis focuses management on the inherent profitability (or lack thereof) of an enterprise.

Let's do a break-even analysis for AppleSeed. The table on the previous page shows AppleSeed Enterprises' annual costs and expenses at various sales and production volumes.

Some of AppleSeed's costs and expenses will not change with its volume of production and sales (fixed costs) and some will change (variable costs).

Fixed Costs. Fixed costs will be the same for AppleSeed, month after month, whether the company makes and sells 5,000 cases, 10,000 cases or even 20,000 cases per month. This fixed cost includes manufacturing costs and also SG&A expenses that are not related to volume. As shown in the table we can see that AppleSeed's fixed costs are $822,898 per year.

Variable Costs. Each time Apple-Seed sells a case of applesauce, it spends $9.483 in variable cost as shown in the

AppleSeed Enterprises Inc. Break-even Chart

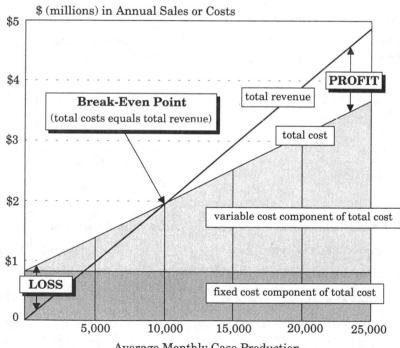

table on page 149. So, if the company sells 10,000 cases per month (120,000 cases per year), total variable cost will be $9.483 per case times 120,000 cases for a total of $1,137,960 variable cost. If AppleSeed sells 20,000 cases per month then the total variable cost will be double to $2,275,920.

AppleSeed's break-even chart on the previous page graphically represents the relationships shown in the table on page 149 between: (1) total revenue, (2) fixed costs, (3) total variable costs, and (4) profit or loss for production volumes from zero to 25,000 cases per month. Review-ing the chart on page 150 shows that AppleSeed turns a profit at a production and sales volume of about 10,700 cases per month. Profitability improves nicely as sales and production reach our 15,000 case per month target.

Note that the difference between total variable cost and total sales is often called *contribution*. That is, the dollar amount that a level of sales "contributes" toward paying for fixed costs and expenses and any profit for the enter-prise. The break-even point occurs when the contribution exactly equals fixed costs.

Profit is the difference between two large numbers: sales *less* costs and expenses. Small changes in either can result in large swings in profit (loss).

Income Statement

for the period including Transactions 1 through 20		prior	+	transaction	=	sum
1	NET SALES	$0	**1A**	15,900		$15,900
2	COST OF GOODS SOLD	6,630	**3B**	10,200		16,830
1 - 2 = 3	GROSS MARGIN	(6,630)				(930)
4	SALES & MARKETING	110,930	**2A**	318		111,248
5	RESEARCH & DEVELOPMENT	0		—		0
6	GENERAL & ADMINISTRATIVE	18,220		—		18,220
4 + 5 + 6 = 7	OPERATING EXPENSE	129,150				129,468
3 - 7 = 8	INCOME FROM OPERATIONS	(135,780)				(130,398)
9	NET INTEREST INCOME	0		—		0
10	INCOME TAXES	0		—		0
8 + 9 - 10 = 11	NET INCOME	($135,780)		5,382		($130,398)

IS Transaction Sum

Cash Flow Statement

for the period including Transactions 1 through 20		prior	+	transaction	=	sum
a	BEGINNING CASH BALANCE	$0				$0
b	CASH RECEIPTS	0		—		0
c	CASH DISBURSEMENTS	211,780		—		211,780
b - c = d	CASH FLOW FROM OPERATIONS	(211,780)				(211,780)
e	PP&E PURCHASE	1,750,000		—		1,750,000
f	NET BORROWINGS	1,000,000		—		1,000,000
g	INCOME TAXES PAID	0		—		0
h	SALE OF CAPITAL STOCK	1,550,000		—		1,550,000
a + d - e + f - g + h = i	ENDING CASH BALANCES	$588,220		0		$588,220

CF Transaction Sum

Balance Sheet

as of this Transaction 20		prior	+	transaction	=	sum
A	CASH	$588,220		—		$588,220
B	ACCOUNTS RECEIVABLE	0	**1B**	15,900		15,900
C	INVENTORIES	577,970	**3A**	(10,200)		567,770
D	PREPAID EXPENSES	0		—		0
A + B + C + D = E	CURRENT ASSETS	1,166,190				1,171,890
F	OTHER ASSETS	0		—		0
G	FIXED ASSETS @ COST	1,750,000		—		1,750,000
H	ACCUMULATED DEPRECIATION	14,286		—		14,286
G - H = I	NET FIXED ASSETS	1,735,714				1,735,714
E + F + I = J	TOTAL ASSETS	$2,901,904		5,700		$2,907,604
				Assets Sum		
K	ACCOUNTS PAYABLE	$469,204		—		$469,204
L	ACCRUED EXPENSES	18,480	**2B**	318		18,798
M	CURRENT PORTION OF DEBT	100,000		—		100,000
N	INCOME TAXES PAYABLE	0		—		0
K + L + M + N = O	CURRENT LIABILITIES	587,684				588,002
P	LONG-TERM DEBT	900,000		—		900,000
Q	CAPITAL STOCK	1,550,000		—		1,550,000
R	RETAINED EARNINGS	(135,780)	**4**	5,382		(130,398)
Q + R = S	SHAREHOLDERS' EQUITY	1,414,220				1,419,602
O + P + S = T	TOTAL LIABILITIES & EQUITY	$2,901,904		5,700		$2,907,604

Liabilities & Equity Sum

T20. A new customer orders 1,000 cases of applesauce. Ship 1,000 cases at $15.90 per case.

It's the moment we have all been waiting for—AppleSeed's Enterprises' very first customer.

Your brother-in-law is the manager of a small convenience store chain. At the instigation of your spouse, he places an order for 1,000 cases to stock applesauce in his northwest region's stores.

Based on past experience, you trust your brother-in-law about as far as you can throw him...and he weighs in at 240 lbs.

You accept the order, but ask him to send a $15,900 prepayment check before you will ship. He says no. You decide to ship on credit and cross your fingers.

Transaction: Receive order for 1,000 cases of applesauce at a selling price of $15.90 per case. Ship product and send a $15,900 invoice to the customer.

1 (1A) Book your first sale of $15,900 as NET SALES on AppleSeed's *Income Statement*. (1B) Add an ACCOUNTS RECEIVABLE for the same amount in the *Balance Sheet*.

2 (2A) Book on the *Income Statement* the 2% commission ($318) for our broker as a SALES & MARKETING expense. (2B) Also book this $318 commission as an ACCRUED EXPENSE on the *Balance Sheet*. The broker does not get paid until we do.

3 (3A) Reduce INVENTORY on the *Balance Sheet* by $10,200— 1,000 cases times standard cost of $10.20 for each case. (3B) Corresponding to the inventory reduction above, increase COST OF GOODS SOLD by $10,200—the standard cost of 1,000 cases of applesauce.

4 Increase RETAINED EARNINGS on the *Balance Sheet* by $5,382—the sale amount, less cost of goods, less the selling commission. That amount is AppleSeed's profit on the sale.

Inventory Valuation Worksheet	RAW MATERIAL	WORK IN PROCESS	FINISHED GOODS
INVENTORY VALUES FROM T18.	$176,600	$8,670	$392,700
R. Ship 1,000 cases of applesauce at $10.20 standard cost/case.	$0	$0	$(10,200)
SUBTOTALS (AS OF THIS TRANSACTION)	$176,600	$8,670	$382,500
		TOTAL INVENTORY	$567,770

Income Statement

		for the period including Transactions 1 through 21	*prior*	+	*transaction*	=	*sum*
1		NET SALES	$15,900		—		$15,900
2		COST OF GOODS SOLD	16,830		—		16,830
1 - 2 = 3		GROSS MARGIN	(930)				(930)
4		SALES & MARKETING	111,248		—		111,248
5		RESEARCH & DEVELOPMENT	0		—		0
6		GENERAL & ADMINISTRATIVE	18,220		—		18,220
4 + 5 + 6 = 7		OPERATING EXPENSE	129,468				129,468
3 - 7 = 8		INCOME FROM OPERATIONS	(130,398)				(130,398)
9		NET INTEREST INCOME	0		—		0
10		INCOME TAXES	0		—		0
8 + 9 - 10 = 11		NET INCOME	($130,398)		0		($130,398)

IS Transaction Sum

Cash Flow Statement

		for the period including Transactions 1 through 21	*prior*	+	*transaction*	=	*sum*
a		BEGINNING CASH BALANCE	$0				$0
b		CASH RECEIPTS	0		—		0
c		CASH DISBURSEMENTS	211,780		—		211,780
b - c = d		CASH FLOW FROM OPERATIONS	(211,780)				(211,780)
e		PP&E PURCHASE	1,750,000		—		1,750,000
f		NET BORROWINGS	1,000,000		—		1,000,000
g		INCOME TAXES PAID	0		—		0
h		SALE OF CAPITAL STOCK	1,550,000		—		1,550,000
a + d - e + f - g + h = i		ENDING CASH BALANCES	$588,220		0		$588,220

CF Transaction Sum

Balance Sheet

		as of this Transaction 21	*prior*	+	*transaction*	=	*sum*
A		CASH	$588,220		—		$588,220
B		ACCOUNTS RECEIVABLE	15,900		—		15,900
C		INVENTORIES	567,770		—		567,770
D		PREPAID EXPENSES	0		—		0
A + B + C + D = E		CURRENT ASSETS	1,171,890				1,171,890
F		OTHER ASSETS	0		—		0
G		FIXED ASSETS @ COST	1,750,000		—		1,750,000
H		ACCUMULATED DEPRECIATION	14,286		—		14,286
G - H = I		NET FIXED ASSETS	1,735,714				1,735,714
E + F + I = J		TOTAL ASSETS	$2,907,604		0		$2,907,604

Assets Sum

			prior	+	*transaction*	=	*sum*
K		ACCOUNTS PAYABLE	$469,204		—		$469,204
L		ACCRUED EXPENSES	18,798		—		18,798
M		CURRENT PORTION OF DEBT	100,000		—		100,000
N		INCOME TAXES PAYABLE	0		—		0
K + L + M + N = O		CURRENT LIABILITIES	588,002				588,002
P		LONG-TERM DEBT	900,000		—		900,000
Q		CAPITAL STOCK	1,550,000		—		1,550,000
R		RETAINED EARNINGS	(130,398)		—		(130,398)
Q + R = S		SHAREHOLDERS' EQUITY	1,419,602				1,419,602
O + P + S = T		TOTAL LIABILITIES & EQUITY	$2,907,604		0		$2,907,604

Liabilities & Equity Sum

T21. Take an order (on credit) for 15,000 cases at $15.66 per case.

Our broker is beginning to do his job. We may soon receive a big order from one of the largest food retailers in the area. We have the goods in inventory, so we promise to ship promptly.

To close the deal we authorize our broker to offer the prospective customer a 1.5% discount. The retailer agrees to purchase 15,000 cases at a discounted selling price of $15.66 per case ($15.90 list less the 24¢ discount).

Transaction: Receive an order for 15,000 cases of applesauce at a selling price of $15.66 per case, $234,900 for the total order.

Note: Receiving an order has no effect on the three major financial statements. Only when the product ordered is shipped to customers do you record a SALE and the associated COST OF GOODS SOLD.

~

Income Statement

for the period including Transactions 1 through 22

		prior	+	transaction	=	sum
1	NET SALES	$15,900	**1A**	234,900		$250,800
2	COST OF GOODS SOLD	16,830	**2A**	153,000		169,830
1 - 2 = 3	GROSS MARGIN	(930)				80,970
4	SALES & MARKETING	111,248	**3A**	4,698		115,946
5	RESEARCH & DEVELOPMENT	0		—		0
6	GENERAL & ADMINISTRATIVE	18,220		—		18,220
4 + 5 + 6 = 7	OPERATING EXPENSE	129,468				134,166
3 - 7 = 8	INCOME FROM OPERATIONS	(130,398)				(53,196)
9	NET INTEREST INCOME	0		—		0
10	INCOME TAXES	0		—		0
8 + 9 - 10 = 11	NET INCOME	($130,398)		77,202		($53,196)

IS Transaction Sum

Cash Flow Statement

for the period including Transactions 1 through 22

		prior	+	transaction	=	sum
a	BEGINNING CASH BALANCE	$0				$0
b	CASH RECEIPTS	0		—		0
c	CASH DISBURSEMENTS	211,780		—		211,780
b - c = d	CASH FLOW FROM OPERATIONS	(211,780)				(211,780)
e	PP&E PURCHASE	1,750,000		—		1,750,000
f	NET BORROWINGS	1,000,000		—		1,000,000
g	INCOME TAXES PAID	0		—		0
h	SALE OF CAPITAL STOCK	1,550,000		—		1,550,000
a + d - e + f - g + h = i	ENDING CASH BALANCES	$588,220		0		$588,220

CF Transaction Sum

Balance Sheet

as of this Transaction 22

		prior	+	transaction	=	sum
A	CASH	$588,220		—		$588,220
B	ACCOUNTS RECEIVABLE	15,900	**1B**	234,900		250,800
C	INVENTORIES	567,770	**2B**	(153,000)		414,770
D	PREPAID EXPENSES	0		—		0
A + B + C + D = E	CURRENT ASSETS	1,171,890				1,253,790
F	OTHER ASSETS	0		—		0
G	FIXED ASSETS @ COST	1,750,000		—		1,750,000
H	ACCUMULATED DEPRECIATION	14,286		—		14,286
G - H = I	NET FIXED ASSETS	1,735,714				1,735,714
E + F + I = J	TOTAL ASSETS	$2,907,604		81,900		$2,989,504

Assets Sum

		prior	+	transaction	=	sum
K	ACCOUNTS PAYABLE	$469,204		—		$469,204
L	ACCRUED EXPENSES	18,798	**3B**	4,698		23,496
M	CURRENT PORTION OF DEBT	100,000		—		100,000
N	INCOME TAXES PAYABLE	0		—		0
K + L + M + N = O	CURRENT LIABILITIES	588,002				592,700
P	LONG-TERM DEBT	900,000		—		900,000
Q	CAPITAL STOCK	1,550,000		—		1,550,000
R	RETAINED EARNINGS	(130,398)	**4**	77,202		(53,196)
Q + R = S	SHAREHOLDERS' EQUITY	1,419,602				1,496,804
O + P + S = T	TOTAL LIABILITIES & EQUITY	$2,907,604		81,900		$2,989,504

Liabilities & Equity Sum

T22. Ship and invoice customer for 15,000 cases of applesauce ordered in Transaction 21.

Although we did lower our price to get this large order, our costs will remain the same. Thus we will garner a lower profit in this transaction than if we had sold at full list price.

AppleSeed's net sales amount will be $234,900 versus the $238,500 if we had sold at list price—a difference of $3,600 in lower sales.

Our gross margin (that is, sales less cost of goods sold) will be $81,900 versus $85,500—again a difference of $3,600 less margin.

In fact, this $3,600 difference in the original selling price will drop all the way to the bottom line as a lower profit. Discounts are dangerous profit-gobblers. Try to use them sparingly.

Transaction: Ship 15,000 cases of applesauce and send a $234,900 invoice to the customer.

 (1A) Book sale of $234,900 as NET SALES on AppleSeed's *Income Statement*. (1B) Make a corresponding entry as ACCOUNTS RECEIVABLE on the *Balance Sheet*.

 (2A) On the *Income Statement* book COST OF GOODS SOLD for this sale of $153,000, equaling a $10.20 standard cost per case times 15,000 cases shipped. (2B) Reduce INVENTORY on the *Balance Sheet* by this same amount.

3 (3A) Book on the *Income Statement* a SALES & MARKETING expense of $4,698 as the 2% selling commission for our broker. (3B) Also book this expense as an ACCRUED EXPENSE on the *Balance Sheet*.

4 Increase RETAINED EARNINGS on the *Balance Sheet* by $77,202—the sale amount less cost of goods less the selling commission.

~

Inventory Valuation Worksheet	RAW MATERIAL	WORK IN PROCESS	FINISHED GOODS
INVENTORY VALUES FROM T20.	$176,600	$8,670	$382,500
S. Ship 15,000 cases of applesauce at $10.20 standard cost.	$0	$0.00	$(153,000)
SUBTOTALS (AS OF THIS TRANSACTION)	$176,600	$8,670	$229,500
TOTAL INVENTORY			$414,770

Income Statement

for the period including Transactions 1 through 23		prior	+	transaction	=	sum
1	NET SALES	$250,800		—		$250,800
2	COST OF GOODS SOLD	169,830		—		169,830
1 - 2 = 3	GROSS MARGIN	80,970				80,970
4	SALES & MARKETING	115,946		—		115,946
5	RESEARCH & DEVELOPMENT	0		—		0
6	GENERAL & ADMINISTRATIVE	18,220		—		18,220
4 + 5 + 6 = 7	OPERATING EXPENSE	134,166				134,166
3 - 7 = 8	INCOME FROM OPERATIONS	(53,196)				(53,196)
9	NET INTEREST INCOME	0		—		0
10	INCOME TAXES	0		—		0
8 + 9 - 10 = 11	NET INCOME	($53,196)		0		($53,196)

IS Transaction Sum

Cash Flow Statement

for the period including Transactions 1 through 23		prior	+	transaction	=	sum
a	BEGINNING CASH BALANCE	$0				$0
b	CASH RECEIPTS	0	**1A**	234,900		234,900
c	CASH DISBURSEMENTS	211,780	**2A**	4,698		216,478
b - c = d	CASH FLOW FROM OPERATIONS	(211,780)				18,422
e	PP&E PURCHASE	1,750,000		—		1,750,000
f	NET BORROWINGS	1,000,000		—		1,000,000
g	INCOME TAXES PAID	0		—		0
h	SALE OF CAPITAL STOCK	1,550,000		—		1,550,000
a + d - e + f - g + h = i	ENDING CASH BALANCES	$588,220		230,202		$818,422

CF Transaction Sum

Balance Sheet

as of this Transaction 23		prior	+	transaction	=	sum
A	CASH	$588,220	**3**	230,202		$818,422
B	ACCOUNTS RECEIVABLE	250,800	**1B**	(234,900)		15,900
C	INVENTORIES	414,770		—		414,770
D	PREPAID EXPENSES	0		—		0
A + B + C + D = E	CURRENT ASSETS	1,253,790				1,249,092
F	OTHER ASSETS	0		—		0
G	FIXED ASSETS @ COST	1,750,000		—		1,750,000
H	ACCUMULATED DEPRECIATION	14,286		—		14,286
G - H = I	NET FIXED ASSETS	1,735,714				1,735,714
E + F + I = J	TOTAL ASSETS	$2,989,504		(4,698)		$2,984,806

Assets Sum

		prior	+	transaction	=	sum
K	ACCOUNTS PAYABLE	$469,204		—		$469,204
L	ACCRUED EXPENSES	23,496	**2B**	(4,698)		18,798
M	CURRENT PORTION OF DEBT	100,000		—		100,000
N	INCOME TAXES PAYABLE	0		—		0
K + L + M + N = O	CURRENT LIABILITIES	592,700				588,002
P	LONG-TERM DEBT	900,000		—		900,000
Q	CAPITAL STOCK	1,550,000		—		1,550,000
R	RETAINED EARNINGS	(53,196)		—		(53,196)
Q + R = S	SHAREHOLDERS' EQUITY	1,496,804				1,496,804
O + P + S = T	TOTAL LIABILITIES & EQUITY	$2,989,504		(4,698)		$2,984,806

Liabilities & Equity Sum

T23. Receive payment of $234,900 for shipment made in Transaction 22 and pay broker his due.

Our big customer is very happy with our applesauce. He says that our brightly colored jars are "walking off the shelves." We're extremely happy that we decided to spend so much money on very fancy packaging.

Although it is true that "all you really need to be in business is a customer," what you really need is a customer who pays. With this transaction we will collect our first accounts receivable and turn it into cash.

Transaction: Receive payment of $234,900 for shipment that was made in Transaction 22. Pay the broker his $4,698 selling commission.

(1A) Book a $234,900 CASH RECEIPT in the *Cash Flow Statement*. (1B) Decrease ACCOUNTS RECEIVABLE on the *Balance Sheet* by the same amount.

(2A) Issue a $4,698 check to our broker and record as a CASH DISBURSEMENT in the *Cash Flow Statement*. (2B) Lower ACCRUED EXPENSE by the amount paid the broker.

3 Increase CASH by $230,202 on the *Balance Sheet* (that is, $234,900 received less $4,698 disbursed).

Note: A customer's cash payment for goods in no way changes the *Income Statement*. The *Income Statement* recorded a sale when first, we shipped the goods, and second, the customer incurred the obligation to pay (our accounts receivable).

Income Statement

for the period including Transactions 1 through 24		prior	+	transaction	=	sum
1	NET SALES	$250,800		—		$250,800
2	COST OF GOODS SOLD	169,830		—		169,830
1 - 2 = 3	GROSS MARGIN	80,970				80,970
4	SALES & MARKETING	115,946	2A	(318)		115,628
5	RESEARCH & DEVELOPMENT	0		—		0
6	GENERAL & ADMINISTRATIVE	18,220	1A	15,900		34,120
4 + 5 + 6 = 7	OPERATING EXPENSE	134,166				149,748
3 - 7 = 8	INCOME FROM OPERATIONS	(53,196)				(68,778)
9	NET INTEREST INCOME	0		—		0
10	INCOME TAXES	0		—		0
8 + 9 - 10 = 11	NET INCOME	($53,196)		(15,582)		($68,778)

IS Transaction Sum

Cash Flow Statement

for the period including Transactions 1 through 24		prior	+	transaction	=	sum
a	BEGINNING CASH BALANCE	$0				$0
b	CASH RECEIPTS	234,900		—		234,900
c	CASH DISBURSEMENTS	216,478		—		216,478
b - c = d	CASH FLOW FROM OPERATIONS	18,422				18,422
e	PP&E PURCHASE	1,750,000		—		1,750,000
f	NET BORROWINGS	1,000,000		—		1,000,000
g	INCOME TAXES PAID	0		—		0
h	SALE OF CAPITAL STOCK	1,550,000		—		1,550,000
a + d - e + f - g + h = i	ENDING CASH BALANCES	$818,422		0		$818,422

CF Transaction Sum

Balance Sheet

as of this Transaction 24		prior	+	transaction	=	sum
A	CASH	$818,422		—		$818,422
B	ACCOUNTS RECEIVABLE	15,900	1B	(15,900)		0
C	INVENTORIES	414,770		—		414,770
D	PREPAID EXPENSES	0		—		0
A + B + C + D = E	CURRENT ASSETS	1,249,092				1,233,192
F	OTHER ASSETS	0		—		0
G	FIXED ASSETS @ COST	1,750,000		—		1,750,000
H	ACCUMULATED DEPRECIATION	14,286		—		14,286
G - H = I	NET FIXED ASSETS	1,735,714				1,735,714
E + F + I = J	TOTAL ASSETS	$2,984,806		(15,900)		$2,968,906
				Assets Sum		
K	ACCOUNTS PAYABLE	$469,204		—		$469,204
L	ACCRUED EXPENSES	18,798	2B	(318)		18,480
M	CURRENT PORTION OF DEBT	100,000		—		100,000
N	INCOME TAXES PAYABLE	0		—		0
K + L + M + N = O	CURRENT LIABILITIES	588,002				587,684
P	LONG-TERM DEBT	900,000		—		900,000
Q	CAPITAL STOCK	1,550,000		—		1,550,000
R	RETAINED EARNINGS	(53,196)	3	(15,582)		(68,778)
Q + R = S	SHAREHOLDERS' EQUITY	1,496,804				1,481,222
O + P + S = T	TOTAL LIABILITIES & EQUITY	$2,984,806		(15,900)		$2,968,906

Liabilities & Equity Sum

T24. Oops! Customer goes bankrupt. Write off cost of 1,000 cases as a bad debt.

Remember back in **Transaction 20** we shipped 1,000 cases of applesauce to your brother-in-law's company? You'll never guess what happened. They went bankrupt! Now he even wants a job.

We will never get paid. And because the goods have already been distributed and sold to applesauce lovers around the northwest, we will never get our product back, either.

Transaction: Write off the $15,900 accounts receivable that was entered when you made the 1,000 case shipment. Also, reduce the amount payable to our broker by what would have been his commission on the sale. If we don't get paid, he doesn't either!

1 (1A) Book the bad-debt expense of $15,900 against GENERAL & ADMINISTRATIVE expense on the *Income Statement*. (1B) Reduce ACCOUNTS RECEIVABLE on the *Balance Sheet* by the $15,900 we will never collect. These entries reverse the sale we had made.

2 (2A) Book a "negative expense" of minus $318 in SALES & MARKETING expense on the *Income Statement*. (2B) Decrease ACCRUED EXPENSE on the *Balance Sheet* by the same amount. These entries reverse the commission that had been due our broker.

3 Reduce RETAINED EARNINGS on the *Balance Sheet* by $15,582, the sale amount we wrote off less the commission no longer due.

Note: Our out-of-pocket loss is really just the $10,200 inventory value of the goods shipped.

Remember that in **Transaction 20** we booked a profit from this sale of $5,382—the $15,900 sale minus the $10,200 cost of goods minus the $318 selling commission. Thus, if you combine the $15,582 drop in RETAINED EARNINGS booked in this transaction plus the $5,382 increase in RETAINED EARNINGS from **Transaction 20**, you are left with our loss of $10,200 from this bad debt.

~

Chapter 10. Administrative Tasks

We've been busy making and selling our delicious applesauce. But having been in business for three months, it's time to attend to some important administrative tasks.

~

Transaction 25. Pay this year's general liability insurance.

Transaction 26. Make principal and interest payments on three months' worth of building debts.

Transaction 27. Pay payroll-associated taxes and insurance benefit premiums.

Transaction 28. Pay some suppliers...especially the mean and hungry ones.

Income Statement

for the period including Transactions 1 through 25		prior	+	transaction	=	sum
1	NET SALES	$250,800		—		$250,800
2	COST OF GOODS SOLD	169,830		—		169,830
1 - 2 = 3	GROSS MARGIN	80,970				80,970
4	SALES & MARKETING	115,628		—		115,628
5	RESEARCH & DEVELOPMENT	0		—		0
6	GENERAL & ADMINISTRATIVE	34,120	**2** 6,500			40,620
4 + 5 + 6 = 7	OPERATING EXPENSE	149,748				156,248
3 - 7 = 8	INCOME FROM OPERATIONS	(68,778)				(75,278)
9	NET INTEREST INCOME	0		—		0
10	INCOME TAXES	0		—		0
8 + 9 - 10 = 11	NET INCOME	($68,778)		(6,500)		($75,278)

IS Transaction Sum

Cash Flow Statement

for the period including Transactions 1 through 25		prior	+	transaction	=	sum
a	BEGINNING CASH BALANCE	$0				$0
b	CASH RECEIPTS	234,900		—		234,900
c	CASH DISBURSEMENTS	216,478	**1A** 26,000			242,478
b - c = d	CASH FLOW FROM OPERATIONS	18,422				(7,578)
e	PP&E PURCHASE	1,750,000		—		1,750,000
f	NET BORROWINGS	1,000,000		—		1,000,000
g	INCOME TAXES PAID	0		—		0
h	SALE OF CAPITAL STOCK	1,550,000		—		1,550,000
a + d - e + f - g + h = i	ENDING CASH BALANCES	$818,422		(26,000)		$792,422

CF Transaction Sum

Balance Sheet

as of this Transaction 25		prior	+	transaction	=	sum
A	CASH	$818,422	**1B** (26,000)			$792,422
B	ACCOUNTS RECEIVABLE	0		—		0
C	INVENTORIES	414,770		—		414,770
D	PREPAID EXPENSES	0	**3** 19,500			19,500
A + B + C + D = E	CURRENT ASSETS	1,233,192				1,226,692
F	OTHER ASSETS	0		—		0
G	FIXED ASSETS @ COST	1,750,000		—		1,750,000
H	ACCUMULATED DEPRECIATION	14,286		—		14,286
G - H = I	NET FIXED ASSETS	1,735,714				1,735,714
E + F + I = J	TOTAL ASSETS	$2,968,906		(6,500)		$2,962,406

Assets Sum

K	ACCOUNTS PAYABLE	$469,204		—		$469,204
L	ACCRUED EXPENSES	18,480		—		18,480
M	CURRENT PORTION OF DEBT	100,000		—		100,000
N	INCOME TAXES PAYABLE	0		—		0
K + L + M + N = O	CURRENT LIABILITIES	587,684				587,684
P	LONG-TERM DEBT	900,000		—		900,000
Q	CAPITAL STOCK	1,550,000		—		1,550,000
R	RETAINED EARNINGS	(68,778)	**4** (6,500)			(75,278)
Q + R = S	SHAREHOLDERS' EQUITY	1,481,222				1,474,722
O + P + S = T	TOTAL LIABILITIES & EQUITY	$2,968,906		(6,500)		$2,962,406

Liabilities & Equity Sum

T25. Pay this year's general liability insurance.

During the first month we were in business many insurance brokers dropped by to try to sell us their wares.

We selected LightningBolt Brokers as our insurance agent. LightningBolt put together a package of building insurance, liability insurance and business interruption insurance that appeared to meet our needs.

We signed up for coverage and the broker said that she would send us a bill for the year, which we just got yesterday.

Transaction: With this transaction we will pay a full year's insurance premium of $26,000, giving us three months' prior coverage (the amount of time we have been in business) and also coverage for the remaining nine months in our fiscal year.

1 (1A) Issue a check for $26,000 to the insurance broker and book as a CASH DISBURSEMENT in the *Cash Flow Statement*. (1B) Lower CASH on the *Balance Sheet* by the amount of the check.

2 Book as a GENERAL & ADMINISTRATIVE expense on the *Income Statement* the $6,500 portion of the premium covering the last three months.

3 Book as a PREPAID EXPENSE on the *Balance Sheet* the remaining $19,500 premium covering the next nine months.

Note: As time goes by, we will take this remaining $19,500 as an expense through the *Income Statement*. The transaction at that time will be to book the expense in the *Income Statement* and at the same time lower the amount of PREPAID EXPENSE in the *Balance Sheet*.

4 Reduce RETAINED EARNINGS in the Balance Sheet by the $6,500 loss due to the expense we have run through the *Income Statement*.

~

Income Statement

for the period including Transactions 1 through 26

		prior	+	transaction	=	sum
1	NET SALES	$250,800		—		$250,800
2	COST OF GOODS SOLD	169,830		—		169,830
1 - 2 = 3	GROSS MARGIN	80,970				80,970
4	SALES & MARKETING	115,628		—		115,628
5	RESEARCH & DEVELOPMENT	0		—		0
6	GENERAL & ADMINISTRATIVE	40,620		—		40,620
4 + 5 + 6 = 7	OPERATING EXPENSE	156,248				156,248
3 - 7 = 8	INCOME FROM OPERATIONS	(75,278)				(75,278)
9	NET INTEREST INCOME	0	**3A**	(25,000)		(25,000)
10	INCOME TAXES	0		—		0
8 + 9 - 10 = 11	NET INCOME	($75,278)		(25,000)		($100,278)

IS Transaction Sum

Cash Flow Statement

for the period including Transactions 1 through 26

		prior	+	transaction	=	sum
a	BEGINNING CASH BALANCE	$0				$0
b	CASH RECEIPTS	234,900		—		234,900
c	CASH DISBURSEMENTS	242,478	**1B**	25,000		267,478
b - c = d	CASH FLOW FROM OPERATIONS	(7,578)				(32,578)
e	PP&E PURCHASE	1,750,000		—		1,750,000
f	NET BORROWINGS	1,000,000	**1A**	(25,000)		975,000
g	INCOME TAXES PAID	0		—		0
h	SALE OF CAPITAL STOCK	1,550,000		—		1,550,000
a + d - e + f - g + h = i	ENDING CASH BALANCES	$792,422		(50,000)		$742,422

CF Transaction Sum

Balance Sheet

as of this Transaction 26

		prior	+	transaction	=	sum
A	CASH	$792,422	**1C**	(50,000)		$742,422
B	ACCOUNTS RECEIVABLE	0		—		0
C	INVENTORIES	414,770		—		414,770
D	PREPAID EXPENSES	19,500		—		19,500
A + B + C + D = E	CURRENT ASSETS	1,226,692				1,176,692
F	OTHER ASSETS	0		—		0
G	FIXED ASSETS @ COST	1,750,000		—		1,750,000
H	ACCUMULATED DEPRECIATION	14,286		—		14,286
G - H = I	NET FIXED ASSETS	1,735,714				1,735,714
E + F + I = J	TOTAL ASSETS	$2,962,406		(50,000)		$2,912,406
				Assets Sum		
K	ACCOUNTS PAYABLE	$469,204		—		$469,204
L	ACCRUED EXPENSES	18,480		—		18,480
M	CURRENT PORTION OF DEBT	100,000		—		100,000
N	INCOME TAXES PAYABLE	0		—		0
K + L + M + N = O	CURRENT LIABILITIES	587,684				587,684
P	LONG-TERM DEBT	900,000	**2**	(25,000)		875,000
Q	CAPITAL STOCK	1,550,000		—		1,550,000
R	RETAINED EARNINGS	(75,278)	**3B**	(25,000)		(100,278)
Q + R = S	SHAREHOLDERS' EQUITY	1,474,722				1,449,722
O + P + S = T	TOTAL LIABILITIES & EQUITY	$2,962,406		(50,000)		$2,912,406

Liabilities & Equity Sum

T26. Make principal and interest payments on three months' worth of building debts.

Review the loan amortization schedule in **Transaction 3**. It shows how we must pay back the money we owe on the purchase of our building. Also, the fine print in the loan documentation says we must pay the principal and interest quarterly.

Three months have gone by since we got the loan, so interest and principal payments are due. According to the amortization schedule, this year we owe a total of $100,000 in principal payments and also $100,000 in interest payments.

Transaction: Make a quarterly payment of $25,000 in principal and also a $25,000 interest payment on the building mortgage.

1 (1A) Lower NET BORROWINGS in the *Cash Flow Statement* by the $25,000 principal payment. (1B) Book a CASH DISBURSEMENT for the $25,000 interest payment. (1C) Lower CASH on the *Balance Sheet* by the total $50,000 in cash that left the company.

2 Lower LONG-TERM DEBT on the *Balance Sheet* by the $25,000 principal payment made above.

3 (3A) Book the interest payment as a negative $25,000 under NET INTEREST INCOME on the *Income Statement*. (3B) Then book the resulting loss in RETAINED EARNINGS on the *Balance Sheet*.

Note: The interest payment entry for this transaction is booked as a negative number. If we had a category INTEREST EXPENSE on the *Income Statement* instead of INTEREST INCOME, then interest payments by the company would be booked as a positive number and interest income would be booked as a negative number.

Got that? It's important to pay attention to the exact account meaning when determining whether an entry should be positive or negative.

~

Income Statement

for the period including Transactions 1 through 27

		prior	+	transaction	=	sum
1	NET SALES	$250,800		—		$250,800
2	COST OF GOODS SOLD	169,830		—		169,830
1 - 2 = 3	GROSS MARGIN	80,970				80,970
4	SALES & MARKETING	115,628		—		115,628
5	RESEARCH & DEVELOPMENT	0		—		0
6	GENERAL & ADMINISTRATIVE	40,620		—		40,620
4 + 5 + 6 = 7	OPERATING EXPENSE	156,248				156,248
3 - 7 = 8	INCOME FROM OPERATIONS	(75,278)				(75,278)
9	NET INTEREST INCOME	(25,000)		—		(25,000)
10	INCOME TAXES	0		—		0
8 + 9 - 10 = 11	NET INCOME	($100,278)		0		($100,278)

IS Transaction Sum

Cash Flow Statement

for the period including Transactions 1 through 27

		prior	+	transaction	=	sum
a	BEGINNING CASH BALANCE	$0				$0
b	CASH RECEIPTS	234,900		—		234,900
c	CASH DISBURSEMENTS	267,478	**1A**	18,480		285,958
b - c = d	CASH FLOW FROM OPERATIONS	(32,578)				(51,058)
e	PP&E PURCHASE	1,750,000		—		1,750,000
f	NET BORROWINGS	975,000		—		975,000
g	INCOME TAXES PAID	0		—		0
h	SALE OF CAPITAL STOCK	1,550,000		—		1,550,000
a + d - e + f - g + h = i	ENDING CASH BALANCES	$742,422		(18,480)		$723,942

CF Transaction Sum

Balance Sheet

as of this Transaction 27

		prior	+	transaction	=	sum
A	CASH	$742,422	**1B**	(18,480)		$723,942
B	ACCOUNTS RECEIVABLE	0		—		0
C	INVENTORIES	414,770		—		414,770
D	PREPAID EXPENSES	19,500		—		19,500
A + B + C + D = E	CURRENT ASSETS	1,176,692				1,158,212
F	OTHER ASSETS	0		—		0
G	FIXED ASSETS @ COST	1,750,000		—		1,750,000
H	ACCUMULATED DEPRECIATION	14,286		—		14,286
G - H = I	NET FIXED ASSETS	1,735,714				1,735,714
E + F + I = J	TOTAL ASSETS	$2,912,406		(18,480)		$2,893,926

Assets Sum

		prior	+	transaction	=	sum
K	ACCOUNTS PAYABLE	$469,204		—		$469,204
L	ACCRUED EXPENSES	18,480	**2**	(18,480)		0
M	CURRENT PORTION OF DEBT	100,000		—		100,000
N	INCOME TAXES PAYABLE	0		—		0
K + L + M + N = O	CURRENT LIABILITIES	587,684				569,204
P	LONG-TERM DEBT	875,000		—		875,000
Q	CAPITAL STOCK	1,550,000		—		1,550,000
R	RETAINED EARNINGS	(100,278)		—		(100,278)
Q + R = S	SHAREHOLDERS' EQUITY	1,449,722				1,449,722
O + P + S = T	TOTAL LIABILITIES & EQUITY	$2,912,406		(18,480)		$2,893,926

Liabilities & Equity Sum

T27. Pay payroll-associated taxes and insurance benefit premiums.

We have some payroll-associated taxes and insurance benefit payments that are due for payment. We had better pay them! The government gets very nasty if we don't pay all withholding and FICA premiums when they are due.

These obligations are some of the few debts that cannot be erased by bankruptcy. Also, if the company does not pay these debts, the IRS often goes after officers of the company personally to collect the government's due.

Transaction: Pay payroll taxes, fringe benefits and insurance premiums. Write checks to the government and to insurance companies totaling $18,480 for payment of withholding and FICA taxes and for payroll associated fringe benefits.

1 (1A) Book a CASH DISBURSEMENT of $18,480 in the *Cash Flow Statement*. (1B) Lower CASH on the *Balance Sheet* by the same amount.

2 Lower ACCRUED EXPENSES on the *Balance Sheet* by the $18,480 amount paid to the government and to various insurance companies.

Note: The *Income Statement* and RETAINED EARNINGS are not affected by this payment transaction. Because AppleSeed runs its books on an accrual basis, we already "expensed" these expenses when they occurred—not when the actual payment is made.

~

Income Statement

for the period including Transactions 1 through 28

		prior	+	transaction	=	sum
1	NET SALES	$250,800		—		$250,800
2	COST OF GOODS SOLD	169,830		—		169,830
1 - 2 = 3	GROSS MARGIN	80,970				80,970
4	SALES & MARKETING	115,628		—		115,628
5	RESEARCH & DEVELOPMENT	0		—		0
6	GENERAL & ADMINISTRATIVE	40,620		—		40,620
4 + 5 + 6 = 7	OPERATING EXPENSE	156,248				156,248
3 - 7 = 8	INCOME FROM OPERATIONS	(75,278)				(75,278)
9	NET INTEREST INCOME	(25,000)		—		(25,000)
10	INCOME TAXES	0		—		0
8 + 9 - 10 = 11	NET INCOME	($100,278)		0		($100,278)

IS Transaction Sum

Cash Flow Statement

for the period including Transactions 1 through 28

		prior	+	transaction	=	sum
a	BEGINNING CASH BALANCE	$0				$0
b	CASH RECEIPTS	234,900		—		234,900
c	CASH DISBURSEMENTS	285,958	**1**	150,000		435,958
b - c = d	CASH FLOW FROM OPERATIONS	(51,058)				(201,058)
e	PP&E PURCHASE	1,750,000		—		1,750,000
f	NET BORROWINGS	975,000		—		975,000
g	INCOME TAXES PAID	0		—		0
h	SALE OF CAPITAL STOCK	1,550,000		—		1,550,000
a + d - e + f - g + h = i	ENDING CASH BALANCES	$723,942		(150,000)		$573,942

CF Transaction Sum

Balance Sheet

as of this Transaction 28

		prior	+	transaction	=	sum
A	CASH	$723,942	**2**	(150,000)		$573,942
B	ACCOUNTS RECEIVABLE	0		—		0
C	INVENTORIES	414,770		—		414,770
D	PREPAID EXPENSES	19,500		—		19,500
A + B + C + D = E	CURRENT ASSETS	1,158,212				1,008,212
F	OTHER ASSETS	0		—		0
G	FIXED ASSETS @ COST	1,750,000		—		1,750,000
H	ACCUMULATED DEPRECIATION	14,286		—		14,286
G - H = I	NET FIXED ASSETS	1,735,714				1,735,714
E + F + I = J	TOTAL ASSETS	$2,893,926		(150,000)		$2,743,926

Assets Sum

		prior	+	transaction	=	sum
K	ACCOUNTS PAYABLE	$469,204	**3**	(150,000)		$319,204
L	ACCRUED EXPENSES	0		—		0
M	CURRENT PORTION OF DEBT	100,000		—		100,000
N	INCOME TAXES PAYABLE	0		—		0
K + L + M + N = O	CURRENT LIABILITIES	569,204				419,204
P	LONG-TERM DEBT	875,000		—		875,000
Q	CAPITAL STOCK	1,550,000		—		1,550,000
R	RETAINED EARNINGS	(100,278)		—		(100,278)
Q + R = S	SHAREHOLDERS' EQUITY	1,449,722				1,449,722
O + P + S = T	TOTAL LIABILITIES & EQUITY	$2,893,926		(150,000)		$2,743,926

Liabilities & Equity Sum

T28. Pay some suppliers...especially the mean and hungry ones.

Several of our raw material suppliers have telephoned recently and asked how we are doing...and by the way, when are we planning to pay their bills?

Because we are in a check-writing mood (and because we will shortly be asking them to send us more apples), we pay a chunk of supplier bills.

Transaction: Pay suppliers a portion of what is due for apples and jars. Cut a check for $150,000 in partial payment.

| 1 | Write a check for $150,000 to pay suppliers. Increase CASH DISBURSEMENTS by that amount in the *Cash Flow Statement*. |

| 2 | Lower CASH by $150,000 in the assets section of the *Balance Sheet*. |

| 3 | Lower ACCOUNTS PAYABLE in the liabilities section of the *Balance Sheet* by the $150,000 that we no longer owe, since we just paid as described above. |

Chapter 11. Growth, Profit and Return

With these transactions we will fast-forward through the rest of AppleSeed's first year in business. We will determine our profit for the year, compute the income taxes we owe, declare a dividend and issue our first Annual Report to shareholders.

Taxes and dividends...one bad, one good? Actually without taxes there would be no dividends. Dividends are paid out of retained earnings. If the business has earnings (and can thus pay dividends), then it will have to pay taxes. Taxes with earnings; no taxes with no earnings. No earnings, then no dividends. Thus, no taxes, no dividends.

But enough of this. Some really exciting events are taking place at our now not-so-little company. We have attracted the attention of a large nationwide food processing conglomerate. The president of the conglomerate particularly likes our applesauce. She may make us an offer to buy the company! How much is it worth?

⁓

Transaction 29. Fast-forward through the rest of the year. Record summary transactions.

Transaction 30. Book income taxes payable.

Transaction 31. Declare a $0.375 per share dividend and pay to common shareholders.

- Changes in financial position

- AppleSeed Enterprises, Inc. Annual Report to Shareholders

- What is AppleSeed worth?

Financial Statements

Income Statement

for the period including Transactions 1 through 29		prior	+	transaction	=	sum
1	NET SALES	$250,800		2,804,760		$3,055,560
2	COST OF GOODS SOLD	169,830		1,836,000		2,005,830
1 - 2 = 3	GROSS MARGIN	80,970		968,760		1,049,730
4	SALES & MARKETING	115,628		212,895		328,523
5	RESEARCH & DEVELOPMENT	0		26,000		26,000
6	GENERAL & ADMINISTRATIVE	40,620		162,900		203,520
4 + 5 + 6 = 7	OPERATING EXPENSE	156,248		401,795		558,043
3 - 7 = 8	INCOME FROM OPERATIONS	(75,278)		566,965		491,687
9	NET INTEREST INCOME	(25,000)		(75,000)		(100,000)
10	INCOME TAXES	0		—		0
8 + 9 - 10 = 11	NET INCOME	($100,278)		491,965		$391,687

IS Transaction Sum

Cash Flow Statement

for the period including Transactions 1 through 29		prior	+	transaction	=	sum
a	BEGINNING CASH BALANCE	$0				$0
b	CASH RECEIPTS	234,900		2,350,000		2,584,900
c	CASH DISBURSEMENTS	435,958		2,285,480		2,721,438
b - c = d	CASH FLOW FROM OPERATIONS	(201,058)		64,520		(136,538)
e	PP&E PURCHASE	1,750,000		—		1,750,000
f	NET BORROWINGS	975,000		(75,000)		900,000
g	INCOME TAXES PAID	0		—		0
h	SALE OF CAPITAL STOCK	1,550,000		—		1,550,000
a + d - e + f - g + h = i	ENDING CASH BALANCES	$573,942		(10,480)		$563,462

CF Transaction Sum

Balance Sheet

as of this Transaction 29		prior	+	transaction	=	sum
A	CASH	$573,942		(10,480)		$563,462
B	ACCOUNTS RECEIVABLE	0		454,760		454,760
C	INVENTORIES	414,770		—		414,770
D	PREPAID EXPENSES	19,500		(19,500)		0
A + B + C + D = E	CURRENT ASSETS	1,008,212		424,780		1,432,992
F	OTHER ASSETS	0		—		0
G	FIXED ASSETS @ COST	1,750,000		—		1,750,000
H	ACCUMULATED DEPRECIATION	14,286		64,287		78,573
G - H = I	NET FIXED ASSETS	1,735,714		(64,287)		1,671,427
E + F + I = J	TOTAL ASSETS	$2,743,926		360,493		$3,104,419
				Assets Sum		
K	ACCOUNTS PAYABLE	$319,204		(82,907)		$236,297
L	ACCRUED EXPENSES	0		26,435		26,435
M	CURRENT PORTION OF DEBT	100,000		—		100,000
N	INCOME TAXES PAYABLE	0		—		0
K + L + M + N = O	CURRENT LIABILITIES	419,204		(56,472)		362,732
P	LONG-TERM DEBT	875,000		(75,000)		800,000
Q	CAPITAL STOCK	1,550,000		—		1,550,000
R	RETAINED EARNINGS	(100,278)		491,965		391,687
Q + R = S	SHAREHOLDERS' EQUITY	1,449,722		491,965		1,941,687
O + P + S = T	TOTAL LIABILITIES & EQUITY	$2,743,926		360,493		$3,104,419

Liabilities & Equity Sum

T29. Fast-forward through the rest of the year. Record summary transactions.

AppleSeed Enterprises, Inc., has been in business for about three months now. We seem to have gotten the hang of recording transactions and manipulating the *Income Statement, Cash Flow* and *Balance Sheet*. It's fun.

With this series of entries we will compress and summarize all the remaining transactions that took place in AppleSeed's next nine months of operations. As you can see from the statements, we sold about $2.8 million in applesauce during the last nine months of the year and a total of $3.1 million for the year.

We also collected a little less than $2.6 million from customers during the year and paid out a little over $2.7 million to suppliers, employees, etc. Significantly, we turned cash flow positive—that is, more cash receipts than cash disbursements—to the tune of over $64,520 during the last nine months of our fiscal year. Note that we were still cash flow negative by $136,538 for the whole year.

The bookings in this summary transaction close out our first year in business. Let's review the bottom line. Income from operations amounted to $491,687. Subtract from this figure the interest paid on building debt and we have a total of $391,687 as our *pre-tax* profit for the year.

A very nice showing. Taxes next.

Transaction: Book a series of entries in the *Income Statement, Cash Flow Statement* and the *Balance Sheet* summarizing transactions that take place in the remaining nine months of AppleSeed Enterprises' first fiscal year.

~

Income Statement

for the period including Transactions 1 through 30

		prior	+	transaction	=	sum
1	NET SALES	$3,055,560		—		$3,055,560
2	COST OF GOODS SOLD	2,005,830		—		2,005,830
1 - 2 = 3	GROSS MARGIN	1,049,730				1,049,730
4	SALES & MARKETING	328,523		—		328,523
5	RESEARCH & DEVELOPMENT	26,000		—		26,000
6	GENERAL & ADMINISTRATIVE	203,520		—		203,520
4 + 5 + 6 = 7	OPERATING EXPENSE	558,043				558,043
3 - 7 = 8	INCOME FROM OPERATIONS	491,687				491,687
9	NET INTEREST INCOME	(100,000)		—		(100,000)
10	INCOME TAXES	0	**1A**	139,804		139,804
8 + 9 - 10 = 11	NET INCOME	$391,687		(139,804)		$251,883

IS Transaction Sum

Cash Flow Statement

for the period including Transactions 1 through 30

		prior	+	transaction	=	sum
a	BEGINNING CASH BALANCE	$0				$0
b	CASH RECEIPTS	2,584,900		—		2,584,900
c	CASH DISBURSEMENTS	2,721,438		—		2,721,438
b - c = d	CASH FLOW FROM OPERATIONS	(136,538)				(136,538)
e	PP&E PURCHASE	1,750,000		—		1,750,000
f	NET BORROWINGS	900,000		—		900,000
g	INCOME TAXES PAID	0		—		0
h	SALE OF CAPITAL STOCK	1,550,000		—		1,550,000
a + d - e + f - g + h = i	ENDING CASH BALANCES	$563,462		0		$563,462

CF Transaction Sum

Balance Sheet

as of this Transaction 30

		prior	+	transaction	=	sum
A	CASH	$563,462		—		$563,462
B	ACCOUNTS RECEIVABLE	454,760		—		454,760
C	INVENTORIES	414,770		—		414,770
D	PREPAID EXPENSES	0		—		0
A + B + C + D = E	CURRENT ASSETS	1,432,992				1,432,992
F	OTHER ASSETS	0		—		0
G	FIXED ASSETS @ COST	1,750,000		—		1,750,000
H	ACCUMULATED DEPRECIATION	78,573		—		78,573
G - H = I	NET FIXED ASSETS	1,671,427				1,671,427
E + F + I = J	TOTAL ASSETS	$3,104,419		0		$3,104,419

Assets Sum

		prior	+	transaction	=	sum
K	ACCOUNTS PAYABLE	$236,297		—		$236,297
L	ACCRUED EXPENSES	26,435		—		26,435
M	CURRENT PORTION OF DEBT	100,000		—		100,000
N	INCOME TAXES PAYABLE	0	**2**	139,804		139,804
K + L + M + N = O	CURRENT LIABILITIES	362,732				502,536
P	LONG-TERM DEBT	800,000		—		800,000
Q	CAPITAL STOCK	1,550,000		—		1,550,000
R	RETAINED EARNINGS	391,687	**1B**	(139,804)		251,883
Q + R = S	SHAREHOLDERS' EQUITY	1,941,687				1,801,883
O + P + S = T	TOTAL LIABILITIES & EQUITY	$3,104,419		0		$3,104,419

Liabilities & Equity Sum

T30. Book income taxes payable.

Taxes are very simple.

For almost all corporations you just take pretax income and multiply it by 34% or so. Then you take out your checkbook and write a check to the government for that amount. If you fail to send in the money on time or if you fudge the books and the IRS catches you, then you go to jail.

See, I told you taxes were simple. With this transaction we will compute and then book the income taxes we owe the government. We will actually pay them later on the tax due date.

Transaction: On a pretax income of $391,687 AppleSeed owes 34% in federal income taxes ($133,173), and $6,631 in state income taxes for a total income tax bill of $139,804. We will not actually pay the tax for several months.

| 1 | (1A) Book an INCOME TAXES expense of $139,804 in the *Income Statement*. (1B) Lower RETAINED EARNINGS by the same amount in the *Balance Sheet*. |

| 2 | Book $139,804 worth of INCOME TAXES PAYABLE in the liabilities section of the *Balance Sheet*. |

Income Statement

for the period including Transactions 1 through 31		prior	+	transaction	=	sum
1	NET SALES	$3,055,560		—		$3,055,560
2	COST OF GOODS SOLD	2,005,830		—		2,005,830
1 - 2 = 3	GROSS MARGIN	1,049,730				1,049,730
4	SALES & MARKETING	328,523		—		328,523
5	RESEARCH & DEVELOPMENT	26,000		—		26,000
6	GENERAL & ADMINISTRATIVE	203,520		—		203,520
4 + 5 + 6 = 7	OPERATING EXPENSE	558,043				558,043
3 - 7 = 8	INCOME FROM OPERATIONS	491,687				491,687
9	NET INTEREST INCOME	(100,000)		—		(100,000)
10	INCOME TAXES	139,804		—		139,804
8 + 9 - 10 = 11	NET INCOME	$251,883		0		$251,883

IS Transaction Sum

Cash Flow Statement

for the period including Transactions 1 through 31		prior	+	transaction	=	sum
a	BEGINNING CASH BALANCE	$0				$0
b	CASH RECEIPTS	2,584,900		—		2,584,900
c	CASH DISBURSEMENTS	2,721,438	**1A**	75,000		2,796,438
b - c = d	CASH FLOW FROM OPERATIONS	(136,538)				(211,538)
e	PP&E PURCHASE	1,750,000		—		1,750,000
f	NET BORROWINGS	900,000		—		900,000
g	INCOME TAXES PAID	0		—		0
h	SALE OF CAPITAL STOCK	1,550,000		—		1,550,000
a + d - e + f - g + h = i	ENDING CASH BALANCES	$563,462		(75,000)		$488,462

CF Transaction Sum

Balance Sheet

as of this Transaction 31		prior	+	transaction	=	sum
A	CASH	$563,462	**1B**	(75,000)		$488,462
B	ACCOUNTS RECEIVABLE	454,760		—		454,760
C	INVENTORIES	414,770		—		414,770
D	PREPAID EXPENSES	0		—		0
A + B + C + D = E	CURRENT ASSETS	1,432,992				1,357,992
F	OTHER ASSETS	0		—		0
G	FIXED ASSETS @ COST	1,750,000		—		1,750,000
H	ACCUMULATED DEPRECIATION	78,573		—		78,573
G - H = I	NET FIXED ASSETS	1,671,427				1,671,427
E + F + I = J	TOTAL ASSETS	$3,104,419		(75,000)		$3,029,419

Assets Sum

K	ACCOUNTS PAYABLE	$236,297		—		$236,297
L	ACCRUED EXPENSES	26,435		—		26,435
M	CURRENT PORTION OF DEBT	100,000		—		100,000
N	INCOME TAXES PAYABLE	139,804		—		139,804
K + L + M + N = O	CURRENT LIABILITIES	502,536				502,536
P	LONG-TERM DEBT	800,000		—		800,000
Q	CAPITAL STOCK	1,550,000		—		1,550,000
R	RETAINED EARNINGS	251,883	**2**	(75,000)		176,883
Q + R = S	SHAREHOLDERS' EQUITY	1,801,883				1,726,883
O + P + S = T	TOTAL LIABILITIES & EQUITY	$3,104,419		(75,000)		$3,029,419

Liabilities & Equity Sum

T31. Declare a $0.375 per share dividend and pay to the common shareholders.

This transaction will be our last for AppleSeed Enterprises this year, just before we close the books. The company has done well in its first year of operation and the board of directors decides to vote a dividend for common shareholders. The question, is how big a dividend?

Dividends are paid out of retained earnings, of which we have more than $250,000 as of the end of the year. We also have a very strong cash position so we can afford the dividend.

After much discussion, a $0.375 per share dividend is voted. With 200,000 shares outstanding, this dividend will cost the company $75,000; $56,250 to the investor group and $18,750 to you, the entrepreneur.

You go out and buy a small boat.

Transaction: Declare and pay a $0.375 per share dividend to Apple-Seed's shareholders.

| 1 | (1A) Book a CASH DISBURSEMENT (see note below) on the *Cash Flow Statement* for the $75,000 dividend payment. (1B) Reduce CASH on the *Balance Sheet* by the same amount. |

| 2 | Reduce RETAINED EARNINGS on the *Balance Sheet* by the dividend payment of $75,000. |

Note: The *Cash Flow Statements* on these transaction spreads are abbreviated. That is, they do not have all the line items that a complete statement would have. The dividend payment should really be placed on a special line titled DIVIDENDS PAID rather than in CASH DISBURSEMENTS. Paying a dividend is not an operating expense and cash disbursements should be reserved for operating expenses.

See the next two pages for a description of the structure of a more complete *Cash Flow Statement*.

~

Statement of Cash Flows

The *Cash Flow Statement* format that we've been using in AppleSeed Enterprises' financial statements is a very simple-to-understand representation of cash movement. We have likened it to a check register, with the "sources of cash" being deposits and the "uses of cash" being checks. However, most accountants would prefer to use another format for cash flow. With this format (shown on

AppleSeed Enterprises, Inc. —for Transactions 19 through 31—	Balance Sheet Element as of T19	Balance Sheet Element as of T31	Cash Flow for the Period T19 thru T31
Cash flows from operating activities:			
Net income (see Note 1)	$(135,780)	$251,883	$387,663
Adjustments to reconcile net income to net cash used in operations:			
Depreciation (see Note 2)	14,286	78,573	64,287
Changes in working capital:			
Accounts receivable (see Note 3)	0	454,760	(454,760)
Inventories (see Note 3)	577,970	414,770	163,200
Prepaid expenses (see Note 3)	0	0	0
Accounts payable (see Note 4)	469,205	236,297	(232,908)
Accrued expenses (see Note 4)	18,480	26,435	7,955
Income taxes payable (see Note 4)	0	139,804	139,804
Net cash used in operating activities			$75,241
Cash flows from investing activities:			
PP&E purchase (see Note 5)	1,750,000	1,750,000	0
Net cash used in investing activities			0
Cash flow from financing activities:			
Sale of stock (see Note 6)	1,550,000	1,550,000	0
Change in debt (see Note 7)	1,000,000	900,000	(100,000)
Dividends paid (see Note 8)			(75,000)
Net cash from financing activities			$(175,000)
Net increase (decrease) in cash (Transactions 19 through Transaction 31)			$(99,760)
Beginning cash (as of Transaction 19)			$588,222
Ending cash (as of Transaction 31)			$488,462

the previous page), the *Cash Flow Statement* is better likened to a "bridge" between the *Balance Sheet* at the start of a period and the *Balance Sheet* at the end of a period. This bridging format specifically shows the asset, liability and equity accounts that change to provide cash, and the accounts that change using cash.

Most of the time when you look at financial statements you will see a statement like the one on the facing page (except the statement will only show the "Cash Flow for the Period" column, not the computational columns we have included as a tutorial).

Both formats allow you to get to the same answer, *Ending Cash Balance*, but in different ways. The format introduced here focuses on cash movements divided into three major categories of interest to anyone reviewing the cash performance of a business:

1. **Cash Flows from Operations.**
   Cash sources (uses) from activities such as making and selling products.

2. **Cash Flows from Investing.**
   Cash uses (sources) from increases (decreases) in the company's productive assets such as property, plant and equipment.

3. **Cash Flows from Financing.**
   Cash sources (uses) from selling stock to investors, borrowing money from a bank and paying dividends.

The Statement of Cash Flows that is shown on the facing page summarizes cash movements for AppleSeed Enterprises between **Transaction 19** and **Transaction 31**. We have selected the period between these two transactions because it provides an informative example; we could have used the period between any two transactions.

If we look on page 146 at AppleSeed's Cash Flow Statement for **Transaction 19**, we see $588,222 as an ending cash balance. Looking at AppleSeed's Cash Flow Statement for **Transaction 31** on page 178, we see $488,462 as an ending cash balance. Subtracting the earlier from the later cash balance, we see that in the time between these two transactions, cash has dropped by $99,762.

Refer to the statement on the facing page and review the following notes to see how this "bridging" Cash Flow Statement is constructed.

~

Note 1. Income for the period is computed from Income Statements by subtracting Net Income as of **Transaction 19** (loss of $135,780) from Net Income as of **Transaction 31** (profit of $251,883).

Note 2. Computed as change in Accumulated Depreciation. Depreciation does not affect cash flow, but because it has been subtracted from the Net Income for the period, it must be added back here to get a true picture of cash movements.

Note 3. Computed as the change in these asset accounts. Note that an increase in an asset account means the company has more working capital and a positive cash flow in that account.

Note 4. Computed as the change in these liability accounts. Note that an increase in a liability account means the company has less working capital and a negative cash flow in that account.

Note 5. Computed as the change in the PP&E Asset. An increase in PP&E takes cash.

Note 6. Computed as the change in the Capital Stock account of Shareholders' Equity.

Note 7. Computed as the change in the Current Portion and Long-term Debt accounts. Lowering of overall debt takes cash. Increasing overall debt increases cash.

Note 8. Dividends paid to shareholders take cash.

Income Statement

for the period including Transactions 1 through 31

NET SALES	$3,055,560
COST OF GOODS SOLD	2,005,830
GROSS MARGIN	1,049,730
SALES & MARKETING	328,523
RESEARCH & DEVELOPMENT	26,000
GENERAL & ADMINISTRATIVE	203,520
OPERATING EXPENSE	558,043
INCOME FROM OPERATIONS	491,687
NET INTEREST INCOME	(100,000)
INCOME TAXES	139,804
NET INCOME	$251,883

Cash Flow Statement

for the period including Transactions 1 through 31

BEGINNING CASH BALANCE	$0
CASH RECEIPTS	2,584,900
CASH DISBURSEMENTS	2,796,438
CASH FLOW FROM OPERATIONS	(211,538)
PP&E PURCHASE	1,750,000
NET BORROWINGS	900,000
INCOME TAXES PAID	0
SALE OF CAPITAL STOCK	1,550,000
ENDING CASH BALANCES	$488,462

Balance Sheet

as of this Transaction 31

CASH	$488,462
ACCOUNTS RECEIVABLE	454,760
INVENTORIES	414,770
PREPAID EXPENSES	0
CURRENT ASSETS	1,357,992
OTHER ASSETS	0
FIXED ASSETS @ COST	1,750,000
ACCUMULATED DEPRECIATION	78,573
NET FIXED ASSETS	1,671,427
TOTAL ASSETS	$3,029,419
ACCOUNTS PAYABLE	$236,297
ACCRUED EXPENSES	26,435
CURRENT PORTION OF DEBT	100,000
INCOME TAXES PAYABLE	139,804
CURRENT LIABILITIES	502,536
LONG-TERM DEBT	800,000
CAPITAL STOCK	1,550,000
RETAINED EARNINGS	176,883
SHAREHOLDERS' EQUITY	1,726,883
TOTAL LIABILITIES & EQUITY	$3,029,419

AppleSeed Enterprises, Inc.

ANNUAL REPORT

To Our Shareholders:

I am happy to have this opportunity to report to you the results of AppleSeed Enterprises, Inc., first year of operation. Your company, in a very short time, has achieved its initial goal of becoming a recognized supplier of very high quality applesauce.

Important Events

At the beginning of the year, AppleSeed raised $1 million through a successful offering of its common stock. This capitalization has allowed us to purchase high-volume production machinery and to maintain sufficient inventory to break into the highly competitive applesauce industry.

Our production continues at over 20 thousand cases per month. As demand increases, we project that the current manufacturing facility can be operated at over twice these levels. Depending, however, on the weather conditions in the northeast, raw material supply may limit our ability to reach increased levels of production.

Financial Results

In AppleSeed's first year of operation, revenues exceeded $3 million. AppleSeed's Net Income for the year was over $250,000 or $1.26 per share with 200,000 shares outstanding.

Our return on sales of 8% exceeds industry averages, as does our 15% return on shareholders' equity. Return on assets was 8%. Our Balance Sheet remains strong. We end the year with $488,000 in cash and cash equivalents.

~

AppleSeed continues to spend heavily in marketing and sales. We believe these investments in the future will pay off

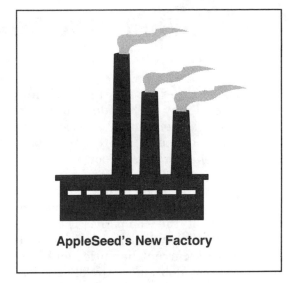

AppleSeed's New Factory

handsomely in significantly improved market position, especially in specialty segments of the applesauce industry.

During the coming year we plan to introduce several new jar sizes and packaging configurations into the gift market. Product testing continues on specialty flavored and colored versions of our basic applesauce. A bright green sauce packaged in a shamrock-shaped jar will be introduced prior to St. Patrick's Day this year. We expect our new products to be well-received in the marketplace.

~

I thank our customers for their continuing confidence in our products and in our ability to serve their applesauce needs. I thank our shareholders for continuing support, and our employees for their productive efforts throughout AppleSeed's first year of operation.

Sincerely,

J. M. Rich

President and CEO

What's the Business Worth?

We've done a super job starting up an applesauce company. What do you think the business is worth now? A good question, one of particular interest to AppleSeed's shareholders. Let's look at several methods of company valuation.

Book Value. Book value represents the value at which assets are carried on the "books" of the company. The book value of a company is defined as its total assets less its current liabilities and less any long-term debt. For AppleSeed Enterprises, Inc., book value can be computed as $1,726,883 (that is, $3,029,419 in total assets less a total of $502,536 in current liabilities less some $800,000 in long-term debt outstanding).

Liquidation Value. The liquidation value is what the company's assets would bring at a forced sale. Normally the liquidation value of a going concern has little relevance since the value of an operating business is much greater than its liquidation value.

For fun (?!) let's compute AppleSeed's liquidation value. Start with the company's book value and then subtract what would lower that amount if, for example, we could only get 10 cents on the dollar for inventory and 50 cents on the dollar for machinery. Using these assumptions AppleSeed's liquidation value would be less than $500,000.

Price-Earnings Multiple. The company has 200,000 shares outstanding and earned a net income of $251,883 last year. Dividing net income by the number of outstanding shares gives a net income of $1.26 per share.

If we assume that companies similar to AppleSeed are currently selling at, let's say, 12 times earnings, then our company is worth $1.26 times this 12 multiple times 200,000 shares outstanding which equals a value of slightly over $3 million.

Market Value. There is no market for AppleSeed's stock. Thus, there is no real "market value" for the company. Selling an untraded company is like selling a house. The business is worth what you can get for it.

Discounted Cash Flow. The discounted cash flow method of valuation is the most sophisticated (and the most difficult) method to use in valuing the business. With this method you must estimate all the cash influxes to investors over time (dividends and ultimate stock sales) and then compute a "net present value" using an assumed discount rate (implied interest rate). There are too many assumptions in this method to make it useful in valuing AppleSeed Enterprises, Inc.

Alternative AppleSeed Valuations

VALUATION METHOD	COMPANY VALUE
Book Value	$1,726,883
Liquidation Value	$467,877
Price-Earnings Multiple	$3,024,000
Market Value	sell to whom?
Discounted Cash Flow	too complex!

Section C. Financial Statements: Construction & Analysis

About this Section

Congratulations! You have accurately kept the books of AppleSeed Enterprises, Inc., for the year. And a good year it was. What follows in this section are some techniques and some details.

Journals and Ledgers. We'll learn about journals and ledgers, the books that accountants use to make transaction entries. Well, accountants did use paper entry books and did sit atop high chairs. Now entries are made in computer memory. Some say that computers have made it easier to commit fraud. (When ledgers were paper books and entries were made with India ink, things were more difficult to fudge.)

Ratio Analysis. Next we will review the common ways of analyzing financial statements to test the financial strength of the enterprise. We will review the liquidity of the company, how efficiently it uses its assets, how profitable it is and how effectively it is using "other people's money," that is, debt.

Accounting Policies. We will review the different, but acceptable, ways to keep the company's books and why companies would want to use them. Note that some of these "creative accounting" techniques can be used to mask problems in the enterprise.

Cooking the Books. Finally, we will discuss the ways of financial fraud and how to detect it. There are some "tried and true" fraudulent techniques that are important to understand whether you are an employee or an investor in the company.

Chapter 12. Keeping Track with Journals and Ledgers

Financial accounting means recording each and every event (transaction) that has a financial impact on the enterprise. By keeping track of these activities just as they happen, the accountant can easily summarize the firm's financial position and issue financial statements. *Journals* and *ledgers* are "the books" in which accountants scribble transaction entries.

A *journal* is a book (or computer memory) in which all of a company's financial events are recorded in chronological order. Everything is there, there is nothing missing. Journal entries can (and must) be made if:

1. We know with reasonable certainty the amount of money involved.

2. We know the timing of the event.

3. An actual exchange between the parties of cash, goods or some formal representation of value (such as stock) has occurred.

A *ledger* is a book of accounts. An account is simply any grouping of items that we want to keep track of. You can think of a ledger as a book with many pages. Each page of the ledger book represents one account.

The main benefit of a ledger system is that it allows us to determine how much we have of any item (account) at any point in time. Immediately after making a chronological journal entry, we update our ledger for each account that has changed as a result of that entry.

Note that every time we make a journal entry, we will be changing the amount that we have in at least two accounts (ledger pages) in order to keep the Balance Sheet and the basic equation of accounting in balance: *Assets equals liabilities plus equity.*

Any event having a financial impact on the firm affects this basic equation. The equation summarizes the entire financial position of the firm. Furthermore, the equation must always stay in balance. To keep this equation in balance, a change in any one number in the equation must change at least one other number. *Accountants call this system of making ledger changes in pairs the double-entry bookkeeping system.*

A *journal* is a book (or computer memory) in which all of a company's financial events are recorded in chronological order. Everything is there, nothing is missing.

A *ledger* is a book of accounts. An account is any grouping of items of which we want to keep track. You can think of a ledger as a book with many pages. Each page of the ledger book represents one account.

Financial Statements

Following are several of the account ledgers for AppleSeed Enterprises. Each ledger shows how our transactions have affected a single account. Note that at all times the ledgers present a current picture of AppleSeed's account balances.

The Cash Ledger shown below lists all transactions that affect the amount of cash in AppleSeed Enterprises' checking account. The *ending cash balance* on the Cash Ledger is the same amount as shown for the CASH account on the *Balance Sheet* for the date of the last transaction.

Shown on the following pages are additional AppleSeed Enterprises, Inc., ledgers.

AppleSeed Enterprises, Inc.

Cash Ledger

	TRANSACTION NUMBER & DESCRIPTION	INCOMING CASH (+)	OUTGOING CASH (-)	ENDING CASH BALANCE (=)
	Beginning of period balance			$50,000
1	Sell 150,000 shares at $10 each	$1,500,000		$1,550,000
2	G&A payroll checks		$3,370	$1,546,630
3	Borrowing to purchase building	$1,000,000		$2,546,630
4	Purchase building for $1.5 million		$1,500,000	$1,046,630
5	SG&A payroll		$7,960	$1,038,670
6	Pay payroll taxes to government		$9,690	$1,028,980
7	Make partial payment for machinery		$125,000	$903,980
8	Make final payment for machinery		$125,000	$778,980
9	Supervisor's payroll		$2,720	$776,260
12	Pay manufacturing payroll		$9,020	$767,240
14	Pay for jar labels		$20,000	$747,240
17	Partial payment to raw material suppliers		$150,000	$597,240
18	Pay manufacturing payroll		$9,020	$588,220
23	Receipts from customer, commission payment	$234,900	$4,698	$818,422
25	Pay insurance premiums		$26,000	$792,422
26	Pay mortgage principal and interest		$50,000	$742,422
27	Pay payroll taxes and benefit premiums		$18,480	$723,942
28	Pay hungry suppliers		$150,000	$573,942
29	Nine months' summary transactions (net)		$10,480	$563,462
31	Dividend payment		$75,000	$488,462

AppleSeed Enterprises, Inc.

Accounts Payable Ledger

	TRANSACTION NUMBER & DESCRIPTION	TRANSACTION AMOUNT	ACCOUNTS PAYABLE
	Opening balance		$0
10	Receive labels	$20,000	$20,000
11	Receive two months' raw materials	$332,400	$352,400
13	Book a month's "all other" mfg. expense	$8,677	$361,077
14	Pay for labels received in Transaction 10	$(20,000)	$341,077
17	Partial payment to raw material suppliers	$(150,000)	$191,077
18-L	Receive additional month's raw materials	$166,200	$357,277
18-P	Book another month's "all other" mfg. expense	$8,677	$365,954
19	Book advertising flier and T-shirt expense	$103,250	$469,204
28	Pay hungry suppliers	$(150,000)	$319,204
29	Nine months' summary transactions (net)	$(82,907)	$236,297

AppleSeed Enterprises, Inc.

Accrued Expenses Ledger

	TRANSACTION NUMBER & DESCRIPTION	TRANSACTION AMOUNT	ACCRUED EXPENSES
	Opening balance		$0
2	Payroll-associated taxes and benefits	$2,860	$2,860
5	Payroll-associated taxes and benefits	$6,830	$9,690
6	Payment of payroll taxes and associated premiums	$(9,690)	$0
9	Payroll-associated taxes and benefits	$2,160	$2,160
12	Payroll-associated taxes and benefits	$8,160	$10,320
18	Payroll-associated taxes and benefits	$8,160	$18,480
20	Sales commission due	$318	$18,798
22	Sales commission due	$4,698	$23,496
23	Payment of sales commission	$(4,698)	$18,798
24	Reversal of sales commission due from T20.	$(318)	$18,480
27	Payment of payroll taxes, fringe benefit, premiums	$(18,480)	$0
29	Nine months' summary transactions (net)	$26,435	$26,435

AppleSeed Enterprises, Inc.

Accounts Receivable Ledger

	TRANSACTION NUMBER & DESCRIPTION	TRANSACTION AMOUNT	ACCOUNTS RECEIVABLE
	Opening balance		$0
20	Applesauce sale - 1,000 cases @ $15.90	$15,900	$15,900
22	Applesauce sale - 15,000 cases @ $15.66	$234,900	$250,800
23	Payment received for Transaction 22	$(234,900)	$15,900
24	Bad debt from Transaction 20 - write off receivable	$(15,900)	$0
29	Nine months' summary transactions (net)	$454,760	$454,760

AppleSeed Enterprises, Inc.

Inventory Ledger

	TRANSACTION NUMBER & DESCRIPTION	BEGINNING INVENTORY	TRANSACTION	ENDING INVENTORY
	Opening balance			$0
10	Receive applesauce jar labels	$0	$20,000	$20,000
11	Receive two months' inventory	$20,000	$332,400	$352,400
12	Pay manufacturing salaries	$352,400	$17,180	$369,580
13	Book depreciation and other mfg. overhead	$369,580	$15,820	$385,400
16	Scrap the value of 500 cases of applesauce	$385,400	$(5,100)	$380,300
18	Mfg another month's worth of applesauce	$380,300	$197,670	$577,970
20	Ship 1,000 cases of applesauce	$577,970	$(10,200)	$567,770
22	Ship 15,000 cases of applesauce	$567,770	$(153,000)	$414,770

Note that for each of AppleSeed's ledgers shown above, the right-most column shows the account value as of the completion of the transaction listed. Ledgers should always be kept current. Then, when statements need to be prepared, the ledgers will always provide correct account values.

Chapter 13. Ratio Analysis

It is not so much the absolute numbers of sales, costs, expenses and assets that are important in judging the financial condition of an enterprise, but rather, the relationships between them.

For example:

- Cash available relative to the level of payables is a good indicator of how easily the company will be able to pay its bills in the future.

- Asset levels relative to sales volume indicates just how efficiently the company's investments in productive assets (machinery and inventory) generate revenue.

- Gross margin as a percentage of sales determines how much the company is able to spend on various selling development and administrative activities and still make a profit.

Ratio analysis (that is, comparing one number on a company's financial statement with another number) is most useful when you wish to: (1) compare year-to-year performance to determine if things are getting better or getting worse

for the enterprise, or (2) compare companies in an industry to see which is performing best given common constraints.

~

In this section we will review AppleSeed Enterprises' first-year financial performance by analyzing the company's Financial Statements and the common ratio indicators of:

- Liquidity
- Asset management
- Profitability
- Leverage

Finally, we will compare ratios across industries. Some businesses are naturally more profitable than others. Some require more capital; some require less.

The ratios computed on the following pages use AppleSeed Enterprises' Inc. *Income Statement* and *Balance Sheet* for the period from **Transaction 1** through **Transaction 31** shown in AppleSeed's Annual Report on page 182.

Common Size Statements

Both the *Income Statement* and the *Balance Sheet* can be converted into "common size" statements for analysis. Common size statements present each item as a percentage of the statement's largest item.

Common Size Income Statement. Normally the largest item in the *Income Statement* is sales. Thus, when the *Income Statement* is converted into a common size statement, all items are presented as a percentage of sales. Reviewing the common size income statement focuses on the proportion of sales dollar absorbed by various cost and expense items. AppleSeed's cost of goods is 34% of sales; operating expense is 18%; net income is 8% and so forth. Not bad percentages for a company such as ours. See AppleSeed's Common Size Income Statement shown at right.

Common Size Balance Sheet. To convert the *Balance Sheet* into a common size statement, all components are expressed as a percentage of total assets. For example AppleSeed's current assets are 44% of total assets; long-term debt is 27% of total liabilities and equity, and so forth.

Common size balance sheets help focus analysis on the internal structure and allocation of the company's financial resources. Common size statements are especially useful for the side-by-side analyses of several years of a company's performance or when two companies of different size are being compared.

Appropriate year-to-year questions to ask are:

- "Why did we do better last year in this area than this year?"
- "How well are we doing when we are compared to other companies in the industry?"

Common Size Income Statement

for the period including Transactions 1 through 31

NET SALES	$3,055,560	100%
COST OF GOODS SOLD	2,005,830	66%
GROSS MARGIN	1,049,730	34%
SALES & MARKETING	328,523	11%
RESEARCH & DEVELOPMENT	26,000	1%
GENERAL & ADMINISTRATIVE	203,520	7%
OPERATING EXPENSE	558,043	18%
INCOME FROM OPERATIONS	491,687	16%
NET INTEREST INCOME	(100,000)	(3%)
INCOME TAXES	139,804	5%
NET INCOME	$251,883	8%

Common Size Balance Sheet

as of this Transaction 31

CASH	$488,462	16%
ACCOUNTS RECEIVABLE	454,760	15%
INVENTORIES	414,770	14%
PREPAID EXPENSES	0	0%
CURRENT ASSETS	1,357,992	45%
OTHER ASSETS	0	0%
FIXED ASSETS @ COST	1,750,000	58%
ACCUMULATED DEPRECIATION	78,573	3%
NET FIXED ASSETS	1,671,427	55%
TOTAL ASSETS	$3,029,419	100%
ACCOUNTS PAYABLE	$236,297	8%
ACCRUED EXPENSES	26,435	1%
CURRENT PORTION OF DEBT	100,000	3%
INCOME TAXES PAYABLE	139,804	5%
CURRENT LIABILITIES	502,536	17%
LONG-TERM DEBT	800,000	26%
CAPITAL STOCK	1,550,000	51%
RETAINED EARNINGS	176,883	6%
SHAREHOLDERS' EQUITY	1,726,883	57%
TOTAL LIABILITIES & EQUITY	$3,029,419	100%

Liquidity Ratios

The so-called liquidity ratios measure the ease with which a company can pay its bills when due. This ability is determined by whether the enterprise has cash in the bank or expects to generate cash (by sale of goods and by the collection of accounts receivable) in sufficient amount to pay its bills as they become due.

There are periods of illiquidity in almost every company's life ... when the company is unable to pay bills on time. Most often this situation is infrequent or only temporary and is usually no major problem. It's happened to all of us at one time or another.

But if a company is illiquid on a regular basis, or for a long period of time, it is likely to find itself *busted, tapped-out, bankrupt.*

Everyone is interested in Apple-Seed's ability to pay short-term debts, including its employees, suppliers and the bank that lent us money for our building. Even our customers care. They need a reliable supply of product.

> *Liquidity* and *profitability* are different. It's possible—and indeed not all that uncommon—for a company to be profitable and illiquid at the same time. A company can show a profit on the *Income Statement* and still have very little cash on hand to pay its bills.

Balance Sheet
as of this Transaction 31

CASH	$488,462	A
ACCOUNTS RECEIVABLE	454,760	B
INVENTORIES	414,770	
PREPAID EXPENSES	0	
CURRENT ASSETS	1,357,992	C
OTHER ASSETS	0	
FIXED ASSETS @ COST	1,750,000	
ACCUMULATED DEPRECIATION	78,573	
NET FIXED ASSETS	1,671,427	
TOTAL ASSETS	$3,029,419	
ACCOUNTS PAYABLE	$236,297	
ACCRUED EXPENSES	26,435	
CURRENT PORTION OF DEBT	100,000	
INCOME TAXES PAYABLE	139,804	
CURRENT LIABILITIES	502,536	D
LONG-TERM DEBT	800,000	
CAPITAL STOCK	1,550,000	
RETAINED EARNINGS	176,883	
SHAREHOLDERS' EQUITY	1,726,883	
TOTAL LIABILITIES & EQUITY	$3,029,419	

Profitability coupled with illiquidity can often occur in companies experiencing unexpected high growth. These companies need increased working capital to finance inventories and accounts receivable. Cash can be very tight. Happily, in these conditions, bankers love to lend money to those companies experiencing illiquidity due to rapid profitable growth.

Current Ratio. The current ratio is one of the oldest and best-known measures of short-term financial strength. The ratio determines whether current assets (cash or assets that are expected to be converted into cash within a year) are sufficient to pay current liabilities (those obligations that must be paid within one year).

A current ratio for a general manufacturing company of 2.0 is considered good. It means that the company has twice the amount of current assets as it has current liabilities. A 1:1 ratio means that a company can *just* meet its upcoming bills. With a 2:1 ratio there is a financial cushion.

Quick Ratio. The quick ratio is an even more conservative measure of liquidity than the current ratio. It is sometimes call the "acid test." The quick ratio is the company's "quick assets" (cash and accounts receivable) divided by current liabilities. Inventories are left out.

As shown in the computations here, AppleSeed Enterprises is quite liquid.

AppleSeed's Liquidity Ratios

$$\text{Current Ratio} = \frac{Current\ Assets}{Current\ Liabilities} = \frac{C}{D} = \frac{\$1,357,992}{\$502,536} - 2.7$$

$$\text{Quick Ratio} = \frac{Cash\ + Receivables}{Current\ Liabilities} = \frac{A\ +B}{D} = \frac{\$488,462\ +\$454,760}{\$502,536} = 1.9$$

Asset Management Ratios

Assets are the financial engine of the enterprise. But how do we know that our assets are being used efficiently? Are we getting the biggest bang for our asset buck? Asset management ratios provide a tool to investigate how effective in generating profits is the company's investment in accounts receivables, inventory and fixed assets.

Inventory Turn. The inventory turn measures the volume of business that can be conducted with a given investment in inventory. AppleSeed "turns" its inventory four times each year. That is, AppleSeed needs to maintain an inventory value level of one-quarter of the total cost of its products sold (COGS) in a year.

Different types of businesses have dramatically different inventory turns. For example, a supermarket may turn its inventory 12 or more times a year while a typical manufacturing company turns its inventory twice.

Because inventory is built in anticipation of sales, inventory turn is especially sensitive to changes in business activity. If sales slow down, inventory can balloon and the inventory turn will increase, a sign of pending trouble.

Asset Turn Ratio. The asset turn ratio is a more general measure of efficient asset use. It shows the sales volume that a company can support with a given level of assets. Companies with low asset turns will require a large amount of capital to generate more sales. Conversely, a high asset turn means that the company can expand sales with a low capital investment.

Receivable Days. Receivables shown as days outstanding is the average length of time the company's accounts receivable are outstanding—that is, how long between when the goods are shipped (on credit) and when the customer pays.

Credit sales create accounts receivable, shown as current assets on the *Balance Sheet*. These accounts receivable represent future cash in-flows into the business. The receivable days ratio (also

Income Statement

for the period including Transactions 1 through 31

NET SALES	$3,055,560	**A**
COST OF GOODS SOLD	2,005,830	**B**
GROSS MARGIN	1,049,730	
SALES & MARKETING	328,523	
RESEARCH & DEVELOPMENT	26,000	
GENERAL & ADMINISTRATIVE	203,520	
OPERATING EXPENSE	558,043	
INCOME FROM OPERATIONS	491,687	
NET INTEREST INCOME	(100,000)	
INCOME TAXES	139,804	
NET INCOME	$251,883	

known as the *average collection period*) just measures how fast, on average, the company gets this cash.

AppleSeed's sales terms state *"net 30."* That means that we expect to receive payment within 30 days after we ship our applesauce. As shown below, Apple-Seeds has a receivable days ratio of 54 days. Generally companies average between 45 and 65 days receivables.

Note that if AppleSeed could get its customers to pay faster—let's say in 35 days on average—and/or if it could get by on less inventory in stock (a higher turn), then a lot of cash would be "freed up" for other uses.

Balance Sheet
as of this Transaction 31

CASH	$488,462	
ACCOUNTS RECEIVABLE	454,760	**C**
INVENTORIES	414,770	**D**
PREPAID EXPENSES	0	
CURRENT ASSETS	1,357,992	
OTHER ASSETS	0	
FIXED ASSETS @ COST	1,750,000	
ACCUMULATED DEPRECIATION	78,573	
NET FIXED ASSETS	1,671,427	
TOTAL ASSETS	$3,029,419	**E**
ACCOUNTS PAYABLE	$236,297	
ACCRUED EXPENSES	26,435	
CURRENT PORTION OF DEBT	100,000	
INCOME TAXES PAYABLE	139,804	
CURRENT LIABILITIES	502,536	
LONG-TERM DEBT	800,000	
CAPITAL STOCK	1,550,000	
RETAINED EARNINGS	176,883	
SHAREHOLDERS' EQUITY	1,726,883	
TOTAL LIABILITIES & EQUITY	$3,029,419	

AppleSeed's Asset Management Ratios

$$\text{Inventory Turns} = \frac{Cost\ of\ Goods}{Inventory} = \frac{B}{D} = \frac{\$2,005,830}{\$414,770} = 4.8 \text{ turn}$$

$$\text{Asset Turn} = \frac{Annual\ Sales}{Assets} = \frac{A}{E} = \frac{\$3,055,560}{\$3,029,419} = 1.0 \text{ turn}$$

$$\text{Receivable Days} = \frac{(Receivables)(365)}{Annual\ Sales} = \frac{(C)(365)}{A} = \frac{(\$454,760)(365)}{\$3,055,560} = 54 \text{ days}$$

Profitability Ratios

Profitability ratios are common *"return on"* ratios: *"return on sales," "return on assets"* and so forth. Profitability ratios relate profits to some other piece of financial information such as sales, equity or assets. These ratios measure some aspects of management's operating efficiency; that is, management's ability to turn a profit given a level of resources.

> **Although the liquidity measures are most important indicators of short-term corporate health, profitability measures are most important in the long term.**

In the long-term, a business must consistently show a profit to remain viable and to provide its owners with a satisfactory return on their original investment.

~

Return on Assets. The return on assets (ROA) ratio measures management's success in employing the company's assets to generate a profit.

Return on Equity. The return on equity (ROE) ratio measures management's success in maximizing return on the owner's investment. In fact, this ratio is often called "return on investment" or ROI.

Return on Sales. A company's return on sales (also called "profit margin") compares what is left over after all expenses and costs are subtracted from sales.

Gross Margin. A company's gross margin (also called "gross profit") measures how much it costs to make a company's products and, consequently, how much the company can afford to spend in SG&A and still make a profit.

Gross margin varies greatly between industries. For example, retail businesses generally have a gross profit of around 25%. Computer software businesses can have a gross profit as high as 80% to 90% of sales. That means that for every dollar in sales the computer software company spends only 10¢ to 20¢ to produce its product.

Income Statement
for the period including Transactions 1 through 31

NET SALES	$3,055,560	**A**
COST OF GOODS SOLD	2,005,830	**B**
GROSS MARGIN	1,049,730	
SALES & MARKETING	328,523	
RESEARCH & DEVELOPMENT	26,000	
GENERAL & ADMINISTRATIVE	203,520	
OPERATING EXPENSE	558,043	
INCOME FROM OPERATIONS	491,687	
NET INTEREST INCOME	(100,000)	
INCOME TAXES	139,804	
NET INCOME	$251,883	**C**

AppleSeed is doing rather well. An 8% return on sales (profit margin) is good for the industry. A 15% return on equity is fine too. The 8% return on assets is rather low, but not all that bad for AppleSeed's first year.

Balance Sheet
as of this Transaction 31

CASH	$488,462
ACCOUNTS RECEIVABLE	454,760
INVENTORIES	414,770
PREPAID EXPENSES	0
CURRENT ASSETS	1,357,992
OTHER ASSETS	0
FIXED ASSETS @ COST	1,750,000
ACCUMULATED DEPRECIATION	78,573
NET FIXED ASSETS	1,671,427
TOTAL ASSETS	$3,029,419 **D**
ACCOUNTS PAYABLE	$236,297
ACCRUED EXPENSES	26,435
CURRENT PORTION OF DEBT	100,000
INCOME TAXES PAYABLE	139,804
CURRENT LIABILITIES	502,536
LONG-TERM DEBT	000,000
CAPITAL STOCK	1,550,000
RETAINED EARNINGS	176,883
SHAREHOLDERS' EQUITY	1,726,883 **E**
TOTAL LIABILITIES & EQUITY	$3,029,419

AppleSeed's Profitability Ratios

$$\text{Return on Assets} = \frac{Net\ Income}{Total\ Assets} = \frac{C}{D} = \frac{\$251,883}{\$3,029,419} = 8\%$$

$$\text{Return on Equity} = \frac{Net\ Income}{Shareholders'\ Equity} = \frac{C}{E} = \frac{\$251,883}{\$1,726,883} = 15\%$$

$$\text{Return on Sales} = \frac{Net\ Income}{Net\ Sales} = \frac{C}{A} = \frac{\$251,883}{\$3,055,560} = 8\%$$

$$\text{Gross Margin} = \frac{Net\ Sales - COGS}{Net\ Sales} = \frac{A-B}{A} = \frac{\$3,055,560 - \$2,005,830}{\$3,055,560} = 34\%$$

Leverage Ratios

Leverage ratios (also called "safety" ratios) measure how much of the company's assets are financed with debt. These ratios (1) reveal the extent of a company's "equity cushion" available to absorb losses, and (2) measure the company's ability to meet its short-term and long-term debt obligations.

Leverage is the use of other people's money to generate profits for yourself. By substituting debt (other people's money) for equity dollars (your own money) you hope to make more profit per dollar that you invest than if you had provided all the financing yourself.

Thus debt "leverages" your investment. The leverage ratios measure the extent of this leverage. The reason that leverage ratios are also called safety ratios is because too much leverage in a business can be risky...unsafe to lenders. A lender may think of these ratios as safety ratios while a business owner may think of them as leverage ratios.

Use too little financial leverage and the firm is not reaching its maximum profit potential for its investors. On the other hand, too much debt and the firm may be taking on a high risk of being unable to pay interest and principle if business conditions worsen. Using just the right amount of debt is a management call.

Debt-to-Equity Ratio. This ratio shows how much debt the company has relative to its investor equity. Lenders want a low level of debt relative to

Balance Sheet
as of this Transaction 31

CASH	$488,462	
ACCOUNTS RECEIVABLE	454,760	
INVENTORIES	414,770	
PREPAID EXPENSES	0	
CURRENT ASSETS	1,357,992	
OTHER ASSETS	0	
FIXED ASSETS @ COST	1,750,000	
ACCUMULATED DEPRECIATION	78,573	
NET FIXED ASSETS	1,671,427	
TOTAL ASSETS	$3,029,419	**A**
ACCOUNTS PAYABLE	$236,297	
ACCRUED EXPENSES	26,435	
CURRENT PORTION OF DEBT	100,000	**B**
INCOME TAXES PAYABLE	139,804	
CURRENT LIABILITIES	502,536	
LONG-TERM DEBT	800,000	**C**
CAPITAL STOCK	1,550,000	
RETAINED EARNINGS	176,883	
SHAREHOLDERS' EQUITY	1,726,883	**D**
TOTAL LIABILITIES & EQUITY	$3,029,419	

equity. It gives them comfort that the loan can be repaid (even out of equity) if things go bad for the company.

Debt Ratio. This ratio measures the amount of debt relative to the total assets of the corporation. The debt ratio is a measure of operating leverage.

AppleSeed's debt-to-equity and its debt ratio are relatively conservative for its type of business.

Leverage Ratios

$$\text{Debt-to-Equity} = \frac{Current + Long\text{-}Term\ Debt}{Shareholders'\ Equity} = \frac{B+C}{D} = \frac{\$100,000 + \$800,000}{\$1,726,883} = 0.5$$

$$\text{Debt Ratio} = \frac{Current + Long\text{-}Term\ Debt}{Total\ Assets} = \frac{B+C}{A} = \frac{\$100,000 + \$800,000}{\$3,029,419} = 0.3$$

Industry and Company Comparisons

Just looking at a single ratio does not really tell you much about a company. You also need a standard of comparison, a benchmark. There are three principal benchmarks used in ratio analysis.

Financial ratios can be compared to the (1) ratios of the company in prior years, (2) ratios of another company in the same industry, and (3) industry average ratios. We'll discuss each.

History. The first useful benchmark is history. How has the ratio changed over time? Are things getting better or worse for the company? Is gross margin going down, indicating that costs are rising faster than prices can be increased? Are receivable days lengthening, indicating there are payment problems?

Competition. The second useful ratio benchmark is comparing a specific company ratio with that of a competitor. For example, if a company has a significantly higher return on assets than a competitor, it strongly suggests that the company manages its resources better.

Industry. The third type of benchmark is an industry-wide comparison. Industry-wide average ratios are published and can give an analyst a good starting point in assessing a particular company's financial performance. The chart on the facing page shows various ratios for a variety of companies in different industries. Note that there can be large differences in ratio values between industries and companies.

～

Review the chart on the facing page. What do the ratios tell us about companies and industries?

Microsoft shows the very high *return on assets* and *return on equity* characteristic of good companies in the computer software industry. In contrast, Boston Edison and ConEd show a lower *return on assets* and *return on equity* that is characteristic of the utility industry.

The *inventory turn* for companies in the pharmaceutical industry is relatively low, meaning a high inventory level in relation to cost of goods. On the other end of the spectrum is McDonald's with an *inventory turn* of almost 90. Such a high turn is characteristic of the restaurant industry where inventory is made up of perishable food "raw materials." McDonald's high *inventory turn* means that the uncooked hamburger waiting to be made into Big Macs is on average only several days old.

Note that grocery stores and restaurants have very low accounts receivables as measured in *receivable days*. Not surprising since both industries are so-called "cash businesses" with little credit given to customers.

The high *debt to equity* ratios for automobile companies and to a lesser extent retail stores indicates use of leverage. By carrying a large amount of debt, these companies can achieve a high *return on equity* in a business that offers only a low *return on assets*.

Note there is not much room for mistakes in businesses with a very low *profit margin*. In grocery stores only 1¢ on a dollar of sales turns into profit. In contrast, Microsoft earns a quarter for every dollar of sales.

Also note that the high *gross profit* in the software and pharmaceuticals industry allows companies to have a high SG&A spending level and still make a healthy profit. Some companies are just inherently more profitable than others, often because of proprietary technology.

Comparative Industry Financial Ratios

	LIQUIDITY RATIO	ASSET RATIOS			PROFITABILITY RATIOS				LEVERAGE RATIO
	CURRENT RATIO	INVENTORY TURN	RECEIVABLE DAYS	ASSET TURNS	GROSS MARGIN	PROFIT MARGIN	RETURN ON ASSETS	RETURN ON EQUITY	DEBT TO EQUITY
AppleSeed	**2.7**	**4.8 turn**	**54 days**	**1.0**	**34%**	**8%**	**8%**	**15%**	**0.5**
Automobile									
General Motors	6.9	11 turn	143 days	0.7	21%	3%	3%	21%	7.7
Ford	1.0	17 turn	9 days	0.6	19%	3%	3%	17%	7.5
Grocery Store									
American Stores	1.2	7.9 turn	6 days	2.4	27%	2%	2%	11%	1.0
Kroger	0.9	11 turn	5 days	4.3	24%	1%	1%	N/A	N/A
Hardware									
IBM	1.2	7.7 turn	79 days	0.9	40%	7%	7%	25%	0.5
Intel	2.8	7.1 turn	65 days	0.9	56%	25%	25%	31%	0.0
Software									
Symantec	2.4	9.6 turn	69 days	1.4	79%	8%	8%	18%	0.0
Microsoft	3.2	4.6 turn	27 days	0.9	86%	25%	25%	29%	0.0
Electric Utility									
Boston Edison	0.6	10 turn	59 days	0.4	65%	8%	8%	11%	0.8
ConEd	0.2	8.7 turn	29 days	0.5	61%	10%	10%	11%	0.7
Food Processing									
Campbell Soup	0.7	5.9 turn	29 days	1.2	43%	10%	10%	29%	0.3
General Mills	0.8	5.7 turn	23 days	1.6	59%	9%	9%	N/A	N/A
Retail Store									
Sears	1.9	5.4 turn	206 days	1.1	35%	3%	3%	26%	3.0
Federated	1.8	2.8 turn	68 days	1.1	39%	2%	2%	6%	1.0
Restaurant									
McDonald's	0.5	88 turn	16 days	0.6	42%	15%	15%	18%	0.6
Wendy's	1.6	43 turn	10 days	1.1	26%	8%	8%	12%	0.2
Petroleum									
Exxon	0.9	11 turn	27 days	1.3	49%	5%	5%	16%	0.2
Mobil	0.8	15 turn	37 days	1.7	41%	4%	4%	16%	0.4
Pharmaceutical									
Lilly	0.9	2.4 turn	73 days	0.5	71%	21%	21%	25%	0.4
Merck	1.6	4.3 turn	49 days	0.8	53%	20%	20%	32%	0.1

Chapter 14. Alternative Accounting Policies and Procedures

Various alternative accounting policies and procedures are completely legal and widely used, but may result in significant differences in the values reported on a company's financial statements. Some people would call this chapter's topic "creative accounting."

All financial statements are prepared in accordance with Generally Accepted Accounting Principals (GAAP). But within these accepted principals are a variety of alternative policies and procedures that may be used.

Selection of one policy over another can depend upon management's judgment and upon circumstance. The financial books can look quite different depending upon which policy is chosen. These alternative accounting policies can be used creatively by management as the "cosmetics" of financial reporting.

The table below shows major alternative accounting policies in use today. Management, with assistance of their auditors will select from this list of acceptable accounting principles those that best suit their particular enterprise and management philosophy. Generally the alternative policies can be grouped into two main categories, those that are financially "aggressive" and those that are financially "conservative."

Conservative Policies. So-called conservative accounting policies tend to understate profits and lower inventory and other asset values. Many accountants think these actions take on a "conservative" posture for the business. Few expenses are capitalized, that is, placing asset value on the *Balance Sheet* and amortizing it over time rather than classifying it as an expense immediately. Thus, expenses are higher and profits are lower in the short term, but more "solid" in the long-term.

Aggressive Policies. The so-called aggressive accounting policies tend to inflate earnings and raise asset values, taking an "aggressive" financial posture. Reserves and allowances are low, which

Alternative Accounting Policies & Procedures

ACCOUNTING POLICY	AGGRESSIVE APPLICATION	CONSERVATIVE APPLICATION
Revenue Recognition	At Sale *(Some Risk Remains)*	After Sale *(Buyer carries all Risk)*
Cost of Goods & Inventory Valuation Method	FIFO *(First-in, First-out)*	LIFO *(Last-in, First-out)*
Depreciation Method	Accelerated *(Faster)*	Straight-Line *(Slower)*
Reserves & Allowances *(Warranty, Bad Debt, Returns)*	Low Estimates *(Higher profit now)*	High Estimates *(Higher profit later)*
Contingent Liabilities	Footnote only *(Postpone bad news)*	Accrue When Known *(Take losses now)*
Advertising & Marketing Expenditures	Capitalize *(Write-off later)*	Expense *(Write-off now)*

keeps profits high. This selection of policy can lead to negative surprises, such as if returns or repairs were seriously underestimated.

Neither conservative nor aggressive policies are "right" or "wrong." They are just different ways of viewing the same financial information but with a different perspective. However, it is important when reviewing financial statements with the purpose of determining a company's financial condition to understand the aggressive or conservative posture the company takes in compiling its books.

With conservative accounting policies, you can take comfort that the profits are real. With aggressive policies, profits may be overstated. *If, however, you see a company change its accounting policies from conservative to aggressive, watch out. This change may be a sign of trouble ahead.*

GAAP does gives management latitude to select certain accounting policies and procedures. But, these policies, once selected, must be used consistently and the year-to-year distortions are usually small. However, in periods of inflation, the difference between common inventory valuation methods can be large.

Inventory Valuation and Costing Methods

No, FIFO is not the name of a dog. It's one of the three methods that accountants use to compute cost of goods sold for the *Income Statement* and the inventory value for the *Balance Sheet*.

Cost of goods sold is most often the single biggest deduction from sales revenue on the way to net profit. How best to value the inventory that makes up this large cost? GAAP offers three basic choices. In an inflationary period or when costs of raw materials fluctuate, these three methods of inventory valuation will yield considerably different values. The three alternative valuation methods are:

1. Average Cost Method. Under the average cost method, the separate purchases of goods placed into inventory are summed to give the total inventory value and are averaged to give a cost of goods

Balance Sheet and Income Statement Effects of Inventory Valuation Method Choice on Inventory Value and COGS

	UNITS	PURCHASE PRICE	AVERAGE COST METHOD	LAST-IN, FIRST-OUT (LIFO)	FIRST-IN, FIRST-OUT (FIFO)
FIRST INVENTORY PURCHASE	1,000	$1,000			
SECOND INVENTORY PURCHASE	1,000	1,050			
THIRD INVENTORY PURCHASE	1,000	1,100			
FOURTH INVENTORY PURCHASE	1,000	1,150			
TOTAL INVENTORY	4,000	$4,300			
AVERAGE COST PER 1,000 UNITS		$1,075			
SALES REVENUE	1,000 units @ $1.50		$1,500	$1,500	$1,500
COST OF GOODS			1,075	1,150	1,000
GROSS PROFIT			$ 425	$ 350	$ 500
STARTING INVENTORY VALUE			$4,300	$4,300	$4,300
LESS COST OF GOODS SOLD VALUE			1,075	1,150	1,000
ENDING INVENTORY VALUE			$3,225	$3,150	$3,300

Summary of FIFO vs. LIFO Financial Statements Effects

	FIFO	LIFO
COST OF GOODS	↑	↓
INVENTORY VALUE	↓	↑
PROFITS	↓	↑

sold value. The average cost method is seldom used, offering no real convenience or added accuracy.

2. FIFO Method. Under FIFO (first-in, first-out) methods of valuation, the costs of the earliest materials purchased are assigned to cost of goods sold and the costs of the more recent purchases are summed and allocated to yield ending inventory values.

This method conforms to the actual flow of goods in a factory with the most recent purchases placed at the back of the fridge, and the oldest purchases placed in front to use before they spoil.

3. LIFO Method. Under LIFO (last-in, first-out) method, costs of the latest purchases become cost of good sold and the cost of the oldest purchases are assigned to inventory. When inventory costs are rising as in a period of inflation, using the FIFO method means higher profits (and higher taxes) than if the LIFO method were used.

The table on the previous page shows *Income Statement* and *Balance Sheet* effects of the three alternative inventory valuation and product costing methods in an inflationary period. Depending on the method used, gross profit can vary from a low of $350 with the LIFO method to a high of $500 with the FIFO method. The average cost method is in the middle of the muddle at $425 in gross profit.

All are "correct" values, they just result from applying different acceptable procedures. The table above summarizes the effects of FIFO and LIFO valuation.

Note that while financial statements most often provide accurate, essential information, they do have limitations:

1. Some important corporate "assets" that are difficult to quantify (valued employees and loyal customers) are disregarded.

2. Only the historic values of tangible assets are presented, not current values.

3. Fallible estimates are made for many important items such as receivables collection, depreciation and the salability of inventory.

4. Profits shown on the *Income Sheet* and inventory values shown on the *Balance Sheet* can be significantly affected by accounting method choices.

Chapter 15. Cooking the Books

The vast majority of audited financial statements are prepared fairly. They are assembled in accordance with GAAP and evidence sound fiscal controls and integrity of management. However, sometimes this is not the case and financial fraud is committed: illegal payments made, assets misused, losses concealed, expenses under-reported, revenue over-recorded and so forth.

The New Shorter Oxford English Dictionary has two definitions for the noun "cook." The first describes a person in the white hat behind the counter. The second definition is more appropriate to our discussion: "A person who falsifies or concocts something." So, the first cook, cooks your lunch; the second cook *eats* your lunch.

"Cooking the books" means intentionally hiding or distorting the real financial performance or financial condition of a company.

～

This chapter will give you recipes for book-cooking. The goal here is *not* to make you able to prepare fraudulent financial statements yourself. Leave this task to trained professionals. Rather, this discussion should make you better able to see the clues of fraud.

Managers most often cook the books for personal financial gain...to justify a bonus, to keep stock prices high and options valuable or to hide a business's poor performance. Companies most likely to cook their books have weak internal controls and have a management of questionable character facing extreme pressure to perform.

Cooking is most often accomplished by moving items that should be on the *Income Statement* onto the *Balance Sheet* and sometimes vice versa. A variety of specific techniques can be used to raise or lower income, raise or lower revenue, raise or lower assets and liabilities and thereby reach whatever felonious objective the business person desires. A simple method is outright lying by making fictitious transactions or ignoring required ones.

Cooking the books is very different from "creative accounting." It is creative to use accounting rules to best present your company in a favorable financial light. It is legal and accepted. Cooking the books is done for a deceptive purpose and is meant to defraud.

Income Statement. Puffing up the *Income Statement* most often involves reporting some form of bogus sales revenue that results in increased profits. See Box A in the chart on the next page.

One of the simplest methods of cooking the books is padding the revenue, that is, recording sales before all the conditions required to complete a sale have

---

"Cooking the Books" means intentionally hiding or distorting the real financial performance and/or financial condition of a company. Whether baked or pan-fried, this cooking is most often performed with a felonious purpose such as to defraud.

Techniques to Puff Up the Income Statement

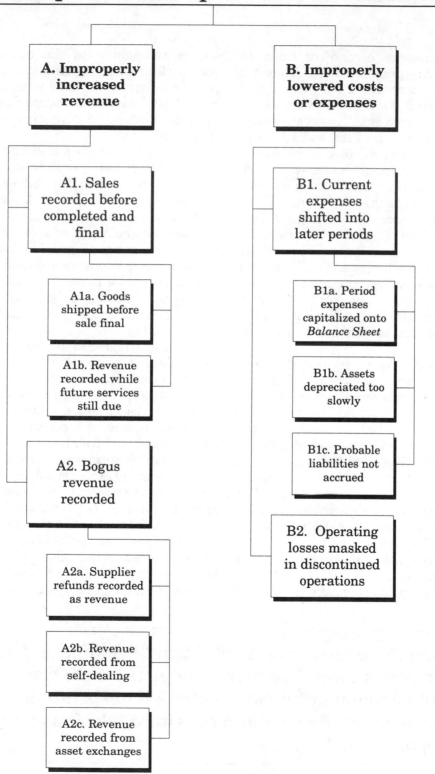

A. Improperly increased revenue

B. Improperly lowered costs or expenses

A1. Sales recorded before completed and final

B1. Current expenses shifted into later periods

A1a. Goods shipped before sale final

A1b. Revenue recorded while future services still due

B1a. Period expenses capitalized onto *Balance Sheet*

B1b. Assets depreciated too slowly

B1c. Probable liabilities not accrued

A2. Bogus revenue recorded

A2a. Supplier refunds recorded as revenue

A2b. Revenue recorded from self-dealing

A2c. Revenue recorded from asset exchanges

B2. Operating losses masked in discontinued operations

occurred. The purpose of this action is to inflate sales and associated profits. A particularly creative technique is self-dealings such as increasing revenue by selling something to yourself *(Box A2b)*.

Revenue is appropriately recorded *only* after all these conditions are met:

1. An order has been received.
2. The actual product has been shipped.
3. There is little risk that the customer will not accept the product.
4. No significant additional actions are required by the company.
5. Title has transferred and purchaser recognizes his responsibility to pay.

The other common route to illegal reporting of increased profit is to lower expenses or to fiddle with costs. *(Box B)* A simple method to accomplish this deception involves shifting expenses from one period into another with the objective of reporting increased profits in the earlier period and hoping for the best in the later period.

Balance Sheet. Most often both the *Balance Sheet* and the *Income Statement* are involved in cooking the books. A convenient cooking is exchanging assets with the purpose of inflating the *Balance Sheet* and showing a profit on the *Income Statement* as well! *(Box D1a.)*

For example, a company owns an old warehouse, valued on the company books at $500,000, its original cost minus years of accumulated depreciation. In fact, the present value of the warehouse if sold would be 10 times its book value, or $5 million. The company sells the warehouse, books a $4.5 million profit and then buys a similar warehouse next door for $5 million.

Nothing has really changed. The company still has a warehouse, but the new one is valued on the books at its purchase price of $5 million instead of the lower depreciated cost of the original warehouse. The company has booked a $4.5 million gain, yet it has less cash on hand than it had before this sell-buy transactions.

Why would a company exchange one asset for a very similar one, especially if it cost them cash and an unnecessary tax payment? The only "real" effect of this transaction is the sale of an undervalued asset and booking of a one-time gain. If the company reports this gain as part of "operating income" the books have been

---

Question: How many sets of books should a company have?
Answer: Generally companies keep three different sets of books, each serving a separate and legitimate purpose:

1. One complete set of books for financial reporting to the outside world and to the owners of the business.
2. One modified set of financial statements focusing on determining and defending tax liability.
3. Other special presentation formats of financial information for management to use as they control the business operations.

Techniques to Sweeten the Balance Sheet

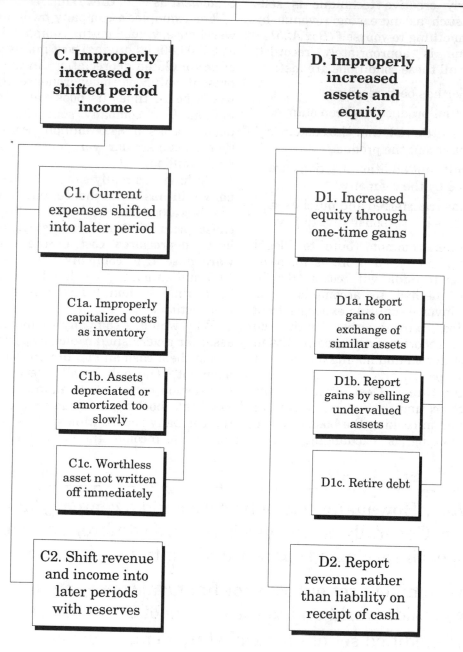

C. Improperly increased or shifted period income

D. Improperly increased assets and equity

C1. Current expenses shifted into later period

D1. Increased equity through one-time gains

C1a. Improperly capitalized costs as inventory

D1a. Report gains on exchange of similar assets

C1b. Assets depreciated or amortized too slowly

D1b. Report gains by selling undervalued assets

C1c. Worthless asset not written off immediately

D1c. Retire debt

C2. Shift revenue and income into later periods with reserves

D2. Report revenue rather than liability on receipt of cash

cooked...income has been deceptively inflated. If the company purports that this one-time capital gain is reoccurring operating income, it has misrepresented the earning capacity of the enterprise.

∽

Just as some people cheat on their tax returns, thinking they will not get caught, some companies "cook the books" hoping auditors and regulators will not catch them either.

Like "borrowing" $20 from the till until payday, and then not being able to repay the "loan," small illegalities can snowball into major fraud.

Remember, an auditor's job is only to review systematically the company's accounting and control procedures and then sample its business transaction to see whether appropriate policies and procedures are being followed in practice. But, it is quite possible for a dedicated and corrupt management to mask transactions and deceive these auditors.

All fast-growing companies must eventually slow down. Managers may be tempted to use accounting gimmicks to give the appearance of continued growth. Managers at weak companies may want to mask how bad things really are. Managers may want that last bonus before bailing out. Maybe there are unpleasant loan covenants that would be triggered but can be avoided by cooking the books. A company can just be sloppy and have poor internal controls.

One key to watch for is management changing from a conservative accounting policy to a less-conservative one, for example changing from LIFO to FIFO methods of inventory valuation or from expensing to capitalizing certain marketing expenses, easing of revenue recognition rules, lengthening amortization or depreciation periods.

Changes like these should be a red flag. There may be valid reasons for these accounting policy changes, but not many. Be warned.

Conclusion

We've come a long way. Our fears of both accounting and financial reporting have melted away. We've learned the vocabulary; we've learned the structure. We know what FASB means and we appreciate the importance of GAAP. We understand:

- That *accrual* has nothing to do with the Wicked Witch of the East. *(pages 58-59)*

- When negative cash flow is a sign of good things happening and when it's a sign of impending catastrophe. *(page 195)*

- Why discounts "drop" directly to the bottom line. *(page 157)*

- The important difference between liquidity and profitably. *(pages 194-195)*

- Those expenditures that are costs and those that are expenses. *(page 50)*

- Depreciation's differing effect on income and on cash. *(pages 118-119)*

- Why product cost always depends on volume. *(pages 148-151)*

- Three common—and different—definitions of what a business is worth. *(page 184)*

- Why assets must always equals liabilities plus shareholders' equity (worth) on the *Balance Sheet*. *(page 16-17)*

- Why working capital is so important and what business actions leads to more and what actions lead to less. *(page 36)*

- The difference between cash in the bank and profit on the bottom line and how they are related. *(page 181)*

We *have* come a long way. We're able to appreciate my young accountant friend's poetic remark:
"It's so symmetrical, so logical, so beautiful and it always comes out right."
It always comes out right.

↩

Index

About the Author

Thomas Ittelson Mr. Ittelson's formal training—as a biochemist, not as an accountant or financial officer—contributes to the unique structure and focus in this book. Necessary vocabulary is introduced and reinforced and transaction structure is emphasized. *Financial Statements* offers a simple step-by-step approach to learning what can be a daunting subject for many people in business.

Mr. Ittelson first learned accounting and financial reporting "on the job," as the strategic planner with a large multi-national corporation and then as the founder, CEO and treasurer of a venture-capital backed high-technology startup company. Currently, he is a principal with The Mercury Group, a Cambridge, Massachusetts based management consulting firm that specializes in market and business strategy development for technology-based companies. His clients range from large industrial enterprises to entrepreneurial startup ventures.

The Mercury Group's intensive, one-day management seminar, ***The Architecture of Financial Statements***, is conducted for business professionals who should know how an Income Statement, Balance Sheet and Cash Flow Statement work...but don't.

Mr. Ittelson lives in Cambridge, Massachusetts, and may be contacted at:

The Mercury Group
P.O. Box 383030
Cambridge, MA 02238

—

Telephone: (617) 576-5713
Facsimile. (017) 954-7007
e-mail: TRIttelson@aol.com